The Killer Concerto

A Shadow Concerto 2

Jill L. Ferguson

red dog press

For information, contact:

red dog press

red dog press, a division of In Your Face Ink LLC Glendale, AZ
www.inyourfaceink.com

ISBN: 979-8-9934752-5-7 Hardback
ISBN: 979-8-9934752-6-4 Paperback
ISBN: 979-8-9934752-7-1 eBook

10 9 8 7 6 5 4 3 2 1
Book design by Rick Schank of Purple Couch Creative

Table of Contents

Chapter 1

Dissonance

THE SNOW HADN'T stopped.

It fell in a relentless, soundless curtain over Brooklyn, thick enough to swallow the footprints thirty-six-year-old Celeste Morgan and Kiril Volkov left behind as they moved through the maze of industrial streets. The flakes were huge and heavy, spun sideways by the wind, clinging to eyelashes and hair, turning each breath into a thin cloud.

Her fingers were numb inside her gloves, but the cold barely registered. Pain was cleaner than thought. She leaned into it.

Two hours ago, she slit Samuel J Harriman's throat. One hour ago, Marcus Vale's penthouse exploded into orange light and black smoke. Now the world felt too quiet, like a concert hall right before a wrong note.

Volkov paced beside her with the steady, predatory ease of someone who had never learned how to walk like a civilian. His boots left neat, efficient tracks. She noticed he didn't seem to shiver. Maybe he was too wired to notice the cold, too.

"You're bleeding," he said, not looking at her.

Celeste's focus flicked down. "Where?"

"Ribs. Right side." He tilted his head slightly toward her. "You're guarding it."

She realized she had been holding her elbow close to her side, unconsciously sheltering the ache. A darker shadow marred the fabric of her coat.

"Just a bruise." She kept walking.

Volkov's hand closed around her forearm and drew her gently to a stop. The contact startled her more than the words. "Let me look."

"Not here," she said. "We're exposed."

"Nobody's watching."

"Everybody's watching," she said. "They always are. That's how I stayed alive."

He didn't let go. His gloved fingers were firm but not harsh. "You'll slow down if it gets worse," he said. "And then you'll die tired. I don't like either option."

She pulled free, sharper this time. "I said I'm fine."

"Stop saying that," he murmured. "You're not."

Snow settled on his lashes, refusing to melt. Under the dim orange of a streetlamp his irises looked almost colorless, pale and intent. She didn't want that gaze on her right now. She didn't want anyone seeing past the shell.

"I'm still walking," she said. "That's enough for tonight."

She pushed forward. He followed without another word, but she felt his attention hovering at the edge of every step, like a shadow that had learned how to worry.

The safehouse was three blocks deeper into the derelict docklands:

an old brick walk-up with one burned-out window and a crooked fire escape clinging to its side. To anyone else, it was another forgotten building in a neighborhood the city had given up on. To Volkov, it was an address, a code, and a history.

He tapped a rhythm on the rusted call box with his knuckles. To Celeste's surprise, the panel's dead green light flickered to life. He keyed in a sequence without looking, and the heavy door buzzed and popped open.

"When did you set this up?" she asked, following him inside.

"Years ago," he said. "I get sentimental about potential exits."

The hallway smelled of old paint, dust, and something indefinable like a faint trace of incense that somebody, sometime, had tried to use to cover up something worse. Their footsteps echoed on worn linoleum. A single bulb burned weakly near the top of the stairwell. It cast long, distorted shadows ahead of them.

The apartment was on the third floor. Volkov unlocked it with a plain metal key. Apparently, not everything in his life required an encrypted protocol. He pushed the door open and stepped aside for her to enter first.

The space was small and bare. Two thin mattresses lay on the floor, parallel but not touching, separated by a crate that held a dented metal lamp. Blackout curtains had been tacked over the windows, blocking the city's glow. A portable gas heater squatted in the corner like an ugly metal toad, emitting a low, steady hiss.

Celeste set her cello down carefully at the end of one of the mattresses. The polished wood looked shockingly out of place like a piece of concert hall grace dropped in a room made of gray.

She straightened slowly, feeling the tight pull at her ribs.

Volkov closed and bolted the door, then crossed the room in three strides. Before she could protest, he knelt in front of her and tugged at the hem of her coat.

She flinched back. "Don't."

"I've seen worse," he said.

"That's not the point."

His eyes lifted to hers, steady. "Let me see, Celeste."

No title. No codename. Just her name.

She exhaled, feeling some part of her resistance surrender—not to him, but to physics. She couldn't maintain tension everywhere all at once. "Fine," she muttered.

He eased the coat aside and lifted her sweater just enough to reveal the dark bloom spreading across her side. The bruise was ugly. It was purple, blue, and sickly yellow at the edges where older impacts still lingered. A shallow cut traced through the center like a grim accent mark.

He whistled softly. "That's from a rifle butt, not a fist."

"One of Harriman's men tried to swing," she said. "I didn't feel like letting him."

"You blocked and let the force carry through," Volkov murmured, his fingers hovering just above the bruise without touching. "You know better."

"I was busy," she said tightly.

"You were angry."

She bit down on a retort. He wasn't wrong.

He stood, dug into his duffel, and came back with a small first-aid kit. The movements were efficient, practiced, almost gentle. He cleaned the cut with antiseptic. It burned. She hissed through her teeth but didn't pull away.

"You've had worse," he said.

"I've had better days."

He smirked faintly. "You think this is a bad day? You killed Harriman. You should be celebrating."

"I killed a symptom," she said. "The disease is still breathing."

He taped gauze over the wound and lowered her shirt. For a moment his hand lingered near her side, not touching, as if he wanted to steady her and didn't know if it would make things better or worse.

He let his arm drop. "How many people have lied to you?" The tone of his voice was low, quiet.

She stared past him at the cracked paint on the wall. "Professionally or personally?"

"Yes."

Her throat felt thick. "Marcus lied about Berlin. He lied about my mother. He lied about Eidolon. But he also… kept me alive. Does that cancel anything out? Does that earn forgiveness?"

"Does it?" Volkov asked.

She shook her head once. "I don't know. That's the problem."

He sat back on his heels, studying her she thought like she was a puzzle that could be solved if he chose the right angle. "How many used you?" he asked.

She let out a breath that almost counted as a laugh. "How many people have I killed because I believed them? I stopped counting both those numbers a long time ago."

He nodded slowly. "Yet here you are. Still standing."

"No thanks to them."

"Some thanks to them," he countered. "They shaped you. But they don't own you anymore."

She almost told him he sounded like Marcus then. The impulse tasted bitter, so she swallowed it whole. She pushed herself to her feet, wincing as the bruised muscles protested. She crossed to the small window and pulled the edge of the blackout curtain aside just enough to peek out.

The street below was empty, just a strip of wet asphalt glowing under a sickly streetlamp. The snow softened the edges of everything, turning cars into low shapeless mounds. No headlights. No shadows moving against the light.

"You're not going to sleep," Volkov said behind her.

"I'm not tired."

"You haven't slept in forty-eight hours."

"I've gone longer," she said.

"That doesn't make it wise."

She let the curtain fall, turning back to face him. "We leave for Tokyo in two days."

A muscle ticked in his jaw. "Are you sure you want to keep traveling with the orchestra?"

"It's the one pattern they expect me to keep," she said. "If I break it, I vanish off the grid. They'll assume I'm running. They know all the places a person like me could hide. They designed half of them."

"And if you stay visible, they'll assume you're still under some control," he finished.

"They built me to be predictable," she said. "I'm going to use that against them."

"Performing onstage while a secret death cult tries to capture you," he said dryly. "Sounds stable."

"It's the only life I know," she said. "Onstage, I decide every note."

He studied her a moment, then gave a short nod. "Fine. Tokyo."

"You can't travel with me. It would draw attention."

He shrugged. "I'm good at folding myself into crowds."

"Not in a tux with a cello section," she said. "You look like someone whose first instrument was a knife."

"For the record, it was a piano," he said.

She blinked. "You're joking."

"One year," he said. "Then things got… louder."

The image of a younger Volkov sitting at a piano, brow furrowed, fingers stumbling through scales, flickered through her mind and did something strange to her ribs that had nothing to do with bruising. "Why are you helping me?" she whispered. "Really?"

He leaned against the wall, folding his arms. "Do you want the professional answer or the honest one?"

"The honest one," she said, surprising herself.

His brow furrowed like he was in thought and then he said, "Because Eidolon took things from me that I can't get back. Because they built something monstrous out of good intentions. Because someone has to burn them down, and you are the only person I've ever seen who might be able to do it."

"That's the professional answer," she said.

A corner of his mouth curved. "The honest one is… I don't like watching you get hunted."

Her pulse stuttered. "Don't," she said. "Don't make this about—"

"About what?" he asked. "Human concern? Attraction? Affection? You can pick whichever one frightens you least."

"All of them," she said.

His gaze softened. "Good. Fear means you haven't shut everything off yet."

"You're intolerable."

"I've been told."

The heater clicked as it cycled, the only sound in the room for a few heartbeats.

She crossed to her cello and ran her fingers over the curved wood. The varnish was cold. The strings were slightly slack from the temperature shifts. She turned the pegs slowly, tightening, listening to the pitch climb.

Volkov watched her. "You going to play?"

"Do you mind?"

He shook his head. "It's better than the heater."

She sat on the edge of the mattress with the instrument between her knees, bow in her right hand. She didn't need sheet music. Her muscles knew more songs than her mind could list. She drew the bow across the strings, soft at first, a low note that filled the small space, vibrating in the air, smoothing the jagged edges of her thoughts without blunting them.

She played something close to Bach, but not quite. The melody kept slipping sideways, minor where it should have been major, dissonant where it should have resolved. It was wrong. It was honest.

Her mother's face flickered in the sound. Marcus's voice surfaced unbidden: *You control the note. You control the space around it. That's all life is, Celeste. Notes and spaces.*

She had believed him. She had built her life around his tempo. The bow quivered in her hand. The note turned rough. She stopped, mid-phrase.

Volkov's voice came softly from the other side of the room. "Why did you stop?"

"Because if I keep going, I might feel something," she said.

"And that's dangerous?"

"Yes."

He considered that. "Play anyway."

She looked up, startled. "You just said feelings will get me killed."

"I said not dealing with them will." He sat on the opposite mattress, forearms on his knees. "You're better with the cello than with words. Let it bleed there instead of on a mission."

She hated that what he was saying made sense. She set her jaw and began again. This time she didn't hold back. The music came out raw and dark, laced with grief and anger and something else she couldn't name, something that felt like the echo of a life she was never allowed to have.

When she finally let the last note die, the room seemed larger somehow. Or maybe she'd just emptied enough of herself to notice its size.

Volkov was looking at her with an expression she couldn't read. His eyes were sharp, but there was something unguarded there too, something almost… reverent. It unnerved her more than any weapon.

"What?" she asked.

"You terrify me more when you play than when you kill," he said.

She snorted. "That's backwards."

"No," he said. "When you kill, I know the stakes. When you play,

I see the parts of you they didn't touch. And that's what makes you dangerous. They tried to turn you into a blade. They forgot you were a whole instrument."

Her throat tightened. She set the cello gently aside and lay back on the mattress, staring up at the water-stained ceiling. The bruise along her ribs throbbed in time with her heart. She folded one arm under her head, letting the other rest flat against her stomach, fingers splayed as if trying to hold something in.

"I'll try to sleep," she said.

"I'll stay up," Volkov replied. "If I hear anything on the street, I'll wake you."

"You really think they'd come that fast?"

"If they know Harriman's dead, yes." He moved to the window and peeled back the curtain just enough to see out. "They don't like loose ends."

"I'm not a loose end," she murmured.

"No," he said. "You're the beginning of something."

She wanted to ask what he meant. She didn't. Exhaustion crept in, slow and sly, filling the spaces the music had hollowed out. She closed her eyes.

Sleep came in fragments. She dreamed she was sixteen again, standing on a Berlin sidewalk, her mother's hand warm around hers. The air smelled like diesel and roasted chestnuts. Street musicians played a Schubert quartet badly at the corner. Her mother laughed and said, "One day you'll play this properly. You'll show them how it's done."

Then the world turned white. Sound became light. Her mother's hand disappeared.

In the dream, Celeste could move. In the real memory, she hadn't.

She woke with a sharp inhale, heart pounding against her bruised ribs, fingers clawing at the thin blanket. The room was gray with pre-dawn light seeping around the edges of the curtains. The heater still hissed. Her cello leaned where she'd left it. For a moment she thought Volkov had gone.

Then she saw him, a dark shape by the door, sitting with his back against the wall, head tipped back, eyes closed. A pistol rested loosely in his hand, angled toward the floor.

He was awake. She could tell by the way his fingers tightened when she shifted.

"Any visitors?" she asked, voice hoarse.

"No," he said without opening his eyes. "They're either regrouping or waiting for a more dramatic stage."

She pushed herself upright slowly. Her ribs complained. "We should assume they'll use Tokyo."

He opened his eyes. "Then we'll be ready."

She stood, feeling the weight of the coming days settle over her like another kind of snow. She had performances scheduled in three major cities. She had an international death cult hunting her. She had an ally she wasn't sure she trusted. And she had a mother's ghost leaning over her shoulder, asking: *What will you do with the instrument I gave you?*

Celeste tightened her jaw, reached for her cello, and began to pack it into its case. "We fly out tomorrow," she said. "We buy the tickets separately. Different routes."

Volkov nodded. "I'll meet you in Tokyo."

She closed the case with a soft click. The sound was almost like a period at the end of a sentence.

No, she thought. Not a period. A breath. The next movement was about to begin. And this time, she would not play what anyone else had written for her.

Chapter 2

Tokyo in Two Keys

THE PLANE DESCENDED into Tokyo at dawn, slicing through a layer of low clouds that turned the world outside her window from gray haze into clean lines: a sprawling city of white and glass, stitched together with highways and rivers like veins.

Celeste pressed her forehead lightly against the cold plexiglass. The view spread out beneath her in quiet, geometric order. Tokyo always felt like a symphony scored by an engineer—every movement precise, every part arranged to the millimeter. It was the opposite of everything her life had become.

"We'll be on the ground in ten minutes," the flight attendant said over the intercom in a bright, practiced tone.

Celeste closed her eyes and pictured the week ahead in measures and bars:

Arrival.

Check-in.

Rehearsal.

Reconnaissance.

Performance.

Survival.

Her cello, checked this time as fragile cargo under her orchestra alias, would be waiting with the instrument handlers. Her passport showed a familiar version of herself, a slightly softer photograph, taken before the last year had carved new lines into her expression. She didn't feel like the woman in the picture anymore.

The plane touched down with a soft jolt. As they taxied toward the gate, Celeste slipped her hand into the inside pocket of her coat and brushed her fingers over the burner phone Volkov had texted coordinates to before their flights parted over the Pacific. He'd taken a different airline, different route, and would arrive hours after her.

They were together. But not. It was safer that way. Safer for him, she told herself, ignoring the echo that whispered safer for you.

The orchestra's tour liaison met her at the gate, a brisk, efficient Japanese woman wearing a perfectly pressed navy blazer and a smile that looked like it had survived a hundred disasters. "Celeste Morgan?" she asked in lightly accented English.

"Yes."

"I'm Aya. Welcome back to Tokyo. Your luggage is already collected. The others are arriving on the afternoon flight from New York. You're on a separate itinerary?"

"Last-minute change," Celeste said smoothly. "I had a… personal matter to attend to."

Aya's eyes flickered with curiosity, but she didn't pry. "Of course.

The van is waiting. We'll take you to the hotel first. Rehearsal at Suntory Hall is scheduled for three p.m."

Celeste nodded and followed her through the immaculate corridors of Narita Airport, letting the rhythm of the language and the flow of the crowds wash over her. Japanese announcements layered over English and Chinese, creating a strange polyphony. Travelers moved like currents in a tide, some fast, some slow, all convinced of their own purpose.

Outside, the air was cold and clean, with a faint hint of jet fuel and winter. The shuttle van was white, spotless, the interior smelling of plastic and citrus cleaner. Tokyo slid past the windows in a blur of neon signs, glass towers, and narrow streets.

Aya pointed out the landmarks as they drove: Tokyo Tower, the Imperial Palace grounds, the endless canopy of apartment blocks that looked identical from a distance and profoundly unique up close.

"You must be tired," Aya said kindly. "You've had quite a tour already. Vienna, Berlin, London, Paris."

Celeste's grip tightened on her bag at the sound of "Berlin." "Something like that," she murmured.

Aya smiled. "The Japanese audience loves you, you know. Your last performance here trended for days." She laughed softly. "My teenage niece tried to dye her hair blonde because of you."

Celeste almost smiled. "Tell her not to. It's a lot of maintenance."

"I told her she doesn't need to look like you to play like you," Aya said. "She didn't listen."

Celeste's fingers twitched, seeking a bow that wasn't there. Compliments on her playing felt off now. They went in, but they didn't land where they were supposed to.

"Do you ever get nervous?" Aya seemed genuinely curious.

"Before performances?"

Aya nodded.

"Not anymore," Celeste said. "Music is the only place my hands know what to do."

"And outside of music?" Aya inquired.

"Outside of music," Celeste said, "is more improvisation."

Aya laughed, accepting that as a joke.

Celeste left it there.

The hotel was a tall, glass-fronted structure in Roppongi: all clean lines and polished marble, the lobby decorated with winter-white flowers and tastefully subtle Christmas lights. Staff bowed as they passed. Everyone moved with the same choreographed efficiency.

Her suite on the twenty-first floor had a view of the city, lines of traffic threading through the streets below like streams of red and white light. She set her carry-on down, walked to the window, and pressed her fingertips against the glass. The city felt distant, like a model constructed, controlled. Somewhere in all of that order, chaos waited with her name printed neatly on its folded hands.

Her phone buzzed.

A message from Volkov, written in a way that could have come from any colleague. **Flight delayed. Landed Haneda. Checking into business hotel nearby. See you at "rehearsal."** The last word was in quotes. They both knew which rehearsal mattered.

She allowed herself one moment to imagine him descending stairs in some anonymous hotel lobby, his expression bored and alert at the same time, eyes scanning the exits. Then she pulled back from the window.

Her cello arrived twenty minutes later with the orchestra gear. She inspected it carefully: no scratches, no cracks, strings still in tune within a half-step. Whoever had handled the instruments this leg of the tour had known what they were doing.

She set the cello upright, ran her fingers over its familiar curves, and felt something in her chest settle. If she didn't think too hard about what else the case had carried in the past year—the rifle, the vial, the syringes—the instrument still looked like an object meant only for beauty.

She showered, letting the hot water try and fail to loosen the clamp on her ribcage, then dressed in rehearsal blacks: fitted black pants, black sweater, hair pulled back into a low twist. The bruise along her side protested, but she ignored it.

By the time she arrived at Suntory Hall, the sun had dipped low enough that the sky was a deep, electric blue. Streetlights flicked on one by one. The hall rose from the surrounding buildings like a modern temple, a geometric façade of brick and glass. Inside, the air hummed with the energy of technicians, ushers, and the first clusters of patrons picking up tickets at the box office for tomorrow night.

Inside the hall, the stage was a warm glow of wood and light. The space was famous among musicians for its acoustic perfection, a place where every note felt like it had been designed to land exactly where it belonged. Celeste walked onto the stage and felt the floor vibrate slightly under her feet, a low, sympathetic resonance from the empty space.

Members of the orchestra were already tuning, their voices rising and falling in friendly gossip. Lena Kovács, the closest thing Celeste had to a friend, wasn't there yet; the orchestra's official plane had just landed. Celeste felt an odd pang of something like loneliness, then pushed it aside.

She set her chair and endpin with the efficiency of ritual and began to tune. The A hummed, then the D, G, and C, each string settling into its familiar relationship with the others. She drew the bow across all four at once, letting the chord ring and fade. For a moment, nothing else existed.

Then she felt it. Someone watching her. Her skin prickled along the back of her neck. She didn't look up immediately. She played an arpeggio instead, letting her peripheral vision sweep the hall. Stagehands, lighting techs, a few early staff in the side aisles.

And—back of the ground floor, just beyond the last row of seats—a man standing alone. Hands in his pockets, posture relaxed, gaze fixed on her. Too still. Too focused. Too calm.

She shifted her bowing to something more lyrical, forcing her body language into the shape of "absorbed artist." The man didn't move. When their eyes met, he smiled faintly. He was in his forties, maybe, with dark hair and a face that was almost forgettable. Almost. His eyes were wrong: pale and flat, like the memory of a color. She had seen eyes like that in too many dossiers.

Aya materialized at the edge of the stage. "Celeste, do you need anything before rehearsal?"

Celeste kept her expression neutral, her bow arm moving. "Who is that?" she asked softly in English, indicating the back of the hall with a glance.

Aya turned. "Oh, that's Mr. Tanaka, I think. He handles security, a liaison for the tour while you're in Japan. The hall staff mentioned he might stop by to observe. Is there a problem?"

Security liaison. Of course. "None," Celeste said. "Just curious."

Aya smiled, reassured, and bustled away to coordinate seating charts.

Celeste let herself look back fully this time.

The man, Tanaka, was gone.

Her stomach tightened.

The conductor arrived ten minutes later. The rest of the orchestra trickled in with the usual blend of jet lag and nervous energy. Lena slipped into her chair beside Celeste, hair slightly frizzed from travel, eyes bright.

"You made it before us," Lena said, bumping Celeste's shoulder lightly. "Show-off."

"They booked me different," Celeste said. "Scheduling issue."

"Or they finally realized you need your rest to continue shaming us," Lena said.

"You play just as well," Celeste said.

"Liar," Lena replied cheerfully, then lowered her voice. "You okay? You look…"

"Haunted?" Celeste suggested.

"Intense," Lena corrected. "Even for you."

"I'm fine." The lie tasted like metal. She swallowed it anyway.

Rehearsal began. Dvořák flowed under her fingers. Shostakovich bristled and bit. The new contemporary piece on the program—an angular, jagged concerto by a young Japanese composer—demanded all of her attention. It was full of syncopations and sudden dynamic shifts, like it had been written by someone trying to turn a panic attack into notation.

She liked it.

The orchestra stopped and started, the conductor calling out corrections, adjusting phrasing, balancing sections. Celeste's world narrowed to bow hair and fingerboard, breath and count, the small nods and glances that made ensemble playing possible.

For two hours, she could almost pretend that this was all she was. Almost.

During a break, she stepped into the wings, taking a bottle of water from a catering table. The backstage smelled of wood, sweat, and coffee. The hum of staff radios buzzed faintly in the distance.

She heard the click of shoes behind her.

"Ms. Morgan," a male voice said in Japanese-accented English.

She turned.

Tanaka stood a few feet away, tie neatly knotted, hands loosely at his sides. His face wore a polite, professional smile.

"Hello," she said. "We didn't get introduced."

He bowed slightly. "Tanaka Hiroshi. I'll be overseeing security coordination for the hall and your ensemble during your visit. I've read about your performances."

"Only good things, I hope." She smiled.

"Very good," he said. "Your discipline is remarkable."

She raised an eyebrow. "You can hear discipline?"

"It shows in posture," he said. "In how you breathe. In where your eyes go when you're not playing."

A small warning flared in her chest. "And where do my eyes go?"

"Places other people's don't," he said comfortably. "Exits. Elevated positions. Corners."

"I tour a lot," she said. "You learn to spot fire and earthquake hazards."

His lips stretched into an almost-smile. "Of course." He stepped a little closer, but not enough to invade her space. "We've had no credible threats reported," he said. "But in light of the incident at the Reznov gala in Vienna, we are taking extra precautions. You understand."

"Of course," she said. "Does my presence here pose a risk?"

His eyes flickered, quick, almost imperceptible. "Your fame always draws attention."

"Fame doesn't kill people," Her volume was just above a whisper.

"No," he agreed. "People kill people." He held her gaze for a beat too long.

She smiled politely. "Thank you for keeping us safe, Mr. Tanaka," she said. "If you need me for anything specific, go through Aya or Maestro Duret. They control my schedule more than I do."

"I already spoke to them," he said. "I'll be positioned near the stage tomorrow in case anything happens."

"I'm sure nothing will," she said.

"I'm sure something will," he replied calmly. He dipped his head again and walked away, disappearing into a maze of staff and music stands.

She watched him go, a cold prickle crawling up her spine. Volkov would want to know about him. She finished her water and went back onstage. The rest of rehearsal slid by in mechanical perfection.

After they were dismissed, Lena invited her to join a group for ramen and drinks. Celeste declined, blaming jet lag. Lena pouted but didn't push.

Outside the hall, the freezing air bit her cheeks. Neon signs painted the wet pavement in blues and pinks. Cabs streamed past. A light sprinkling of snow had started again, dusting suits and umbrellas.

Her phone buzzed in her pocket.

Lobby.

No name. No punctuation. Just a location. She turned and went back inside.

Volkov sat in an armchair in a quiet corner of the main lobby, looking completely out of place and yet somehow invisible. He wore a dark coat over a simple black shirt and jeans, posture relaxed, one ankle resting over his knee. To most people, he'd just be another slightly bored man waiting for someone else to finish up whatever art they were pretending to appreciate.

To her, he was a smudge of intent in a room full of passive observation. She sat down in the chair next to him, not quite facing him.

"How was the rehearsal?" he asked.

"Musically satisfying," she said. "Existentially unsettling."

"So… normal," he said.

"Tanaka Hiroshi," she said quietly. "Security liaison. Too observant. Too comfortable talking about violence."

"Agency?" Volkov asked.

"Feels more like subcontracted muscle. But I don't like his eyes."

"He clock you?"

"Everywhere I looked."

"Then we watch him," Volkov said.

"Thought you said I need rest."

"You can rest while we watch him," he said. "Delegation."

"Nice to see you embracing management," she murmured.

He huffed a faint laugh. "You holding together?"

"No," she said. "But I'm moving. That's enough."

He looked at her profile, his gaze lingering on the shadow under her eyes. "You dreamed?"

"Berlin," she said.

"And?"

"And nothing I can change now." She shook her head slightly. "What did you find?"

"Eidolon has a shell company with partial control of ticketing and event logistics here," he said. "On paper it's a security consultancy. In reality, it's a funnel."

"A funnel for what?"

"Money. Personnel. Data." He gave a small shrug. "They're piggybacking on legitimate cultural institutions. It gives them prestige and plausible deniability."

She huffed. "Of course, they're laundering through art."

"Saints launder through churches," he said. "Monsters launder through beauty. It makes them feel sophisticated."

"Any names?" she asked.

"None that matter yet," he said. "But I did find this." He slid his phone across the small table between them. A photograph on the screen: a grainy security cam still of Tanaka shaking hands with a man whose face was turned away. "Pulled from a private feed," Volkov said. "Location: Berlin. Date stamp: two months ago. Tanaka met with Harriman. Twice."

Celeste's chest went cold and hot at the same time. "So, Tanaka isn't just a liaison," she said. "He's a node."

"And he knows you're here," Volkov said.

"We knew they'd come," she said. "I just didn't expect them to be early for the performance."

He studied her for a moment. "We can pull you from the concert."

"No," she snapped. "If I cancel, they know I'm onto them. If I stay, I control the stage."

"Control is an illusion," he said.

"It's the only one I have," she replied.

They sat in silence for a moment, watching the lobby thin as staff finished their shifts and left. A few tourists trailed through, taking photos of the hall. No one paid attention to the man and woman sitting together and saying nothing.

"Are you scared?" Volkov asked suddenly.

"Yes," she said.

The honesty must have surprised them both because she saw his eyebrows raise in response.

"Good," he said.

"Why is that good?" she asked.

"Because fear means you still want to live," he said. "People who stop being afraid do stupid things."

"Like walking into Eidolon headquarters alone?" she asked.

"That was calculated risk," he said.

"That was suicidal impulse dressed up as strategy," she corrected.

"You're still here," he pointed out.

"So are you."

"For now," he said.

She looked at his hands. There was a faint burn near the base of his thumb she hadn't noticed before—old, healed, pale against the rest of his skin. She wondered if it was from fire, a weapon, or something else entirely. She wondered why she cared. "I hate all of this," she said quietly.

"I know," he replied.

"I hate that my mother built them. I hate that Marcus sharpened me for them. I hate that the only way to stop them now is to become something even worse."

"You're not them," he said.

"I'm made of them," she countered.

He paused. "You're made of a lot of things. They're just the ones that branded you the deepest."

"A poetic assassin," she deadpanned. "How unnerving."

"If you think this is my poetic setting, you haven't seen me drunk," he said.

She almost laughed. It came out like a breath with a sharper edge.

"I'll tail Tanaka tonight," he continued. "See where he sleeps, who he talks to. You go back to the hotel. Rest. Play. Do whatever it is you do when you're not orchestrating murder."

"You think he'll move tonight?" she asked.

"Even if he doesn't, I will," Volkov said. "They think they're conducting this. I'd like to change the tempo."

Her fingers tapped a silent rhythm on the arm of the chair.

"Don't kill him yet," she said. "He might know where the other branches are."

"I wasn't going to kill him," Volkov said, paused, and then added, "yet."

She stood. "Then I'll see you tomorrow. Before the concert."

He rose as well. For a moment they stood too close in the muted light of the lobby, both of them angled half-away as if pretending they weren't sharing the same air.

"Celeste."

"Yes?"

"If something happens tomorrow and we don't get a second chance, you should know..."

She tensed. "Don't."

His mouth quirked. "You don't even know what I was going to say."

"You were going to say something that makes the air heavier," she said. "Save it."

"For when?" he asked.

"For when we're not dying," she said. "Or trying not to."

He studied her, then nodded. "Okay. Later, then."

The word later hung between them like a possible note in an unwritten measure.

She turned and walked out into the Tokyo night. The air was cold enough to sting, neon bright enough to make everything feel hyperreal. The city thrummed with life: snatches of laughter, the click of shoes, the distant echo of a street musician playing a shakuhachi flute somewhere in the maze of side streets.

Back in her room, she set her cello in its stand by the window. The city glowed behind it with skyscrapers reflected in the varnished wood. She drew the curtains halfway, leaving the instrument silhouetted against the lights, and sat on the edge of the bed.

On the desk, a folded paper had been left by hotel staff, a printed program draft for tomorrow's concert. Her name was listed under "Featured Soloist," bracketed by Japanese characters that translated to "world-renowned" and "rare appearance."

Her thumb brushed over the print. Her identity, on paper. Half true. Half weapon.

She took out the burner Volkov had given her and typed a message. **If they come during the concert, they'll aim for offstage. Intermission. Back corridors.**

A beat later, his reply blinked in. **Then don't go offstage alone.**

She considered that, then typed: **What if the danger is onstage?**

His answer came quickly. **Then I hope your bow is as sharp as your aim.**

She set the phone down and reached for her cello. Tomorrow, she would step into the light again. Tomorrow, she would play for an audience that had no idea what kind of war was happening in the wings. Tomorrow, Eidolon would make a move.

She rested the instrument against her shoulder, closed her eyes, and drew the bow across the strings. The note that filled the room was dark, resonant, and edged with something almost like resolve.

She didn't know who she was anymore. But she knew exactly what she was about to do. And that, for now, was enough.

Chapter 3

Broken Applause

THE AIR IN Suntory Hall tasted different on performance nights. It wasn't anything obvious. There was still the familiar mix of wood polish, dust, and faint perfume that clung to the red seats and velvet curtains. But layered over it was something electric and almost metallic, the charged stillness of a thousand people holding their breath at the same time.

Celeste stood alone in the soloist's dressing room, staring at her reflection. The mirror showed a woman in black: sleek floor-length gown, fitted bodice, simple lines that allowed her arms and shoulders to move freely. Her hair was twisted into a low chignon, a few loose strands framing a face that looked calm, composed, and entirely under control.

She didn't feel under control.

She leaned closer to the mirror, studying her eyes. They were the only thing that betrayed her. Light caught in the blue-green irises, turning them almost glassy, like the surface of water just before it breaks.

On the dressing table, a printed setlist lay beside her bow and rosin cake. *Mozart. Intermission. Contemporary concerto. Encore dependent on audience response.* Everything predictable, everything scheduled, everything tidy.

Except the part where a shadow organization wanted to test their newest acquisition in front of a live audience.

There was a soft knock on the door.

"Come in," she said.

Lena slipped in, already in concert black with a knee-length dress, dark tights, her hickory hair in a hasty twist that didn't quite restrain her curls.

"Oh good," Lena said. "You look like the embodiment of terrifying elegance. Everything is normal."

Celeste lifted a corner of her mouth. "Is that a compliment?"

"It's the only kind I know how to give," Lena said. She shut the door and leaned back against it, exhaling. "The hall is full. Totally sold out. People are scalping tickets outside. One guy offered me his watch for a chance to sit in the wings."

"You should've taken it," Celeste said. "Resell the watch, pay your rent."

Lena laughed. "Tempting." Her smile faded slightly as she took in Celeste's posture. "How are you? Really?"

Celeste smoothed an imaginary crease in her gown. "Focused."

"Focused is good," Lena said. "Focused means you're not about to have a breakdown in the middle of the adagio."

"I don't have breakdowns mid-phrase," Celeste said. "It's unprofessional."

Lena shook her head affectionately. "Only you could sound

arrogant and self-blaming at the same time." She hesitated. "You know if something is wrong… you can tell me, right?"

That was the problem. Too many things were wrong. All of them too big to fit into one sentence.

Celeste met Lena's eyes in the mirror before she said, "Something is always wrong. Tonight, at least, I know my part."

Lena sighed. "Mystery answer. Very on brand." She pushed away from the door and stepped closer, reaching for Celeste's shoulders. "Listen. Whatever is chewing you up inside, when you walk onstage, it's just you and the cello. Okay? The rest of us are just trying to keep up."

Celeste swallowed. "You keep up just fine."

"Lie better," Lena said. She squeezed Celeste's shoulders, then leaned down and kissed the top of her head in a quick, affectionate gesture. "You'll be brilliant. Try not to obliterate us emotionally. Some of us have fragile hearts."

"Yours?" Celeste asked.

"Mine is bulletproof," Lena said. "It's the audience I'm worried about."

Someone knocked again, more briskly. "Five minutes, Ms. Morgan," came Aya's voice through the door.

"Thank you," Celeste replied.

Lena blew an exaggerated kiss toward the ceiling and backed out. "See you out there, assassin of feelings."

The door shut.

Assassin. The word hung in the air like a joke with teeth.

Celeste picked up her bow. Her hand shook once. She stared at it until the tremor stopped. She had faced harder rooms than this. She had aimed at more dangerous targets. Tonight, though, she was both performer and hunted, and there was no clean way to separate those roles anymore. She lifted her instrument, felt the familiar pull in her shoulder, and walked out.

Backstage, the air was cooler, threaded with the rustle of fabric and the soft clink of instruments being adjusted. Stagehands murmured into headsets. An usher whispered to another near the curtain, which Celeste overheard: "Is she nervous? She never looks nervous."

Celeste took her place among the wings, waiting for her cue. The orchestra filed onstage to polite applause, the conductor following with his usual sweeping charm.

She scanned the hall from the shadows. Tanaka was standing in the aisle near the first exit on the left, wearing a dark suit and a barely-there earpiece. His attention moved across the crowd, lingering on nothing and everything. To anyone else, he looked like dedicated security.

To her, he looked like a fixed point in a pattern she didn't understand yet.

Where are your eyes when you're not playing? he had asked.

On you, she thought.

She searched for any sign of Volkov. He'd promised not to be obvious, but she knew how he moved; she could recognize his presence in the tilt of a stranger's shoulders, the way someone leaned just wrong at the edge of a crowd.

Nothing.

Good. That meant he was working.

The house lights dimmed. The murmurs softened into silence.

The conductor lifted his hands. The first notes of Mozart rose into the air—light, clear, deceptively simple. The orchestra followed, a single living organism breathing together.

Celeste closed her eyes for a second behind the curtain and matched her breath to theirs.

Then she stepped onstage. The applause rose as soon as she appeared, then swelled when she walked to the soloist's chair and sat, adjusting the endpin, letting the orchestra finish their opening movement.

She felt it. Not just the sound, but the collective focus, the way a thousand people aimed their attention like a single spotlight. It was a different kind of weapon, and she knew how to wield it.

She waited for her first entrance.

The cello slid in under the violins—low, warm, a thread of gravity pulling the music toward something deeper. Her bow moved like it belonged there. Whatever turmoil had been in her chest shifted, reshaping itself into sound.

She played with a clarity she hadn't felt in weeks. Every note was the exact weight she wanted. Every shift of her left hand found the pitch dead center. Her body knew the piece so well that her mind had space to drift, to watch.

She watched the balcony, the exits, the backstage door where a faint sliver of light indicated movement in the wings.

She watched Tanaka. At first, he remained at his post with his hands clasped loosely, gaze sweeping the audience with almost bored professionalism. Then, halfway through the slow movement, he lifted a hand to his ear and his lips moved as his chin dipped to his mic. He stepped away from the aisle and disappeared into the rear of the hall.

Her fingers didn't falter, but her pulse changed tempo.

Intermission, she had told Volkov. Offstage. Back corridors. *But what if the danger is onstage?*

For the rest of the piece, she split herself in two. The musician half surrendered to the music; the assassin half counted exits, routes, timing.

The last movement ended on a shimmer of sound. The final note hung, then died, and the audience erupted. People stood. Shouts of "bravo" cut through the applause.

She rose, bowed, smiled.

The lights were bright. The stage felt suddenly too exposed. She left the stage with the rest of the orchestra, stepping into the relative darkness of the wings. The noise of the hall became muffled, like a storm heard from underwater.

Lena grabbed her arm. "Oh my God, Celeste. You just made three first violins cry."

"You're exaggerating," Celeste said.

"Am I?" Lena gestured back toward the stage. "We're all wiping their eyes. It's like a funeral for composure."

Someone laughed too loudly. People always joked more when they were moved and didn't know what to do with it.

Aya appeared, beaming. "Exquisite," she said. "Truly. Press requests are already coming in. The audience is going crazy."

"Please tell them no until after the concert," Celeste said. "I still have to play the concerto."

"Of course," Aya said. "You have fifteen minutes before the second half. Do you need anything?"

Celeste wanted to say, *Yes. I need a blueprint for a shadow organization and a list of everyone who wants me dead.* Instead, she said, "Water would be great."

Aya nodded and hurried off.

Lena slipped away to flirt with the second clarinetist, leaving Celeste alone near the instrument cases. She set her cello down and took a slow breath.

Footsteps approached on her right. They were soft, measured.

She spun.

"Easy," Volkov murmured, fading out of the shadow of a support pillar. He wore a plain black suit, no tie, his hair slightly damp as if from the snow. His presence blended with the backstage chaos so well that for a second, she wasn't sure if he was actually there or something her mind had conjured.

"You shouldn't be back here," she said.

"Neither should half these people," he replied. "They'll assume I'm with one of the sponsors."

"Did you follow Tanaka?" she asked.

"Yes," he said. "He met someone at the loading dock. Tall, Western, expensive coat. Didn't get close enough for a clear face. They exchanged something. A drive, most likely, from what I could tell. Then Tanaka came back inside."

"Is that all?"

"Not quite." Volkov glanced toward the hall. "There's a secondary security team here. Not Japanese, not local. Their stance is wrong. Too many ex-military habits."

"Agency?" she asked.

"Maybe. Maybe not," he said. "Could be Eidolon contractors."

"They like outsourcing." Her fingers twitched.

He studied her carefully. "You're playing beautifully."

"Now is not the time for flattery."

"It's not flattery," he said. "It's an observation. It means your hands are steady. Your head… maybe not."

"My head is fine."

"You told me backstage in New York that if you kept playing, you might feel something you couldn't control."

"And?" she asked.

"And you're about to play the most exposed piece of the night," he said. "If they hit you during the concerto, they won't just be aiming for your body. They'll be aiming for your mind."

She swallowed. "Good thing they don't know how many layers that has."

A stagehand walked by, glancing at them briefly before moving on. To him, they were just two people having an intermission conversation.

Volkov lowered his voice. "If something goes wrong, what's your exit?"

"There's a service door off stage right," she whispered. "Leads to a stairwell, then a side alley. The orchestra will bottleneck in the main corridor. If I move fast, I can be outside before anyone notices I'm not with them."

"I'll be in the balcony," Volkov said. "Left side. If I see anything, I'll signal."

"And what will that look like?" she asked.

"You'll know," he said.

She hated that she believed him.

Aya returned with a bottle of water and a small towel. "Five minutes," she said cheerfully. "They're still buzzing."

Celeste took the water, unscrewed the cap, and drank. The coolness slid down her throat, anchoring her for a moment.

"Break a leg," Volkov murmured.

She gave him a look. "In my line of work, we don't use that phrase."

"You'll be fine," he said. He stepped back into the shadows and was gone.

She wasn't sure if he'd ever really been there.

The call for places came. Musicians filed back into the wings, adjusting jackets and dresses, telling half-hearted jokes. The conductor strode past, offering Celeste a nod and a quiet, "Ready?"

"Yes," she said. This was the one place she still told the truth easily.

They took the stage again. The applause rose, then settled into expectant hush.

The contemporary concerto was written to begin with the cello alone: a whisper of sound emerging from silence, no orchestral cushion. Celeste lifted her bow. The first note was barely more than a breath. It hovered on the edge of audibility, thin and almost fragile. Then she drew more weight into it, the sound swelling, stretching, pulling the hall into focus.

The piece built in sharp, asymmetrical phrases with bursts of notes, then sudden emptiness, like someone talking in fragments between heartbeats. It demanded risk. It punished hesitation.

She leaned into it, and her world narrowed to the arc of her bow and the distances between her fingers. The orchestra joined in, first as dissonant accents, then as a rolling tide beneath her, pushing and pulling the melody in unexpected directions.

She forgot about Tanaka. She forgot about Harriman, Marcus, her mother, Eidolon. For a few measures, there was only intention and response, tension and release.

Then, in one of the quieter passages, she saw movement in the balcony.

Left side.

A man stood up mid-row, jostling others. People frowned. The usher moved toward him, whispering. He ignored her. His hand dipped into his jacket.

Volkov rose three seats away, hand already moving.

Celeste's bow hit the wrong string for the first time in years, and the dissonant scrape slashed through the hall.

She caught herself instantly, folding the mistake into the next gesture, turning it into an intentional, jagged accent. Most listeners wouldn't notice. Musicians would raise an eyebrow and call it interpretive choice.

Her heart pounded.

The man pulled something out of his jacket. Small. Black. Rectangular.

A device. Not a gun. Too flat for that. A jammer? A trigger?

Volkov moved toward him, fast.

The house lights flickered.

The sound system crackled.

Her ears popped, as if a pressure wave had rolled through the hall.

Suddenly, the orchestra's sound blurred in her monitoring earpiece, warping at the edges. The acoustics shifted. The hall felt… wrong. As if the room itself had changed shape.

The conductor's baton faltered for a fraction of a second, then drove forward with more force.

The device in the man's hand blinked once, then went dark. Volkov seized his wrist, twisted, and the device clattered to the floor.

Two "patrons" near the back row stood simultaneously, hands going to their belts.

Volkov dropped, pulling the first man with him, using his body as a shield.

A moment later, nothing visible happened. No gunshots. No obvious attack. But Celeste felt it—a rip in the air, a tension that hadn't been there before.

Tanaka was suddenly at the rear aisle, moving faster than a hall security officer should. He spoke into his earpiece, eyes scanning.

Celeste kept playing. She poured the spike of adrenaline into the next passage, turning fear into ferocity. The piece called for aggression; she delivered it like a threat.

She played knowing someone had just tried something in her presence. She played knowing Volkov was three seconds from death or killing or both. She played because stopping would cause more questions, more panic, more eyes on the wrong things.

The concerto hit its most violent section: strings slashing, brass blaring, percussion hammering like a migraine. Her bow arm felt like fire. The bruised ribs screamed.

She rode it.

In the balcony, ushers ushered, security clustered, whispers broke out. But no one rushed the stage. No one pointed a weapon at her. Whatever the device had been meant to do, it had failed or misfired, and now Eidolon would be recalculating.

The piece ended not with a triumphant shout but with a strangled, unresolved chord that hung in the air and then dropped away, leaving a raw silence.

For a breath, no one clapped. Then the hall erupted. People shot to their feet. Shouts, whistles, applause that felt like a physical force hit the stage. The conductor signaled for her to stand.

Celeste rose slowly, bow in her hand, cello resting against her hip. She bowed.

She was vaguely aware that her vision was narrowed, as if she were looking through a lens that cut off the edges. Her heart pounded in her ears. Her hands shook.

She masked it in another bow. Then she left the stage.

Backstage, the sound of applause became a muffled roar.

Lena caught her as soon as she cleared the curtain. "What happened?"

"What do you mean?"

"You did something weird in the middle." Lena's eyes were wide. "It was amazing. Terrifying, but amazing. I thought Maestro was going to swallow his baton."

"New interpretation," Celeste said.

"Right," Lena said. "Your fans are going to lose their minds."

Aya ran up, phone in hand. "Are you okay?" she asked.

"Yes," Celeste said.

"There was some… disturbance in the balcony," Aya said. "Security handled it. Some kind of equipment failure or medical episode, they're not sure yet. But the audience barely noticed."

"Good," Celeste said.

"The reviews are going to be insane," Aya said breathlessly. "That last movement, I thought the hall might explode."

Celeste almost laughed at that. "Excuse me," she said. "I need a minute." She slipped down the side corridor before anyone else could intercept her.

Volkov was waiting at the far end, near the service door, his suit jacket slightly askew, a faint red mark blooming along his jaw where someone's fist had connected. He raised an eyebrow. "Nice improvisation."

"You tackled a man in the balcony," she said. "That wasn't exactly subtle."

"No one saw me," he said. "They saw commotion. They'll fill in their own story."

"What was the device?" she asked.

"A kind of acoustic jammer," he said. "Would've blown the hall's sound field, disrupted communications, maybe triggered a panic. And it was broadcasting before I shut it down."

"To where?" she asked.

"Good question," he said.

She exhaled. "Tanaka?"

"Acted surprised," Volkov said. "Too surprised."

"Meaning?"

"Meaning if he's Eidolon, he's not low-level. He didn't expect this particular move."

"So, whose move was it?" Celeste asked.

Volkov's gaze held hers. "The new conductor."

"You think there's someone above Harriman?" she asked.

"There was always someone above Harriman," Volkov said. "He was a manager. Not a visionary."

She felt suddenly cold, despite the heat from the stage lights still clinging to her skin. "Wonderful. So, we just decapitated the middle."

"Think of it as warming up," Volkov suggested.

She frowned. "How did you get up there so fast?"

He shrugged. "I picked a good seat."

Her eyes flicked to the reddening mark on his jaw. "How many did you take down?"

"Two and a half," he said.

"Half?"

"One tripped on his ego and did my job for me."

She almost smiled. The knot in her chest loosened half a fraction.

"Did they see your face?" she asked.

"One of them might have," he said. "But I made sure he was unconscious before he could appreciate it."

"We can't keep playing whack-a-mole in every city," she whispered. "This was testing. Next time, they'll escalate."

"I know," he said.

She leaned back against the wall, feeling her heartbeat begin to slow. "They wanted to see how I'd react onstage."

"They saw," he said. "You didn't break."

"Inside, I did," she said.

He stepped closer. Not touching. Just near. "Good. It means you're not a machine."

"Eidolon would disagree," she said.

He studied her face, searching. "What do you want to do?"

"Keep playing," she said. "Then leave Tokyo. Barcelona is next."

"You really want to stay with the orchestra?" he asked.

"Yes," she said. "The itinerary is the only thing about my life that still makes sense on paper. And if Eidolon thinks they can rattle me off this tour, they're wrong."

He nodded slowly. "Then I'll meet you in Barcelona."

"You'll follow Tanaka?"

"And anyone else who moves when he does," Volkov said. "They lit their first flare here. I want to see who gathers around it."

She straightened, pushing away from the wall. "When you said you'd see me in Tokyo, you asked if I was scared."

"I did," he said.

"I still am," she said. "But not of them. Not exactly."

"Then what?" he asked.

"Of what I'll do to them when I finally stop holding back."

Something dangerous flickered in his eyes. "I'm looking forward to it." There was a hint of warmth in his tone that had nothing to do with violence.

It rattled her more than the device, more than Tanaka, more than the nearly-ruined concert. "Don't," she said.

"Don't what?" he asked.

"Don't make this about anything but survival," she said.

He held her gaze. "We're past just survival, Celeste."

She shook her head. "Not yet. Not while they still think they're writing the score." She turned toward the stairwell, where the noise of the dispersing audience filtered faintly through the walls.

"Celeste," he said.

She paused.

"You were magnificent," he said. "As a musician. Not as a weapon. Don't lose that."

For a moment, she wanted to lean into the words, to let them sink into the part of her that still believed in beauty for its own sake.

Instead, she said, "I'll text you flight details." Then she walked away, back toward the dressing rooms, back toward the version of herself the world expected to see.

Behind her, in the quiet corridor near the service door, Volkov stayed where he was for a long time, listening to the applause fading overhead, the tick of cooling lights, and the soft echo of notes that weren't his but had somehow lodged themselves under his skin.

Outside, Tokyo glittered, oblivious.

Inside, the next city waited on the itinerary: Barcelona. Another hall. Another stage. Another opportunity for Eidolon to test their creation.

And for Celeste to start testing them back.

Chapter 4

Ghost Notes in Barcelona

THE MEDITERRANEAN LIGHT was wrong for her mood.

Barcelona glowed in late afternoon with warm, honeyed sun sliding over terracotta roofs and wrought-iron balconies, over laundry strung between buildings and graffiti that looked more like declarations than vandalism. The air smelled like salt, diesel, coffee, and something sweet from a nearby bakery.

It should have felt like a holiday. It felt like a stage set.

Celeste stepped out of El Prat's arrivals into the brightness, blinking. A soft breeze tugged at her hair, carrying snippets of Catalan and Spanish conversation. Taxi drivers held signs, tourists clustered with rolling suitcases, locals moved with the relaxed impatience of people who lived in a beautiful city and needed to get on with their day.

Her cello case was a familiar weight across her back. A new bruise had bloomed along her shoulder from the way she'd gripped it during the Tokyo incident, a little souvenir from the night someone tried to fracture reality with a device in a concert hall.

She moved through the crowd with the unconscious alertness that had become muscle memory: cataloguing angles, scanning hands and eyes and posture. No one paid her more attention than she paid them. That meant either she was safe or they were better at this than she was. She didn't like either possibility.

The orchestra's Spanish liaison, who was short, efficient, wearing a blazer the color of Rioja, met her near the doors. "Señorita Morgan?" the woman asked in lightly accented English.

"Yes."

"I'm Teresa. Welcome. The others arrive from Tokyo tonight. You are… avant-garde." Teresa smiled.

"My itinerary got changed," Celeste said. "Jet lag roulette."

Teresa laughed. "Barcelona is good for jet lag. Sun, wine, good coffee, bad decisions. You will see."

"I'll stick with coffee," Celeste said.

"We all lie to ourselves," Teresa enthused. "Come, the car is this way. You're at a hotel near Plaça de Catalunya, very central. Rehearsal at Palau de la Música Catalana tomorrow morning."

The name sent a small thrill through Celeste despite everything. She'd always wanted to play the Palau, a jewel box of stained glass and carved stone, a place where music and architecture blurred. The first time she'd seen photos of it she'd thought, this hall understands excess.

She followed Teresa to a waiting black car. The driver loaded her cello gently. They drove through the city, past palm trees and apartment blocks, past a sudden glimpse of the sea glittering between buildings, past a Gaudí façade that looked like a melted cathedral.

"First time in Barcelona?" Teresa asked.

"Second," Celeste said.

"Ah. So, you know to keep one hand on your bag and one on your heart," Teresa said. "The city might steal either."

"You make a good case for staying indoors," Celeste said.

"That would be a waste," Teresa replied. "Besides, indoors is where the dangerous people are. Out here, it's just thieves."

Celeste smiled faintly. "I'll keep that in mind."

Her phone vibrated. A message on the encrypted app flashed briefly before auto-deleting. **Landed earlier. Watching from the cheap seats. –V**

She didn't look around for him. If Volkov wanted to be seen, he'd appear. If he didn't, she'd only waste energy searching shadows.

The hotel was, as promised, near Plaça de Catalunya: tall ceilings, old tile floors, heavy wooden doors. The elevator was the creaky cage kind that seemed cosmetically updated but mechanically ancient. The room was small but bright, a balcony overlooking a narrow street where people leaned out of windows and scooters whined past.

She put her cello on the bed and stepped out onto the balcony.

Below, a man in his sixties watered plants on his own balcony, humming. A group of students passed, laughing, backpacks bouncing. Somewhere nearby, a radio played a flamenco-inflected pop song. Laundry fluttered on a line like Tibetan prayer flags.

For a moment—just a thin sliver of one—she felt an ache for a life that might have been hers: small, ordinary, defined by practice schedules and neighbors and arguments over trash collection.

It lasted three heartbeats.

Then she saw the black motorcycle idling at the corner. The rider wore a helmet with the visor down, all in black. Hands relaxed on the handlebars. The bike pointed the wrong way for traffic. Just waiting.

Her muscles tightened. She went back inside, closing the balcony doors.

Her phone buzzed again. **Don't panic. That one's ours. —V**

She exhaled, halfway between annoyance and relief.

She typed back: **You're enjoying this too much.**

His reply came quickly. **Not even a little. But I'm not letting you walk around this city alone.**

We're in the same hotel? She asked and then she watched the three dots blink, vanish, return.

No. Across the street. Third floor. Nice curtains.

She glanced at the building opposite. Neutral blinds. No sign of him.

She set the phone down and unpacked.

This was how her life worked now: half musician, half fugitive, entirely surrounded by people who either wanted to use her, kill her, or keep her breathing long enough to finish some unspeakable plan.

She loosened her bow hair, checked the instrument again, cleaned resin dust from the bridge. The mostly mundane ritual grounded her. It was something her mother had taught her, long before the words Eidolon or asset meant anything. *Always take care of the instrument first. People will tell you that you are the instrument, but they're wrong. You hold the bow. Remember that.*

She ran her thumb along the bow's ebony frog and thought, I'm trying.

The next morning, the Palau de la Música Catalana was more impossible in person than in photographs. From the outside, it looked like a building that had gotten drunk on its own reflection: columns of mosaic, sculpted figures bursting from brick and stone, wrought-iron and stained glass everywhere your eye could land.

Inside, it was even more absurd. The concert hall was a riot of color. Stained glass dripped from the ceiling in the form of an inverted dome, like a sun trying to fall into the room. Every surface was carved or painted or tiled. The stage was framed by muses and horses and busts. It was as if someone had tried to carve music into architecture and never stopped.

Celeste stood in the center of the stage during a lull in rehearsal setup and turned slowly, taking it in.

"If Austrians built concert halls with this much personality," Lena said beside her, "we'd never leave."

"You're assuming you'd survive the visual overstimulation," Celeste said.

"I'd die happy," Lena said. "Look at that ceiling. It's like God hired Gaudí as his interior designer."

Celeste's lips quirked. "Blasphemy before rehearsal. Bold move."

"The day I stop blaspheming is the day you've been body-snatched," Lena said.

Teresa appeared in the aisle, waving a clipboard. "We're starting in ten minutes! Please, everyone, if you're not tuning, pretend you are."

The orchestra filtered onto the stage: brass players blowing warm air into their instruments, woodwinds chirping scales, violins fussing over string tension. The conductor strode in, clapped his hands, and brought order to the chaos.

Celeste sat, cello between her knees, bow poised. The first note she played blended with the hall in a way that felt almost obscene, as if the building itself were an instrument, responding. She focused, letting the space teach her its timing. Between notes, her eyes traveled.

Exit doors. Upper balconies. Sight lines. On the highest balcony, to the left of the stained-glass sunburst, someone sat alone in the front row, elbow resting on the velvet railing, head tilted.

Volkov. He inclined his chin a fraction when their eyes met.

She shifted her gaze before anyone else followed it.

The rehearsal ran in long, exhausting stretches: Spanish repertoire this time—Falla, Granados, Albéniz arranged for orchestra. The conductor fussed over idiomatic phrasing, insisting on color and rhythm, on "sun in the sound."

Celeste gave him sun, but internally, she felt more like storm.

At the first break, she slipped offstage, into the warren of corridors that tunneled through the building. The backstage area of the Palau was smaller than most halls. Stone walls, narrow passages, a lingering smell of old wood and dust. It felt like walking inside the skeleton of something ancient.

She found Volkov leaning against a wall in a side hallway, hands in his pockets, blending as well as a tall, scarred man who radiated threat could. "How are the acoustics?" he asked.

"Ridiculous," she said. "If I breathe too loudly, the room writes it down."

"Careful," he said. "You're starting to sound like a romantic."

She rolled her eyes. "What did you find?"

"Eidolon's shell company in Barcelona is called Fundación Orfeó," he said. "Officially, they support young musicians. Scholarships, rehearsal spaces, mentorship."

"Of course, they do," she said. "Corrupt power loves philanthropy."

"On paper, they're saints," he said. "In reality, they launder money and talent. The foundation has sponsored three players in your orchestra's recent auditions."

A chill slid down her spine. "Who?"

"Two violists and a percussionist," he said. "All turned down in the final round. But they were in the building. They had access. They learned things."

"So, they're recruiting near the orchestra," she said.

"It would be stupid of them not to," he replied.

Her fingers tightened on her bow. "Any of them in the city now?"

"One," Volkov said. "The percussionist. A woman named Aria Kovalenko."

The name hit her like a punch. She leaned back against the opposite wall, the breath gone from her lungs for a second. "Aria is here?"

Volkov's attention sharpened. "You know her."

"We trained together," Celeste said.

Memories surfaced uninvited: a training range in an anonymous facility; the humidity of a concrete hallway; a young woman with dark hair and laughing eyes lying on her stomach, rifle steady, hitting target after target.

Aria had been good. Almost frighteningly so.

"She disappeared after one mission," Celeste said. "I assumed she was dead. Or retired."

"No one retires from Eidolon," Volkov said.

"Then she's working for them," Celeste said.

"Or rebelling," he said.

"You don't know her," Celeste said. "Aria loves a cause. They probably gave her one."

"Either way, she's here," Volkov said. "She played in a small percussion ensemble last week. I got a photo from a contact." He pulled out his phone and showed her.

Aria looked older, sharper. Her hair was shorter, cut to her jaw, streaked with blonde at the ends. Her expression in the candid shot was focused, alert, amused by something off-frame.

Celeste's throat felt tight. "She was always better at feeling things than at hiding them."

"She's dangerous," Volkov said. "Anyone who trained with you is."

"She may not know I'm the target," Celeste said. "She might think she's saving me."

"Do you believe that?" he asked.

She shook her head slowly. "No."

"Then assume she'll strike," he said.

"In the hall?" she asked.

"Or outside it," he said.

Footsteps echoed in the corridor. They shifted just enough to look like colleagues in conversation.

Lena appeared around the corner, then halted. "Oh," she said. "Sorry, I didn't mean to interrupt your… secret meeting." Her eyes flicked between them, curiosity flaring.

"Not secret," Celeste said smoothly. "Volkov's with one of the sponsors."

Lena raised an eyebrow. "Is he sponsoring emotional trauma or string sections?"

"Security consulting," Volkov said easily, his accent softened. "Hall asked me to review their procedures."

"Ooh." Lena grinned. "Are we safe?"

"Not from each other," he said.

She laughed. "Good. It would be a shame if we were." She jerked her head back toward the stage. "Maestro's calling us. Ten more rounds of arguing about tempo." She looked at Celeste more closely. "You okay?"

"Just stretching my legs," Celeste said.

"Your legs look stretched," Lena said. "Don't disappear at lunch. I found a place around the corner that sells churros so good they're probably illegal."

"I'll try," Celeste said.

"Try harder than that," Lena said, then vanished back toward the stage.

Volkov waited until her footsteps faded. "She likes you," he said.

"She likes everyone," Celeste said. "It's her fatal flaw."

"It may become yours." He breathed the words.

"That sounds like a threat," she said.

"It's a warning," he replied. "Eidolon hunts in concentric circles. They rarely kill the center first."

"Use the people around you to pressure you."

"Or to punish you," he said.

She clenched her jaw. "I won't let that happen."

"You may not get a vote," he said.

She met his gaze. "Then we make sure they never get close enough to try."

After rehearsal, the orchestra scattered into the city like marbles dropped on a map. Small groups went in search of tapas, wine, and sunshine. Someone mentioned the beach. Someone else mentioned a nap.

Celeste begged off again with a quiet excuse about fatigue. Lena threatened to stage an intervention if she didn't "start acting like a human being" soon.

"If I start acting like a human being," Celeste said, "you'll regret it."

"You can't scare me," Lena said. "I grew up with four brothers."

"Then you're already damaged," Celeste said.

"Exactly," Lena said cheerfully, and disappeared into a crowd of violinists.

Celeste walked alone toward the older part of the city, letting the streets narrow and twist beneath her feet. The Gothic Quarter wrapped around her in stone and shadow. Sinuous alleys opened onto small plazas where children played and old men argued on benches.

She felt oddly more at ease here than she had in the gleaming predictability of Tokyo. Chaos made sense. Straight lines didn't.

Her phone buzzed. **Left at the next corner. −V**

She followed the instruction, turning into a narrower street. Laundry overhead, the distant smell of grilled fish, the echo of a busker's guitar.

He stepped out from a doorway a moment later, merging with her stride as if they'd done this a thousand times. "Aria's been here for at least three days," he said without preamble. "Checked into a hostel near the university under a false name. Print records match. She's not exactly hiding."

"She wants to be seen," Celeste said.

"Or she thinks she's invisible," he said. "Fanatics often do."

They walked past a small church whose door stood open, candles flickering in the dim interior. "You're sure she's on assignment?" she asked.

"She met with someone last night at a bar near the port," he said. "Older man. Military posture. They parted without shaking hands."

"Details?" she asked.

"Too dark. Too crowded." He gave a small shrug. "I'll find him."

"And tonight?" she asked.

"Tonight, she has a small percussion recital at a conservatory hall," he said. "Public. Ten euros at the door. I bought us tickets."

"You're taking me to a concert?" she asked.

"It's called reconnaissance," he said. "Don't get sentimental."

The conservatory hall was modest compared to the Palau, but it had good bones: wooden seats, decent acoustics, a stage framed by plain curtains. The audience was mostly students and teachers, with a handful of older patrons sitting with the air of people who donated more money than time.

Celeste sat in the middle rows with Volkov on the aisle.

When Aria walked onstage, the past punched her. Same posture. Same way of scanning the room once and then pretending she hadn't. Her hair was shorter, yes, and there were new lines at the corners of her mouth, but the core was the same: coiled energy, precise focus, and that unnerving combination of warmth and calculation.

She played a solo marimba piece that sounded like rain turned into arithmetic. Every note was placed exactly where it needed to be, but there was something feral in the phrasing, a wildness barely contained.

Celeste listened with her hands folded in her lap, fingers pressing into her palm hard enough to leave crescent marks.

"What do you hear?" Volkov murmured.

"Control," Celeste said softly. "And anger."

"At whom?"

"Hard to say," she said. "Maybe everyone."

When the recital ended, Aria bowed, smiled, and left the stage.

"Now?" Volkov asked.

"Now," Celeste said.

They moved quickly but not hurriedly, out into the lobby where students clustered, praising or critiquing performances. Aria stood near a column, laughing with a young man holding a snare drum case. Up close, the changes in her were more obvious: her eyes were harder, her smile shorter, the aura around her edged with something cold.

Celeste approached until she was a few feet away. "Nice rhythmic precision," she said in Russian.

Aria froze. Then she turned slowly. For a heartbeat, her expression was blank. Then recognition hit. Her eyes widened. "Celeste," she said.

The sound of her name in Aria's voice dragged the years away for a second. Celeste remembered shared cigarettes on training breaks, whispered jokes, a hand on her shoulder when she'd missed a shot for the first time. "Hello, Aria," she said.

The young man with the drum case looked between them. "You know each other?"

Aria's smile returned, but it was brittle now. "We trained together. A lifetime ago." She switched to English. "You're famous now. The killer cellist, yes?"

"That's one way of putting it," Celeste said.

"You were always the favorite," Aria said lightly. "Even when we were just sweating and bleeding in the same concrete box."

"Some of us still are," Celeste said.

Aria's gaze flicked to Volkov, assessing. "And you are…?"

"Bored," Volkov said. "And trying to stay that way."

Aria laughed once, sharp. "You pick interesting company, Celeste."

"So do you," Celeste said. "Barcelona's a long way from home."

"Home," Aria repeated, tasting the word. "That's cute." She dismissed the young man with a touch to his arm. "I'll find you later, Luca."

He nodded and retreated, like he sensed something above his pay grade.

Aria turned fully to Celeste. "So. To what do I owe this nostalgic reunion?"

"You know why I'm here," Celeste said.

"Concert at the Palau," Aria said. "Big career moment. I saw the posters." Her smile turned sly. "Don't worry. I bought a ticket."

"That's not what I meant," Celeste said.

"I know." Aria's eyes cooled. "You're here because they pointed you here. Just like they point you everywhere."

"They are the reason my mother is dead," Celeste said. "And the reason yours is probably scared."

"My mother's proud," Aria said sharply. "Her daughter is changing the world."

"By killing for Eidolon?" Celeste asked.

Aria arched a brow. "We never called it that when we begged them for assignments."

"I begged them for purpose," Celeste said. "Not ownership."

"And did you get what you wanted?" Aria asked.

No, Celeste thought. "Yes," she said.

Aria's mouth curved. "Liar."

They stood there, in the middle of a small conservatory lobby, the noise of ordinary people swirling around them, and it felt like an old training ground again with two operatives circling, no weapons visible, all of them drawn.

"Why are you in Barcelona?" Celeste asked.

"Why are you?" Aria countered.

"Because the orchestra is touring," Celeste said. "Because I still have a life that isn't theirs."

"Is that what we're calling it?" Aria asked. "A life?"

Celeste's temper flickered. "You don't get to stand there and act like you're the one who broke free, Aria. You're still theirs. You just like the leash."

"Leash?" Aria's eyes flashed. "You think you're off it?"

"I cut Harriman's throat," Celeste said. "Their middle man is dead."

Aria's expression didn't change. For a second, Celeste wondered if maybe she didn't know. Then Aria smiled slowly. "Yes," she said. "That was… messy."

"You knew," Celeste said.

"Of course, I knew," Aria replied. "We get memos about these things. 'Asset X eliminated Node Y, proceed with caution.' It's very corporate."

"You're all right with that?" Celeste asked. "You're all right with being in their newsletter?"

"I'm not in their newsletter," Aria said. "I'm at the strategy table."

The words landed like a slap. "You're what?" Celeste asked.

"You think they only wanted you?" Aria said. "You think your mother built all of this just for you?"

Celeste's heart stuttered. "What did you say?"

Aria's smile widened. "They never told you, did they? Of course, they didn't. Poor Celeste. Always shielded." She leaned in slightly. "We're not your competition, *celistka*. We're your cohort."

"Meaning?" Volkov cut in, voice flat.

Aria glanced at him, amused. "Meaning there are more of us. Trained, shaped, tuned. Different specialties. Different cities. Same origin."

"You're lying," Celeste whispered.

"Ask your mother," Aria said.

"She's dead," Celeste said.

"And yet she left so many little legacies walking around," Aria replied. "You killed Harriman. That shakes the tree. But the roots are still strong. Some of us like the fruit."

The lobby noise seemed to recede into a dull roar.

"How many?" Celeste asked.

Aria tilted her head. "Enough to replace you if you break."

There it was, naked.

"You're here to test me," Celeste said. "Like Tokyo."

"Tokyo was amateur hour," Aria said. "Barcelona is midterm exams."

"You going to be grading me from the balcony?" Celeste asked.

"I prefer closer seats," Aria said. "I like seeing the strain in the hands."

"You don't have to do this," Celeste said softly. "You could walk away."

Aria laughed with no humor. "Walk where? Into some soft, civilian life where I pretend the things I did don't follow me into every grocery store? No. I know what I am. That's the difference between us."

"What am I?" Celeste asked.

"Confused. Lonely. Dangerous. Useful." She stepped back, her expression turning crisp. "See you at the Palau, *celistka*. Try not to disappoint." She turned and walked toward the doors, disappearing into the flow of students leaving, her posture casual, her purpose anything but.

Volkov watched her go, jaw tight. "I don't like her."

"You shouldn't," Celeste said.

"She rattled you," he said.

"She told me there are others like me," Celeste said. "Of course, I'm rattled."

His voice softened. "Does it matter?"

"Yes," she said. "If there are more, Eidolon doesn't just want to use me. They want to compare me."

"And?"

"And I don't intend to be measurable," she said.

He studied her profile. "What are you going to do?"

She looked down at her hands, fingers that had killed and played and held too much. "I'm going to perform at the Palau. I'm going to let her watch. And then I'm going to show her what happens when you try to turn me into a test subject."

A slow, dark smile ghosted the corner of his mouth. "Now that's a concert I'd pay to see."

"You already have tickets," she said.

"I was hoping for backstage access," he replied.

She gave him a look that was half warning, half something else. "We'll see if you survive the balcony again first."

They walked out of the hall together into the gathering dusk. The sky over Barcelona was streaked pink and gold, buildings outlined in warm shadow.

Somewhere in the city, Aria was preparing her own performance.

At the Palau, a sun of stained glass waited overhead.

And in Celeste's chest, something sharp and new began to tune itself: Not just anger. Not just grief. Something like rivalry. Something like defiance. Something like resolve so strong it felt almost like joy.

The next movement would not be subtle.

Chapter 5

The Test

ON THE NIGHT of the Palau concert, Barcelona felt like it was holding its breath.

The streets outside the hall were slick with recent rain, cobblestones reflecting the glow of streetlights and the kaleidoscopic façade of the building. People clustered under umbrellas, talking, laughing, posing for photos with the Palau rising behind them like a fever dream carved in stone and glass.

Celeste stepped out of the car into the soft, damp air, her black gown sweeping the ground, the cello case a familiar weight across her back. A low murmur of recognition rippled through the waiting crowd as some audience members spotted her.

"Es ella."

"Celeste Morgan."

"She's incredible, you'll see——"

She kept her expression neutral, the same faint, distant half-smile she used for fans and donors and anyone else who loved the version of her that existed only in recordings and carefully curated interviews. Inside, the lobby was a bright whirl of colors and sound: jewel-toned dresses, dark suits, the clink of glasses from the bar, the rustle of programs. The mosaic walls and carved columns made everything feel like it was happening inside a cathedral designed by someone who'd never heard of restraint.

"Ms. Morgan." Teresa materialized at her elbow, clipboard in hand. "You look stunning. Reviews from Tokyo have arrived, by the way. Hysterically enthusiastic. You're the 'soul-shredder of the century.'"

"That sounds unsanitary," Celeste joked.

Teresa laughed. "There is also a rumor you had a small… episode… middle of the piece. People are calling it 'the Tokyo fracture.'"

"That was an acoustic malfunction. Someone mishandled the sound tech."

"Of course," Teresa said with a conspiratorial wink. "Geniuses fracture reality. It sells tickets." She gestured toward a staff-only corridor. "Dressing room's ready. Maestro is already pacing."

"Is he ever not?" Celeste muttered.

As Teresa guided her away from the lobby, Celeste glanced up at the balconies ringing the hall. On the highest one, in the shadow of the stained-glass sunburst, a figure leaned against the railing. Too far to identify clearly, but the tilt of the head was unmistakable.

Aria.

Their gazes caught for half a heartbeat, even at that distance. Aria lifted two fingers to her temple in a lazy half-salute.

Celeste looked away.

The soloist's dressing room at the Palau was small but ornate with ceramic tiles, an old wooden dressing table with a big mirror framed in dark wood, a vase of white flowers on the side. Someone had left a plate of fruit and a carafe of water.

She set her cello case down and opened it carefully, checking the instrument. No cracks, no new scratches, strings still where she left them. She ran a clean cloth over the wood anyway, more as ritual than necessity.

Her phone vibrated. **Third balcony. Rear column, stage left. Aria's people. –V**

Another message followed a second later. **Two exits at the back blocked. Saw men checking them "for safety." It's not safety.**

She typed with her thumb, fast. **Tanaka**?

Response: **Not here. Either he backed off or they moved him to another city. Means whoever's running this wants their own team.**

Her reflection in the mirror looked calm. Her stomach felt like it was tightening around a fist. She set the phone down and picked up her bow. Her hand was steady. Good.

A knock at the door.

"Come in."

The conductor poked his head in, tux immaculate, white hair more disheveled than usual. "There she is," he said. "Our star. Ready to make Spain cry?"

"Spain seems resilient," Celeste said.

"Not when you play like you do," he replied. His smile softened. "You look tired."

"That's an occupational hazard."

"Music or travel?" he asked.

"Yes," she said.

He chuckled. "Don't overthink it. Open your heart. The hall will take care of the rest."

Men always said things like that—open your heart—as if they hadn't spent years encouraging her to weaponize her control instead.

"I'll do my best," she said.

When he left, she adjusted the bodice of her dress, checked the pins in her hair, and forced herself to take three slow, full breaths.

Fear means you still want to live, Volkov had said.

She wanted to live. She also wanted to stop running. Maybe tonight would decide which one she got.

A stagehand's voice came from the corridor. "Ten minutes, Ms. Morgan."

She lifted the cello, felt its familiar weight settle against her, and stepped into the hallway.

Backstage, the Palau was cramped but buzzing. Musicians in black milled around in narrow corridors. Stagehands squeezed past with hurried apologies. Someone tuned a horn in a corner; somewhere else, a bassoon played a fragment of something that sounded like a question.

Lena appeared beside her, breathless, cheeks flushed. "I thought you were going to hide again."

"Not tonight," Celeste said.

"Good," Lena said. "I refuse to witness greatness without a pre-show snark exchange." She eyed Celeste's face critically. "You look like you're about to walk into a battle or a marriage."

"Those are similar things," Celeste smirked.

"Depends on the spouse," Lena said. "Break everyone's heart out there, okay?"

"I'll try not to kill anyone," Celeste murmured.

"What?" Lena asked.

"Nothing," Celeste said.

They were called to places. The orchestra filed onstage. Applause rose, warm and immediate. Celeste stayed in the wings during the opening piece, listening, her body swaying almost imperceptibly in time with the music she knew by heart.

She scanned the audience sidelong. Third balcony, left she found Aria, seated near the aisle, leaning forward on her elbows, eyes fixed on the stage even when she had no reason to be watching yet. Three men sat spaced out behind her, too still for casual patrons.

Near one of the rear exits, two ushers stood with their hands folded in front of them, their posture just slightly wrong for ushers. Too balanced. Too alert.

She didn't see Volkov.

Good, she told herself again. *That meant he was where he needed to be.*

When it was time for her, she stepped out. The audience's applause folded around her. The hall seemed to inhale with her. She bowed, sat, and adjusted her endpin on the worn wooden stage floor.

The first piece she played in Barcelona was a romantic concerto, lush and melodic, a crowd-pleaser. No sharp edges, nothing like the fractured modern work from Tokyo.

As the orchestra settled into the opening tutti, she let the music wash over her and through her. Her fingers flexed on the fingerboard. The bow balanced perfectly in her hand.

She thought of Aria, watching from above, waiting to see if Celeste would slip. She thought of her mother, designing projects she never told her daughter about. She thought of Marcus, teaching her how to aim not just with her hands but with her whole life.

Then she played. Sound poured out as if it had been waiting for a crack to escape through. She didn't hold back. Every line was shaped with fierce tenderness, every phrase dipped and rose like a tide. She let the hall's extravagant acoustics carry her, riding the resonance instead of fighting it. The orchestra bloomed beneath her, never drowning her, always pushing.

For a little while, she forgot that Aria was watching as an examiner and not just another musician. For a little while, she just was.

At the end of the first movement, she heard it: a gasp, somewhere in the hall. She couldn't tell if it was pain or wonder or both.

The second movement was slower, more exposed. She leaned into the long lines, letting vibrato widen and narrow like breath. The hall was so quiet she could hear a distant cough, the rustle of a program, the soft whir of the ceiling fan.

In the third row, a woman wiped her eyes.

On the third balcony, Aria's face was still and intent.

This is what you can't replicate in a training room, Celeste thought grimly. This fragile, dangerous thing where people give you their hearts for an hour and trust you not to break them too badly.

At the end of the concerto, the applause felt bigger than the hall. People stood. Someone shouted something in Spanish that made others laugh and cheer louder.

She rose, bowed, and accepted the flowers handed to her by a young usher. She smiled the performance smile, but inside, she was already bracing for the second movement of the real evening.

Offstage, in the narrow corridor, the noise muffled.

Lena grabbed her and hugged her roughly, nearly crushing the bouquet. "You homicidal goddess," Lena said into her shoulder, "you're going to ruin music for everyone else."

"Just doing my job," Celeste said.

Teresa appeared, clapping her hands. "We have critics here from Madrid, London, Berlin," she said. "They're all losing their minds. I've already had four texts from people asking if you plan to stay in Europe."

"I have a commitment in Istanbul," Celeste said automatically. "And then New York."

"We'll talk after," Teresa said, eyes gleaming with plans. "Right now, bravo. Really."

She moved on to congratulate others.

Lena squeezed Celeste's hand once, then went back onstage for the final piece.

Celeste slipped away. The service stairwell behind the stage was narrow and lit by harsh fluorescent bulbs. The sounds of the orchestra tuning for the next piece floated faintly up through the walls.

Halfway up the stairs, she heard a footstep behind her. She turned, body shifting without conscious thought into a defensive stance.

Aria stood three steps below, one hand on the rail, expression open and amused. "Careful," Aria said. "You almost broke my nose with that last cadenza."

"How did you get back here?" Celeste asked.

Aria rolled her eyes. "Please. You think I haven't gotten past more complex barriers than a Catalan stagehand?"

Celeste's fingers itched to reach for something that wasn't there. No gun. No knife. Just her own hands and the muscle memory of a thousand training hours.

"You played beautifully," Aria said, "for someone conflicted."

"I'm fine," Celeste said.

"There it is," Aria said lightly. "The lie you tell everyone. Including yourself."

"What do you want?" Celeste asked.

Aria's smile thinned. "To see whether you break the way they're afraid you will."

"Afraid?" Celeste repeated.

"Oh yes," Aria said, "you should hear the way they talk about you. The 'prodigal asset.' The 'unstable composition.' The one thing they built that might grow a conscience and destroy the rest of us."

"Us," Celeste said. "So, you do consider yourself theirs."

"I consider myself aligned with them," Aria said. "Mutual goals. Mutual enemies. It's convenient."

"And what are those goals?" Celeste asked.

"Removing rot," Aria said. "The world is full of it. Governments that pretend to be stable, corporations that pretend to be ethical, people who pretend to be good. We cut out tumors. Someone has to."

"And who decided they were tumors?" Celeste asked.

"The people who built us," Aria said. "Your mother. Harriman. Others. You liked that when it meant killing men like Reznov, didn't you?"

Celeste's jaw hardened. "Reznov sold bioweapons and people. He deserved to die."

"Exactly," Aria said. "And you were happy to be the knife. The only reason you're shaking now is because the blade is looking back at the hand that holds it and asking uncomfortable questions."

"You think you're so certain," Celeste seethed. "You think believing in something makes it pure."

"I think knowing what you are makes you stronger," Aria said. "You're dangerous when you're decisive. You're pathetic when you hesitate."

"I slit Harriman's throat," Celeste said. "Does that sound like hesitation?"

"It sounds like rage," Aria said. "Not conviction."

Celeste took a slow step down, closing the distance between them by one riser. "What are you supposed to do with me tonight?" she asked. "Recruit me? Kill me? Evaluate me?"

Aria looked almost disappointed. "I was hoping you'd guess."

"Humor me," Celeste said.

Aria leaned a shoulder against the wall. "Officially? I am to observe and report. Unofficially? I was curious whether you're still as precise as they say."

"And?" Celeste asked.

"And you didn't miss a single note," Aria said.

"That's not the precision they're talking about," Celeste said.

Aria's eyes glittered. "No. They want to know if you can still execute in the field when you know where you come from. When you know who your mother really was. When you know Marcus wasn't your savior, but your sculptor."

"Why do you think I can't?" Celeste asked.

"Because you're already different," Aria said. "You care about these musicians. About that girl with the curls who keeps orbiting you. About the man in the balcony who keeps pretending he's not always six steps from wherever you are."

Celeste stiffened. "You've been watching him."

"Of course," Aria said. "He's interesting. I like interesting men. They die with better last words."

"You won't touch him," Celeste said, voice dropping.

Aria's smile was slow. "See? There it is. Attachment. You think they won't use that?"

"I think you underestimate what I'll do to stop them," Celeste said.

"And I think you underestimate what you'll do when they make you choose," Aria replied.

"Choose what?"

"Between your orchestra and the world," Aria said. "Between your friends and your purpose. Between the life you pretend to have and the one you were built for."

"I'm not built for anything," Celeste said through her teeth. "I'm not a device you can program."

"You're already programmed," Aria said gently. "You're just refusing to read your own code." She moved up one step, until they were almost eye level. "They're accelerating things," Aria said, her voice lower. "You killed Harriman. It rattled them. They want you evaluated, contained, or corrected. Quickly."

"Corrected," Celeste repeated. "Is that the new euphemism?"

"For some, yes," Aria said. "For you? It might mean something else."

"And what's that?"

"Leadership," Aria said.

The stairwell seemed to constrict around them for a second. "You're lying," Celeste whispered.

Aria shook her head. "I've sat in rooms you never got into. I've read files you didn't even know existed. Your mother didn't build Eidolon just to clean up messes. She built it to create a new structure of control. Harriman was a phase. Marcus was a phase. You are supposed to be the next phase."

"No," Celeste said.

"Denial doesn't change blueprints," Aria said.

"I'm not interested," Celeste said. "Tell them the position is filled."

"They don't ask," Aria said. "They don't recruit. They shape. They apply pressure until you move the way they need."

"Then they don't understand me at all," Celeste said. "I break under pressure. I don't bend."

Aria's smile returned, slight and almost affectionate. "Oh, *celistka*. They are counting on that."

Footsteps echoed faintly below: someone passing through the corridor. Aria stepped back down a stair, already half turning away. "Enjoy your encore," she said. "The audience will demand one. They always do when you bleed like that."

"I didn't bleed," Celeste said.

Aria's gaze dipped briefly to her hands. "Not yet." She disappeared around the bend.

Celeste stayed where she was for a long moment, the hum of the building vibrating through the metal railing under her fingers.

Leadership. The word felt obscene in connection with Eidolon. Her mother's face flashed in her mind again—not the woman in grainy declassified photos, the one in a blazer at conference tables, but the woman at their old kitchen table, laughing over sheet music.

Would you be proud of this? she wondered. Of this thing you built out of whatever you thought justice was?

A soft ping from her phone pulled her back. **In the wing behind stage right. Something's off with the rear exits. Hurry. −V**

She shook the numbness out of her fingers and moved.

Backstage, the orchestra was lining up for the final bow. The last piece, a fiery, rhythmic showpiece, had just ended. The audience was already clapping, chanting something like *"una altra"* for an encore.

She slipped into her place near the wing. Volkov stood just beyond the curtain, dressed like an off-duty tech in all black, headset hanging loose around his neck as camouflage.

"What's wrong with the exits?" she asked under the cover of applause.

"Back doors are chained from the outside," he said. "Fire code violation. Also, a good way to funnel everyone out through one route."

"A kill box," Celeste said.

"Or a capture box," he said.

"For whom?" she asked. "Me?"

"Maybe," he said. "Or someone close enough that you'd break for them."

Her mind flashed to Lena, to Teresa, to the conductor, to the random violinist who'd shared her music stand in Paris and chatted about cats.

"I'm not letting them touch anyone," she said.

"Then we get ahead of it," Volkov said.

The conductor turned, scanning the wings. His eyes found Celeste and he gestured urgently. "Encore," he mouthed. "Something solo. Give them a memory."

Of course. The tradition in such halls was for the star to offer something intimate and unexpected, a quiet piece after the fireworks, a last sip after the main course. The audience was already clapping in unison.

Celeste's stomach turned. "This is their moment," she said to Volkov. "While everyone's looking at me."

"Yes," he said. "So, make sure they're only looking at you."

"What?" she asked.

"Give them something they can't look away from," he said. "Something big enough that any move they make looks like an interruption of history."

"That's a ridiculous strategy," she said.

He smiled tightly. "It's your specialty."

Her heart pounded. "You'll cover the exits?"

"I always do," he said.

She stepped onto the stage. The hall's roar swelled, then softened into expectant hush. She didn't sit. Instead, she walked to the very front of the stage, cello in one hand, bow in the other, and spoke into the space in English, then repeated in Spanish. "Thank you for being here," she said. "Tonight has been… complicated. For me. For the world. I'd like to play something that was important to my mother."

The audience quieted further. A wave of attention rushed forward and wrapped itself around her.

On the third balcony, Aria sat forward.

In the wings, Volkov went still, watching her with an intensity that felt like a physical touch.

Celeste sat, adjusted, and lifted the cello.

She began to play a Bach Sarabande—simple, solitary, haunting. Her mother had played it on Saturday mornings when Celeste was small, moving around their kitchen with a cup of coffee in hand, humming. Later, when life became sharper, she'd played it as a kind of prayer. Celeste had learned it long before she was technically ready, fingers too small at first, heart already understanding the shape of the sorrow in it.

Now, in the riotous jewel box of the Palau, she stripped everything else away and gave them this: bare, unaccompanied melody; no tricks, no fireworks, just the line of thought and feeling. It was the most vulnerable thing she'd ever done in public, and that scared her more than any gun.

She played it like confession. Like accusation. Like an elegy for a woman who might have been both savior and architect of a machine that swallowed people whole.

As she played, she watched. She saw ushers freeze, captivated, forgetting to nudge people toward the proper doors. She saw the men at the rear exits frown, their gaze pulled unwillingly toward the stage, fingers loosening on their radios. She saw Aria's face flicker and something complicated passing through her eyes, something that looked uncomfortably like grief. She saw Volkov move along the side aisle, almost invisible, slipping behind a column near one of the exits.

When the last note dissolved into the hall, there was a long, long silence.

Then the applause came—less explosive than before, but deeper, tidal, people rising to their feet not with excitement but with something heavier.

Celeste stood, bowed once, and left the stage.

Backstage, everything sped up at once. Stagehands rushed to clear the sets. Musicians began packing instruments. Voices rose, excited, overlapping.

"Celeste!" Teresa called. "BBC wants an interview. *El País* too. They'll come backstage in ten minutes."

"No," Celeste said.

Teresa blinked. "No?"

"Tell them I'm ill," Celeste said. "Tell them I fainted. Tell them I fled. I don't care. Not tonight."

Teresa's brows knit. "But the publicity—"

"Not tonight," Celeste repeated, sharper.

Something in her tone made Teresa back off. "Okay. I'll… manage. Are you all right?"

"No," Celeste said. "But I will be. Hopefully." She turned away before Teresa could answer.

In the far corner, near a door marked EMERGÈNCIA, Volkov waited, eyes scanning.

"The chains?" she asked.

"Cut," he said. "Quietly. If they had a plan, they lost their window."

"And Aria?" she asked.

"She stayed in her seat until the very end," he said. "Then she left through the main doors like any other fan. No tail. No meeting. She wanted to see what you'd do. Nothing more. Tonight."

"Tonight," Celeste echoed.

He looked at her for a long second. "You did it."

"I played a piece of Bach," she said.

"You took their moment," he said, "turned it into yours. They can't risk acting in public when you've turned the room into an altar."

"That's dramatic," she said.

"That's true," he replied.

She leaned back against the rough backstage wall, feeling the energy drain out of her all at once. Her hands trembled. She clenched them into fists. "Aria says there are others, others like me. Built. Tuned. Waiting."

"There probably are," he said. "But there's only one you."

"That's exactly their problem," she said.

His gaze softened. "It may be their problem. It might be their mistake."

She let her head tip back, eyes closing for a moment. The sounds of the hall—applause fading, people starting to leave, the faint words of staff—blurred into a distant hum.

"When we get to Istanbul," she said, "we're not just reacting anymore. We go hunting."

"We already are," Volkov said.

"No," she said softly. "Until now, I've been trying to survive their tests. I'm done with that. Istanbul is not their stage. It's ours."

He smiled, slow and fierce. "Now you're thinking like a composer."

She opened her eyes. "Don't ever compare me to my mother," she said.

"I didn't," he replied. "I meant you."

The words landed somewhere she didn't have language for yet. She pushed off from the wall. "I need to get out of here before Teresa drags me into a press ambush."

"I'll clear a path," Volkov said.

"You always do," she said.

They slipped out through the side exit he'd unchained, into the cool Barcelona night. The air outside felt different now, less like a city at leisure, more like the space between one movement and the next.

Behind them, the Palau glowed, stained glass alive with internal light.

Above them, on some rooftop or balcony or shadowed edge, Aria might still be watching. And far beyond, in offices and bunkers and hidden rooms, people who thought they owned Celeste Morgan were already revising their plans.

Let them, she thought. The next piece would be hers. Istanbul was waiting.

Chapter 6

The Vanishing

THE FLIGHT FROM Barcelona to Istanbul left just after dawn, the kind of hour that made airports look like liminal spaces that were too bright and too tired and filled with people moving through them like specters carrying coffee.

Celeste sat by a window again, cello safely on the seat next to her. Her eyes were on the tarmac. The condensation on the glass blurred the wing of the plane into a hazy white shape. She traced a tiny circle in it with her fingertip, then wiped it away.

Barcelona still clung to her: the fever dream of the Palau, Aria's words in the stairwell, the feeling of playing Bach like a confession in front of more than a thousand strangers. She hadn't slept afterward.

When she finally reached the hotel, the city had been pulsing with late-night energy, bars spilling music and laughter into the streets. She'd watched from her window until the sky began to pale.

A soft chime sounded as the fasten seatbelt sign blinked on.

"We're third for takeoff," the pilot's voice said. "Weather is clear all the way to Istanbul."

Celeste closed her eyes and tried to picture "clear" as something that existed beyond meteorology.

She and the orchestra were on their private plane this time. A cluster of woodwinds were two rows ahead, already deep into a card game. The violas were arguing quietly about a tempo marking. Somewhere in the back, a brass player snored.

Across the aisle, Lena watched Celeste over the top of a paperback thriller. "You're doing the face again," Lena said.

"What face?" Celeste asked without opening her eyes.

"The one where you look like you've just solved the meaning of life and it disappointed you," Lena said.

"I didn't realize I had that face," Celeste said.

"You have a rich face vocabulary," Lena replied. "Most of them are deeply concerning."

Celeste cracked one eye open. "And yet you sit next to me voluntarily."

"You're good for my ego," Lena said. "Every time I play sharp, I tell myself, 'At least I'm not Celeste-level tragic.'"

Celeste huffed a small laugh. "Tragic doesn't sell tickets."

"After Barcelona?" Lena countered. "I beg to differ. People were leaving with wet eyes and existential crises."

"You're welcome," Celeste said.

Lena put the book down, expression softening. "Seriously. Are you okay? I know I keep asking, but you haven't been yourself."

"I don't know who that is anymore," Celeste whispered.

Lena frowned. "Do you ever want to… I don't know… stop?"

"Stop what?"

"Touring. Performing. The whole 'being a myth' thing," Lena said. "Move to a small town. Teach. Get a dog. Hex your enemies with scales and music theory."

The idea made something in Celeste's chest ache. A small town. A dog. A life measured in semesters and recitals, not targets and extractions. "They wouldn't let me," she said before she could censor herself.

"Who?" Lena asked.

Celeste opened her eyes fully. "My agents. My manager. Everyone who has a financial stake in me being exhausted and visible."

Lena stuck out her tongue like a five-year-old before she said, "Fire them."

"It's not that simple," Celeste said.

"Sure, it is," Lena said. "You're terrifying and talented. You could walk away, write your own ticket. People would follow you."

Celeste turned her gaze back to the window. "You overestimate my freedom."

Lena stared at her for a long moment. "Maybe or maybe, you underestimate it." Her voice was soft and held no rancor.

The plane began to move, rolling toward the runway. Celeste felt the familiar lift of her stomach as the engines roared and the ground dropped away. She watched Barcelona shrink, the roofs and streets and people becoming patterns, then colors, then nothing.

She didn't look down again until the shimmer of water and dense sprawl of Istanbul appeared beneath the plane's wing. From above, the city looked like someone had spilled two continents and then stitched them together with bridges and ferries. Minarets and skyscrapers shared the skyline. The Bosphorus cut through it all, a silver ribbon catching the afternoon light.

As they descended, Celeste caught a call to prayer through the aircraft's thin skin. The distant, wavering sound somehow felt louder than the engine's drone.

She inhaled. The air here would taste different. It always did.

The Turkish liaison met them at the airport: a tall woman in a slate-gray coat, hair tucked neatly under a silk scarf, posture straight enough to make conductors jealous.

"Welcome to Istanbul," she said in flawless English. "I'm Esra. I'll be assisting your orchestra while you're here."

Lena leaned across Celeste's shoulder as they walked. "She looks like she could single-handedly organize world peace and a bake sale."

"I'd attend for the efficiency," Celeste said.

Their luggage and instruments were shepherded with surprising care. Istanbul, at least, respected musicians. The cello's case was cool against her palm.

"It's beautiful," Lena said as they stepped outside, eyes on the skyline. "Look at that." Mosques dotted the horizon with their blue tiles, domes, sharp minarets piercing the sky. Ferries moved across the water below like small, determined animals. The air smelled of sea salt, exhaust, roasted chestnuts, and something spiced from a food cart. Celeste took it in, cataloguing everything.

Esra glanced at her. "You've been here before?" she asked.

"Once," Celeste said. "Years ago. Short trip."

"Tour?" Esra asked.

"Something like that," Celeste replied.

Esra watched her for a beat longer, then nodded, as if filing that away.

The hotel was in Beyoğlu, near Istiklal Avenue, a stretch of shops, restaurants, and too many people. Celeste's room faced a side street, mercifully quieter, with a view of tangled electrical wires and laundry and, in the distance, a slice of water. She checked the door, the windows, the fire exit. Old habits, never optional.

Her phone was already waiting with a message when she pulled it out. **Room two floors below yours. End of hall, right-hand side. They put me with the "technical team." I'm offended. –V**

She exhaled, tension easing slightly.

She answered: **Technical seems accurate. You fix things.**

His reply came before she finished unzipping her suitcase. **I break things. Different department. Rehearsal location?**

She typed: **Aya Sofia Concert Hall. Tomorrow, 10 a.m. It's near the old city walls.**

A moment. Then his reply came: **Good. Lots of exits. And hiding places. Get some sleep.**

Sleep. She shook her head before she lay on the bed in her rehearsal clothes, staring at the ceiling, listening to the muffled noise from the street below. Car horns, laughter, the occasional bark of a dog.

Her mother had once called Istanbul a city of thresholds. Always between: East and West, old and new, sacred and profane. It felt right that the next phase of this unwanted war would happen here.

The Aya Sofia Concert Hall was modern, despite its name. It was a large, graceful building with glass walls that reflected the old stone of nearby structures. Inside, the stage was wide and simple, the seats steeply banked. The acoustics were still being debated in music circles: some said the hall was too dry, others said it was perfect for clarity. Celeste liked clarity.

During rehearsal, she tested the way sound responded to her bow, how far she had to push to make the hall bloom, how much she could pull back before it turned unforgiving.

The orchestra sounded tired but determined. Tour life was catching up with them. Istanbul was the last major stop before they returned to New York. You could hear the fatigue in the brass, the small lapses in the woodwinds' focus, the slight raggedness at the edges of the strings.

Celeste played as if she were fresh. Drive mattered more than honesty sometimes. Between pieces, she caught sight of Volkov walking along the back row of the hall, a clipboard in hand, fake badge clipped to his belt. Esra walked beside him, listening as he gestured toward fire exits and aisles.

He'd gone all in on the "security consultant" cover.

Good.

At the break, Celeste went backstage, poured herself a paper cup of terrible coffee, and stood near an open loading bay door where the cold air seeped in. Volkov appeared a moment later, the clipboard now tucked under his arm. "You've sounded worse," he said.

"You've heard me sound worse?" she asked.

"Once," he said. "You were eighteen. Some benefit concert in Prague. You'd just finished a job two hours earlier."

The memory flashed to rain on cobblestones, the smell of wet stone, a man's body cooling on a balcony, her bow hand shaking minutely on an encore. "You were there?" she asked.

"In the balcony," he said.

"I didn't know."

"You weren't supposed to," he replied. "I wasn't working for you."

She took a sip of the coffee. It tasted like burnt dirt. "Are you working for me now?"

"He considered that. "I'm working with you."

"Semantics," she said.

"Semantics keep you alive in my line of work," he said.

"In ours," she corrected.

"You don't work," he said. "You do something beyond that."

"That sounds like flattery," she said.

"It's an observation," he said. "Also, a tactical assessment. They can't replace you easily. That's why they haven't killed you."

"Aria implied they don't need to," Celeste said. "She says there are others."

"Lower-tier," Volkov confirmed, though she countered with: "You don't know that."

"I've seen Eidolon's files," he said. "You're red-flagged. The others are orange at best."

"Comforting." Sarcasm seeped into the word.

He nodded toward the hall. "You saw anyone?"

"Not yet," she said. "But Aria likes to make an entrance."

"And an exit," he said.

Lena stuck her head through the doorway. "Hey, tragic duo. Esra says they're bringing in Turkish pastries. If you don't get in there now, the brass will eat them all."

"Go," Volkov said. "You need sugar."

"You're not coming?" Celeste asked.

"I've eaten food that didn't come in anonymous packages before," he said. "It was unsettling. I'm not repeating the experience."

Lena rolled her eyes. "Your commitment to misery is impressive."

"Thank you," he said, as if she'd complimented his tie.

Celeste followed Lena back inside. The pastries were indeed under siege. Someone had set up a table laden with baklava, simit, and small cups of strong Turkish tea. Musicians circled like sharks at a feeding frenzy. Lena grabbed a simit and tore it in half, offering a piece to Celeste. "You need carbs. You burn through calories like a furnace."

"Your medical opinion is noted." Celeste took part of the simit.

"I've seen how you play," Lena said. "Your bow arm is doing the work of four normal humans."

They found a spot near the wall, backs against the cool plaster, watching the chaos. "Do you ever think about staying in one place?" Lena asked suddenly.

"New topic," Celeste said.

"Same one, really," Lena said. "You're always… distant. Like your body's here but your mind is scanning the exits. And now it's worse. I'm starting to wonder if you actually like any of us."

"I like you," Celeste said, surprising herself with the ease of it.

"Yeah?" Lena asked, eyebrows rising.

"Yes," Celeste said. "You're annoying. It helps."

Lena laughed. "You know how to flatter a girl."

Celeste bit into the simit. It was chewy, sprinkled with sesame seeds, tasting vaguely of something toasted and sweet.

"I worry about you," Lena's voice was low. "You don't have to tell me what's going on, but I'd like to know if I should start learning krav maga."

"You play the violin," Celeste said. "You're already dangerous."

"Flattery again," Lena said. "Careful, you'll ruin your reputation."

Esra clapped her hands. "Five minutes! Back onstage, please."

The second half of rehearsal was focused on logistics: entrances, exits, bowing, curtain calls. The kind of mundane detail work that made performances look effortless. Celeste moved through it in a mild haze, her body doing what it knew, her mind drifting. She caught sight of the rear exits in her peripheral vision. No chains. No added locks. *For now.*

After rehearsal, Esra announced an informal group dinner. "Traditional meze," she said. "Near the Galata Bridge. You should see the city at night at least once while you're here."

The orchestra responded with tired enthusiasm. Free food was free food, especially when per diems barely covered decent coffee. "I'm in," Lena said immediately. She poked Celeste's shoulder. "You're coming too."

"I was going to practice," Celeste said.

"You've practiced since the womb," Lena said. "You can spare one evening."

Celeste hesitated.

Volkov appeared just inside the stage door, listening without pretending not to. "Go," he said when she caught his eye.

"I don't like being separated from you," she teased.

"You won't be," he said. "I'll be at the restaurant. Different table. Pretending to judge the hummus."

"Is that in your job description now?"

"It will be when I write it," he said.

She sighed. "Fine. One dinner."

Lena cheered.

The meze restaurant near the bridge was crowded and loud, filled with a mix of locals and tourists. Long tables had been pushed together for the orchestra. Plates of hummus, baba ghanoush, grilled vegetables, cheeses, and bread covered the surfaces. Raki flowed freely for those not performing tomorrow.

Celeste sat midway down the table, Lena on one side, a second violinist on the other. The air was warm with spice and laughter, the kind of convivial chaos she usually avoided. Tonight, she let herself sink into it, just a little. She listened to stories about missed cues and travel mishaps. She watched a cellist and a trombonist argue about football teams. She watched Lena flirt shamelessly with a waiter who brought extra olives.

Across the room, at a small table near the wall, Volkov sat alone, a glass of tea in front of him, eyes half-hooded as he watched everything casually and nothing casually.

Our cohort, Aria had said.

These people didn't know they were in the blast radius of something enormous and invisible. They were just living, making music, complaining about jet lag. Celeste felt a surge of protective fury so strong it made her grip her fork too tightly.

"You okay?" Lena asked, noticing.

"I'm fine," Celeste said automatically, then grimaced at herself. "I hate that phrase."

"Me too," Lena said. "It's like putting a bandage on a broken leg."

The night wore on. Food was replaced with more food. Some people began to drift out in small groups, heading back to the hotel or deeper into the city.

"I'm going to get some air," Lena said, pushing back her chair. "You want to come?"

"I'll stay a bit longer," Celeste said. "Finish this and then go practice."

Lena rolled her eyes affectionately. "Of course, you will. It's your love language." She squeezed Celeste's shoulder. "Don't stay too late. Istanbul eats people who wander alone at night."

"Noted," Celeste said.

Lena grabbed her coat and bag, waved at a few colleagues, and slipped through the restaurant's front door into the cool night.

Twenty minutes later, when Celeste decided she'd had enough of pretending to be normal, she stood, nodded to Esra, and made her way outside. The air hit her like a gentle slap—cool, carrying the smell of water and grilled fish from the vendors on the bridge. The city glowed with lights reflecting on the Bosphorus, mosques lit from below like stone lanterns, traffic crawling in bright lines.

She checked her phone.

No messages from Lena.

Odd. There was usually at least a "I'm alive, don't worry, this city is gorgeous" text by now, even if Celeste hadn't asked for one.

She sent a quick message. **At hotel?**

No response.

She waited a minute, then tried calling.

The line rang once and then went dead, replaced by a flat, electronic tone.

A prickle crawled up her spine. She walked back into the restaurant, scanning. No Lena. She caught Esra's eye. "Have you seen Lena?" Celeste asked.

"She left about half an hour ago," Esra said. "Said she was tired. Why?"

"She's not answering her phone," Celeste said.

"Maybe she fell asleep," Esra said. "Or is flirting with a street musician."

Celeste's mind was already moving. "Which way did she go?"

Esra pointed. "Left, toward the tram stop."

Celeste stepped back outside. Volkov was already there, leaning against the building, as if he'd grown out of the stone.

"You saw?" she asked.

"Her leave? Yes," he said, "I let her go."

"I shouldn't have," Celeste said.

"You're not responsible for every adult who decides to walk in a city at night," he said.

"Yes, I am," she said.

He studied her face. The tension there was enough. "What happened?" he asked.

"She's not answering," Celeste said. "Call dropped."

"Could be nothing," he said, even as his voice lost any trace of casualness. "Could be bad reception."

"In a major city? Near a tram stop?" Celeste shook her head. "No."

He straightened. "Then we find her."

They moved together down the street, past the line of restaurants and vendors, toward the tram. Istanbul bustled around them: couples walking arm in arm, teenagers in clusters, tourists pausing to take photos of the illuminated mosques.

"Do you have her location?" Volkov asked.

Celeste swallowed. "Her phone pings to the hotel when the Wi-Fi is on. But if they've disabled it…"

"Then we check physical routes," he said.

They reached the tram stop. The platform was sparsely populated now, just a few people waiting, eyes on the tracks.

"Excuse me," Celeste said to a middle-aged woman in a headscarf. "Did you see a woman about this tall"—she gestured—"curly hair, black coat, violin case?"

The woman blinked, then nodded slowly. "Yes. She was here. Ten, fifteen minutes ago. Two men talked to her. Asked for directions, I think. Then she walked with them." The woman frowned. "Seemed strange."

"Which way?" Volkov asked.

The woman pointed toward a side street that angled down toward the water.

"Thank you," Celeste said. Her pulse thudded in her ears. "Two men," she echoed. "Directions."

"That's classic," Volkov said. "Approach with low threat, create a vector, isolate, then—"

"Then what?" she snapped.

"Then vanish," he said.

They turned down the side street which was darker, lit only by a few lamps and the glow from windows above. The cobblestones were uneven. A stray cat darted across their path, pausing to glare with luminous eyes before disappearing into an alley.

Halfway down the block, Celeste saw something glint near a doorway. She crouched. A small, dark object lay on the ground. She picked it up.

Lena's phone.

Her breath caught. The screen was cracked, as if it had been dropped or stepped on. It lit briefly as she pressed the side button, then went dark again. Beside it, scuffed into the dust, was the faint outline of a struggle: drag marks, a heel streak, an odd scuff that might have been a knee hitting the ground.

Celeste's stomach turned. "This is my fault," she said.

"No," Volkov said. "This is theirs." He scanned the area, eyes narrowing. "Look."

On the wall above the doorway, someone had taped an envelope. Plain, white, nearly invisible in the gloom. Volkov plucked it down and handed it to Celeste.

Her hands were steady as she tore it open. Inside was a single sheet of paper, folded twice. She unfolded it:

THE WORLD LOVES YOUR MUSIC.

WE LOVE YOUR POTENTIAL.

YOU HAVE SOMETHING WE WANT.

NOW WE HAVE SOMETHING YOU CARE ABOUT.

COME TO US ALONE.

TOMORROW NIGHT, AFTER YOUR PERFORMANCE.

THE CISTERN UNDER THE OLD CITY.

FIND THE STAIRS BEHIND THE CLOSED GATE.

NO SECURITY.

NO COMPANIONS.

IF YOU COME, SHE LIVES.

IF YOU DON'T, SHE BLEEDS.

YOU KNOW WE KEEP OUR PROMISES.

The signature was a simple symbol, printed in red ink: a stylized mask with no features. *Eidolon.*

Celeste read it twice. The words blurred at the edges, but the meaning pressed in with brutal clarity.

Lena. They had taken Lena. She felt something in her chest that wasn't panic, wasn't fear—something colder.

Volkov watched her, face unreadable. "Well," he said quietly, "they finally made a personal move."

"This was always where it was going." Her voice sounded like it belonged to someone else. "Aria warned me. And you said it, they hunt in circles."

"They picked her because they saw how you look at her," he said. "She matters to you."

"Everyone in that orchestra matters to me," Celeste said. "They're… proof."

"Of what?" he asked.

"That I could've had a life that didn't involve blood," she said.

He stepped closer, close enough that she could feel the heat of him, the steadiness. "You know it's a trap," he said.

"Of course, it's a trap," she said. "That doesn't matter."

"It matters if you plan to walk into it alone," he said.

"Their note says—"

"I don't care what their note says," Volkov cut in. "You're not walking into their ground solo. That's how people die. Or worse."

"Worse?" she asked.

"Get turned," he said. "Rewired. Used."

She folded the paper carefully, once, then twice. "They already tried to turn me. They failed."

He searched her face, frustration and something like panic, she thought, flashing in his eyes. "Don't make me watch you sacrifice yourself for someone who was just in the wrong restaurant."

"She's not just anything," Celeste seethed. "She's… good."

"Good people die all the time," he said. "If we let them dictate our moves, we'll never get ahead."

"You think I don't know that?" she asked, incredulous. "You think I haven't watched collateral pile up so some man in a suit could feel safer? This is not that. This is my choice."

His jaw clenched. "Your mother would say—"

"Don't," she hissed. "Don't bring her into this. She chose her experiments. I choose my loyalties."

He stared at her for a long beat. Then his shoulders dropped a fraction. "I won't let you go alone," he said.

"You might not have a choice," she replied.

"Don't underestimate what I'll do to keep you breathing," he said.

"Don't underestimate what I'll do to get her back," she shot back.

They stood there, in the dim side street, the city's symphony around them, Lena's broken phone in Celeste's hand and Eidolon's letter folded in her pocket. Above them, somewhere in the vast sprawl of Istanbul, mosques called the faithful to prayer.

Celeste wasn't sure who she believed in anymore. But she believed this: She would walk into the cistern. She would face whatever waited there. She would not let Lena die for knowing her. Even if it meant becoming something she didn't recognize.

Volkov must have seen that decision settle into her bones, because he exhaled slowly, a sound almost like surrender. "Fine," he said. "We'll use their trap."

"How?" she asked.

He looked toward the distant silhouette of the old city, where domes and minarets etched the sky. "We turn the cistern into a stage," he said. "And we make sure we're the ones writing the ending."

His eyes met hers. She saw equal parts steel and something softer.

"Tomorrow night," he said. "After the performance."

She nodded once. The vanishing had begun. Now they would see what kind of music she could make underground.

Chapter 7

Under the City

THE LETTER BURNED in Celeste's pocket all night. She didn't sleep. She lay on the hotel bed fully dressed, eyes open, watching the shifting patterns of light on the ceiling as car headlights swept past outside. The sounds of Istanbul crept in around the edges of the windows, the distant traffic, an occasional shout, the low rumble of a tram.

Somewhere in that vast city, Lena was in a room that didn't belong to her, listening to sounds she couldn't interpret as either salvation or danger. Celeste's mind kept trying to imagine it and kept flinching away.

She got up when the sky was still dark, showered too hot, dressed in rehearsal clothes, and drank coffee that tasted like regret. By the time the orchestra began gathering in the lobby to head to the hall, she looked exactly the way she always did before a performance day: composed, pale, dangerous in a way most people mistook for focus.

"Has anyone heard from Lena?" She kept her voice calm and casual, as they loaded into the buses.

"Her roommate says she never came back last night," the second violinist said. "Probably found some cute musician and crashed."

There was a round of knowing laughter, the kind that assumed the world was essentially safe.

Celeste smiled like she agreed. "She'll probably crawl in halfway through rehearsal," she said. "Looking smug."

On the bus, Esra moved down the aisle, ticking names off on a tablet.

"Lena?" Celeste asked when the woman reached her row.

"Doesn't answer her phone," Esra said, frowning. "No answer at her room either. I've alerted the hotel to notify us when she appears. If she doesn't arrive by this afternoon, I'll contact local authorities."

"Good," Celeste said. Her voice sounded like it was coming from somewhere behind her. "She's probably fine."

"Probably," Esra echoed, but her eyes said she was already calculating scenarios, which made Celeste wonder if Esra was more than the handler of guest musicians.

Celeste sat in the third row of the bus, with her hands folded. Outside, the city rolled by in a blur of stone and metal and color. She caught a glimpse of the Galata Tower, then a flash of water, then the walls of the old city.

Her phone buzzed once in her pocket. **Meet me under the stage after sound check. Boiler room. −V**

Sound check bled into rehearsal, rehearsal into a blur of instructions from the conductor and adjustments from Esra and the hall's staff. Celeste played cleanly, hands on autopilot, mind holding two parallel scores: the music and the plan.

By the time they ran the last piece, her bow arm ached in a way that felt more like proof of life than fatigue. She packed up slowly, letting the crowd thin, then slipped through the maze of corridors to the heavy metal door marked MAINTENANCE.

Nobody paid attention to her. Soloists were allowed to be eccentric about their pre-show rituals.

The boiler room was two levels down, a concrete cavern of pipes and rusted machinery. The air was warm and slightly damp. The low hum of the building's systems reverberated in the floor. Volkov was there, leaning against one of the bigger pipes, arms folded. He'd swapped his "security consultant" jacket for a plain black shirt and jeans. It made him look simultaneously more dangerous and more like a man you'd forget seeing in a crowd.

He watched her cross the room without speaking. When she was close enough to see the tightness at the corners of his mouth, he said, "You didn't sleep."

"Neither did you," she replied.

"True," he said. "But I look better tired."

"Lies," she said.

Some of the tension in his posture eased. It didn't leave, but it eased, she noted.

He pulled a folded map from his back pocket and spread it out on the only clear patch of workbench. "The Basilica Cistern," he said, tapping a shaded area. "Tourist entry here." His finger shifted. "But the note says 'behind the closed gate.' That suggests one of the old service stairwells. There are at least three, all currently sealed off."

"You got plans?" she asked.

"Turkish infrastructure is full of pride and paranoia," he said. "If it's old and important, someone's drawn too many maps of it. I called in a favor." Lines and levels crisscrossed the paper—chambers, support columns, access points. "There," he said, pointing at a narrow shaft labeled with a notation in Turkish. "Old maintenance stairs. Closed to the public thirty years ago. Above ground, it's a metal gate on a side street, chained. Matches the letter."

"And down there?" she asked.

"A platform just off the main cistern," he said. "Above the waterline. Big enough for twenty people. Or four, depending on how theatrical they're feeling."

"They're feeling theatrical," Celeste said.

"Yes," Volkov agreed. "They always are when they give instructions in red ink."

She looked at the narrow lines of the stairwell, the rectangular platform. "They'll have vantage points. High spots. Elevated walkways?"

"Here, here, and here," he said, tapping. "They can control line of sight. Cameras are easy to hide in that stone. Sound carries weird in there, too. Echoes. You'll be at an acoustic disadvantage."

"I'll manage," she said.

"I know," he said. "But I still hate it."

She placed her fingertip on the drawn platform. "They'll expect me here, alone."

"They won't trust you to follow directions," Volkov said. "But they're hoping your attachment to Lena overrides your training."

"They're right," she said.

He nodded once, as if he'd been waiting for her to say it.

"Then we play offense," he said. "You show up exactly where they want you, exactly when they asked. I get in earlier, through another access point. There are old drainage tunnels leading into the cistern from the north side. Small, but not impassable."

She raised an eyebrow. "You planning to swim?"

"Not if I can help it," he said. "But I've done worse. Once, I spent eight hours in a sewer—"

"Stop," she said. "If this story involves rats, I'm leaving."

"Just painting a picture." His voice lacked inflection. "Point is, they're not the only ones who know how to use the old parts of a city."

She stared at the map. "What about Lena?"

"They'll use her as leverage," he said. "They'll want you close enough to see she's alive, far enough that you can't reach her without obeying some instruction."

"Could they have moved her?" she asked.

"Probably," he said. "But logistics matter. Moving a live hostage around a city is risky. If they picked the cistern, odds are she's there now or will be shortly before the meeting."

"Then we find her," Celeste said.

"We try," he corrected.

She looked up sharply. "Try?"

"I won't lie to you," he said. "They may never intend to let her leave. Even if you play along. Especially if you play along."

"You're terrible at reassurance." She frowned at him.

"I'm not trying to reassure you," he said. "I'm trying to keep you from breaking the plan the second you see her face."

She inhaled slowly, count of four in, count of four out. Then she asked, "What's the plan?"

"You go in without visible weapons," he said. "They'll scan you, pat you down, maybe have you step through some jury-rigged detector. You give them nothing."

"I'm not walking in empty-handed," she said.

"I didn't say 'empty-handed,'" he said. "I said 'without visible weapons.'" He pulled a small case from his bag and opened it. Inside were devices that looked like jewelry and buttons: a ring, a thin bracelet, two tiny earpieces, a pendant on a fine chain.

"Please tell me you didn't raid a spy movie prop department," she said.

"One of my contacts in Berlin owes me more than money," he said. "These are prototype toys."

He picked up the ring. "This emits a short-range EMP burst. Two-meter radius, three-second duration. Fries most unshielded electronics including cameras, comms, jerry-built traps. One-time use. The gem is the trigger."

He set it down and held up the bracelet. "This is a contact mic. It picks up vibrations through surfaces you touch and transmits to a receiver. Useful for hearing conversations through walls and floors."

"And the pendant?" she asked.

"Flashbang," he said. "Low-yield, directional. Pull the chain twice; you get light and sound enough to disorient in a ten-foot cone. Won't kill anyone. Will make them regret being awake."

"Cute," she said. Her hand hovered over the pendant. "Won't they notice?"

"It looks like a piece of modern jewelry," he said. "Lena would approve."

Her throat tightened. "And the earpieces?" she asked, forcing her voice steady.

"One for you, one for me," he said. "Encrypted. Short range. Stone will interfere, but we'll get enough to coordinate. Unless the cistern walls are thicker than this hall's management's skulls."

She almost smiled. "What's your entry vector?"

He pointed at the map again. "There's an old drainage access here. It's supposed to be sealed. It isn't. I'll get in before you arrive, find a vantage point, and wait."

"They wrote 'no companions,'" she said. "They'll expect me to obey."

"They designed you to obey," he said. "That's not the same thing."

The words landed somewhere deep and raw. She let herself feel that for half a second, then set it aside. "All right," she said. "Timeline?"

"You perform tonight," he said. "You make it convincing. No hint of what's coming. No missed notes, no trembling hands, no haunted-stare-at-the-middle-distance more than usual."

"I don't tremble onstage," she said.

"I know," he said. "That's one of the reasons they're so fascinated by you." He tapped the letter, folded neatly beside the map. "They'll have eyes in the audience, gauging your reaction to their threat. You show them control. You show them the version of you they think they built."

"And afterward?" she asked.

"You slip away from the orchestra in the post-concert chaos," he said. "No goodbyes. No explanations. You go to the gate. Alone."

"And you?" she asked.

"I'll already be under their feet," he said. He folded the map and the letter together and handed them to her. "Burn these before you leave the hotel."

She took them. "What if they're expecting you, too?"

"They don't know about me," he said.

"Aria does," she said. "She watched us together in Barcelona."

"She knows I exist," he said. "She doesn't know what I can do."

"You're very confident," she said.

"It's that or collapse," he said. "And I don't collapse."

She studied him for a long moment. "You're not doing this because of some noble desire to protect the innocent," she said.

"Partly," he said. "And partly because I'm invested now."

"In what?" she asked.

"In seeing whether you decide to let them make you into what they want," he said.

"And if I do?" she asked.

"Then I'll stop you." His voice was soft but filled with confidence.

She didn't flinch. "You think you could?"

"I hope I never have to find out," he said.

The boiler room suddenly felt too small. She stepped back. "I have to get ready."

He nodded. "I'll see you at the hall. And then... under it."

She left without another word.

The hours before a performance always blurred with hair, makeup, last-minute changes, warm-ups. Tonight, they felt like moving through a dream where everything was slightly off-key. Celeste sat in the dressing room, the same generic cream walls and mirror bulbs as every other hall in the world. A makeup artist had offered to do her face; she'd declined, sticking to eyeliner and a touch of color on her lips. Her reflection looked pale and composed. Only her eyes betrayed the storm.

Esra knocked and stepped in. "How are you feeling?" she asked.

"Focused," Celeste said.

"Have you heard from Lena?" Esra asked.

"No," Celeste said.

Worry flickered across Esra's face. "I've filed a missing person report," she said. "The police say it may be too soon, but… I pushed. I've also asked the hotel to check security cameras."

"Good," Celeste said. "She's hard to lose."

"You're sure she didn't just… spend the night with someone?" Esra asked delicately.

"Lena texts," Celeste said. "Even if she's mid-sin."

Esra snorted despite herself. "I see." Her expression sobered. "If there's anything you need…"

"There is," Celeste said, "I need you to pretend everything is normal tonight. No announcements. No panic. Nothing to suggest anything strange is happening."

Esra studied her. "You think this is connected to us? To the orchestra?"

"I think everything is connected to everything," Celeste said. "But tonight is not the night to unravel it."

Esra hesitated, then nodded slowly. "As you wish. Just don't ask me to stand down if something dangerous happens in this hall."

"I wouldn't," Celeste said. "You're better at your job than most people I've met."

Esra's lips quirked. "Flattery. I had heard you were emotionally stunted."

"I am." Celeste flashed her a smile. "Don't tell anyone."

When Esra left, Celeste picked up her cello and felt the familiar grounding weight of it. She rested her forehead against the curve of the instrument for a moment, eyes closed. "If I get you killed," she murmured to the wood, "my entire life will have been inaccurately marketed."

Someone knocked again. "Five minutes," a voice called.

She stood, smoothed her gown, and walked into the noise and light.

The stage at the Aya Sofia Concert Hall was awash in warm illumination. The seats were full of locals, tourists, expats, dignitaries. The low hum of pre-concert chatter dipped and rose like an orchestrated murmur. She could almost feel Eidolon's eyes among them.

The orchestra tuned. The conductor walked onstage to applause. Celeste stood in the wings, watching. On the second balcony, to the right, she saw a figure standing in the shadows behind a pillar. Aria. She recognized the posture, the cut of her jacket. Their gazes met for a brief, sharp second. Aria smiled, small and satisfied, then melted back into the darkness.

Celeste's skin crawled.

Her cues came. She stepped out. The applause that greeted her was enthusiastic, admiring, sincere. These people had come for music. For escape. For a few hours of beauty in a world that didn't offer enough of it.

She was about to use that trust as cover for something else entirely.

She sat, set her endpin, and lifted her instrument. The first piece demanded brilliance; she gave it. Whatever turmoil lived inside, her body refused to betray it onstage. Her fingers moved with practiced grace, her bow arm precise and fluid. The orchestra followed, ebbing and surging under her.

She thought of Lena's laugh over late-night coffee, the way she rolled her eyes at certain conductors, the way she'd said, "You could walk away if you wanted." She thought of a basement cistern under the old city, dark and echoing, waiting. She thought of Volkov, somewhere in the hall, watching the exits, counting security, planning his own descent.

At intermission, she returned to the dressing room. Staff buzzed around her, praising, offering water, asking if she needed anything. She put on her performer's smile and said no.

When they left, she allowed herself one small crack. Her hands shook. She gripped the back of the chair until her knuckles turned white, forcing the tremor out through static muscle tension. Then she reached into her bag.

The ring, bracelet, and pendant lay where she'd hidden them. She slipped the ring onto her right hand, the bracelet onto her left wrist, the pendant around her neck. They felt lighter than their purpose. The earpiece slid into place behind her ear, hidden by her hair. "Check," she whispered.

Volkov's voice came back, faint but clear. "I hear you."

"Where are you?" Her voice was barely above a whisper.

"Heading to the old city now," he said. "I'll be underground before the end of your encore."

"You sound very cheerful about that," she said.

"I'm not," he said. "My shoes are going to hate me."

She almost smiled. "Stay alive," she said.

"Only if you do," he replied.

"Is that sentiment?" she asked.

"Shut up and play." His tone was gentle, gentler than the words of the command.

She took a breath that felt like diving and walked back out.

The second half of the concert felt like moving through a dream. She played with the same precision, the same artistry, but somewhere underneath, a timer had started ticking.

The audience didn't notice. They cheered, they clapped, they shouted for more.

She gave them an encore, something bright and fierce that didn't cut as deep as Bach. She bowed, accepted flowers, accepted their applause like a wave she had no choice but to ride one last time.

Then she left the stage. Backstage was chaos again, the usual post-concert mess of congratulations and logistics. Esra tried to catch her eye; Celeste slipped around her, murmuring something about needing to change.

In the dressing room, she didn't sit. She didn't remove her makeup. She only swapped her gown for dark, nondescript clothes: black pants, gray sweater, black coat. She left the pendant and bracelet on, the ring still on her finger.

She opened the hotel-style safe and took out the letter one last time. Red ink, simple words, ugly promises.

"It's your turn," she whispered before she tore it into small pieces, held them over the sink, and lit them with a cheap disposable lighter. The paper curled and blackened, the red ink turning into nothing.

When only ash remained, she ran water, watched it all swirl down the drain, and turned off the tap.

Then she picked up her cello case, slung it over her back—empty, this time, just wood and strings—and walked out of the hall through a side door.

No one stopped her.

The night air was sharp and cool against her face. The lights of the old city glowed ahead: the outlines of Hagia Sophia, the Blue Mosque, the ancient walls. She walked toward them, boots quiet on the pavement.

Traffic thinned. Tourists grew fewer. The streets narrowed, stone and shadow pressing closer.

"Talk to me." She barely moved her lips.

"I'm in," Volkov's voice came, distorted slightly by interference. "North access tunnel. It smells like history and mold."

"Any movement?" she asked.

"Not yet," he said. "They're either very early or very confident in their schedule."

"Both," she said immediately before she spied the gate exactly where the map and letter said it would be: a heavy metal barrier set into an old stone wall in a small, unremarkable side street. Closed, chained, a "NO ENTRY" sign bolted crookedly across the middle.

It looked like something the city had forgotten; she knew better. Her heart was beating very fast now, but her hands were steady.

"Any eyes?" Volkov asked in her ear.

She turned slowly, scanning shadowed doorways, dark windows, parked cars. Nothing. "Probably cameras," she murmured. "Hidden."

"Assume you're onstage," he said.

"I always do," she replied as she stepped up to the gate and wrapped her fingers around the chain. Before she could tug, a hidden lock clicked. The chain loosened on its own, slithering down like a metal snake to coil at her feet. The gate swung inward a few inches, as if opened by an invisible hand. "Showtime," she breathed.

"Celeste—" Volkov began.

She stepped through before he could finish, and the gate closed behind her with a soft, final clang.

Chapter 8

The Cistern

THE DARKNESS TOOK her like a curtain. On the other side of the gate there was no street light, no city light, just a stone stairwell dropping steeply into shadow. The air was colder, damp, carrying the faint smell of algae and old water.

Celeste stood still for a moment, letting her eyes adjust. The only light came from above, a thin gray wedge leaking in around the edges of the gate. It was already shrinking as her pupils widened.

"Talk to me," Volkov's voice said in her ear, faint but present. "What do you see?"

"Stairs," she whispered. "Stone. No rail. No visible cameras, but they're here."

"They know you're in," he said. "They won't rush. They want you to feel it."

She put one hand against the wall, fingertips brushing rough, cool stone, and began to descend. The steps were uneven, worn by centuries of feet before hers. Each one echoed softly, a small hollow sound swallowed by the depth below. The stairwell curved, cutting her view of the gate, then kept dropping.

"Signal's degrading," Volkov said, his voice fuzzing at the edges. "Stone's thicker than the map—" His words dissolved into a burst of static.

"Volkov?" Celeste's voice barely audible.

Silence. Just the sound of her own breathing and the rasp of her boots on stone. *Of course.*

She kept going. The air grew colder and wetter the deeper she went. Somewhere far below, she heard water: dripping, trickling, the slow, steady sound of something that had been moving for a very long time.

After what felt like too many turns, the stairwell widened. A faint orange glow seeped up from below, not natural, not bright, but enough to pull her down like a thread.

She stepped off the last stair onto a small landing. The cistern opened before her. Columns, dozens of them, rose from dark water to a low vaulted ceiling. Their reflections trembled in the black surface, turning each pillar into a long, ghostly twin. The air hummed faintly with the subtle acoustics of stone and liquid, a space built for silence, not sound.

Small lamps had been mounted in discreet places along the columns, casting pools of amber on the water. It wasn't enough to dispel darkness; it only rearranged it. A narrow walkway of stone led from the base of her stairs out into the cistern, stretching between columns toward a larger platform in the distance. That platform was better lit; she could see the edge of it, the suggestion of crates, a low table.

And a chair.

Her throat tightened.

There was a figure in the chair. She knew the shape before her mind had time to argue. *Lena.*

Her friend was tied at the wrists and ankles, arms lashed to the chair's arms, head bowed. Her dark hair fell forward, hiding her face, but Celeste could see a strip of tape across Lena's mouth.

Celeste's hands curled around the cello case straps until her knuckles ached. She took one step onto the walkway. The stone was slick with condensation, faintly green in patches where moss had crept up from the waterline. Her footfalls echoed: once off the stone, once off the water, once off the ceiling.

She felt eyes on her long before she saw anyone else.

"Welcome, Celeste." The voice came from everywhere at once, bouncing off stone and water. Male, low, with the kind of calm that made her skin crawl. Amplified, she decided, coming through small speakers hidden among the columns.

She didn't stop.

"You came alone," the voice observed. "Good. I wasn't sure you would."

"You gave me a choice," she said. Her words came back to her slightly late, distorted by the space. "You know what I do with those."

A soft chuckle, echoing. "Your reputation suggested as much."

She kept walking, one measured step after another. The water beside the walkway was still, black, hinting at unfathomable depth. She could feel it pulling at the edges of her awareness.

"You can remove the case," the voice said. "We've already scanned you. You're remarkably… clean."

"I don't take orders from disembodied audio," she said, and kept the case on her back.

"Defiant," the voice said. "Good. Leadership requires that."

She ignored that. As she drew closer, more details of the platform emerged. A portable floodlight stood near the edge, directed inward, leaving the water around it dark. Crates that were metal, military-grade lined one side. A laptop sat open on the table. A camera on a tripod pointed toward the chair.

And there were people. Four of them, at least, that she could see immediately: two flanking Lena, rifles slung low in a way that suggested comfort, not nerves; one near the crates, leaning against a column; one to the far side of the platform, perched almost casually on a stone ledge, legs dangling.

Aria. Her former fellow trainee wore black pants, a dark shirt, and an expression that was almost bored. Her hair was damp at the ends, as if she'd come in through a less civilized route. She lifted a hand in a small salute when she saw Celeste watching.

"So predictable," Aria said, her own voice carrying without amplification. "You always did show up when someone you cared about was in trouble."

"I considered sending flowers instead," Celeste said. "But you're hard to shop for."

"Violence is fine," Aria said. "We have similar taste."

Celeste reached the edge of the platform and stopped.

Up close, Lena looked smaller. Her face was pale under the harsh floodlight, a bruise blooming along one cheekbone. Her eyes were open, wide and furious above the tape. When she saw Celeste, they flared with something like relief and terror all at once.

Celeste let herself look, absorbing the sight, the fact of Lena's breathing, the way her chest rose and fell, the tension in her hands as she flexed against the restraints.

"I'm here," Celeste said quietly, not caring if the microphones picked it up. "I won't let them hurt you."

Lena made a muffled sound behind the tape, eyes blazing.

"That depends entirely on her," the disembodied male voice said pleasantly.

"Come closer," Aria said. "You're too far away for this to be intimate."

Celeste stepped onto the platform.

Nothing exploded. No guns went off. No trapdoors opened. The restraint was almost more unnerving than any immediate violence would've been.

She turned in a slow, controlled arc, taking everything in. The four visible operatives. The crates. The laptop. The camera. The columns rising into darkness. No sign of the speaker's physical source.

"Where are you?" she asked.

"Everywhere," the male voice said. "Nowhere. For tonight, you may call me Maestro, if you like."

"Already taken," she said. "Pick another title."

"I see humor is still your default defense," he said. "Your handlers always admired that."

"You knew my handlers," she said.

"And your mother," he replied.

Her pulse picked up. "Of course, you did," she said. "This is your moment to tell me how visionary she was."

"Visionary and flawed," he said. "Like most composers."

"She raised me," Celeste said. "She made grilled cheese sandwiches and threatened to throw my cello out the window when I refused to practice scales. She smelled like coffee and rosin. Whatever else she was, she was human."

"Yes," he said. "And humans break. That's why she wanted something better."

Aria swung her legs idly, watching them like this was a show, before she said, "Enough nostalgia. We brought her here for a reason. We don't have all night."

"We have as much time as it takes," the Maestro replied. "This is an audition."

Celeste took a step closer to Lena.

One of the guards shifted, raising his rifle a hair.

Aria held up a hand. "Let her look," she said. "She earned that much."

Celeste knelt, slowly, careful not to make any sudden movements that might spook anyone. She met Lena's eyes.

The fear there wasn't for herself. It was for Celeste. *Good. That meant she hadn't broken yet.* "Blink once if you're hurt badly," Celeste said softly. "Twice if you're just scared and angry."

Lena stared at her, then blinked twice, deliberately.

Celeste exhaled, something in her chest unclenching an infinitesimal amount. She rose. "Let her go," she said, turning toward the camera. "You have me. You don't need her."

"Oh, but we do," the Maestro said. "She is the lever that finally made you move according to our tempo. Do you have any idea how long your mother worked to find the right variable?"

"My mother is dead," Celeste said flatly.

"Death is a state," he said. "Not an absence. She left so much behind."

Aria hopped down from her perch and strolled to the laptop. She pressed a key. The camera's red light shifted, and the laptop's screen flickered. For a moment, there was just static. Then an image resolved. A woman sat at a table, hands folded, expression calm.

Celeste's world narrowed to a point.

"Hello, Celeste," said her mother.

The voice was wrong and right at the same time. The woman on the screen looked younger than Celeste remembered, like the version from her childhood, not the one from photographs in classified files. Her hair was pulled back. She wore a simple blouse, no jewelry. In the background, there was no kitchen, no window, just a blank wall.

"It's not live," Aria said. "Don't get too excited."

"Quiet," the Maestro said. "Let her listen."

The recorded woman's eyes seemed to look straight at her. "If you are seeing this," her mother's voice said, "then a number of things have gone wrong, and at least one has gone very right."

Celeste couldn't breathe.

"You were always going to be remarkable," the recording continued. "I knew that from the moment I first watched you reach for sound as if it were something you could mold. Your brain… it sees patterns other people don't. That's why the project made sense."

Project. Celeste felt herself go cold.

"We live in a world full of systems," her mother said. "Political, economic, criminal. They entrench themselves; they protect themselves. You can't fix them from the outside. You have to infiltrate, reshape, and conduct."

Celeste could feel Aria watching her face like a scientist observing a reaction.

"I joined Eidolon because I believed it could be that force," her mother said. "A conductor for a broken world. I helped design frameworks. Training regimes. Selection criteria. I made mistakes. I trusted the wrong people. Harriman, most of all. But I did one thing right."

She leaned slightly closer to the camera before saying, "I built you."

The words hit like physical blows.

"Not in the genetic sense," her mother said with a smirk. "I didn't tinker with your DNA. I mean I built your environment. Your training. Your inputs. Music, discipline, languages, problem-solving under pressure. You were my hypothesis: that a human mind could be both art and weapon, empathy and precision, if shaped carefully enough."

"You were an experiment," Aria hissed, off to the side. "A successful one."

Celeste's hands ached from how tightly she was gripping the cello case strap. She forced her fingers to loosen.

"I am not sorry," her mother said on the screen. "For that. For building you. I am sorry for what it cost you. Secrets. Lies. The absence of choice. If you are watching this, you have discovered enough to resent me. I understand. Resentment is a form of engagement. It means you're still thinking about the problem." She smiled then, a small, sad smile that Celeste remembered from the quiet hours after late rehearsals.

"You are not meant to be a tool," her mother said. "You are meant to be a conductor. Harriman will tell you we need to stay in the shadows. Others will tell you we need to cut deeper, faster. I am telling you: if you want this machine to do any good, you must stand at its center and demand that it answers to you. Otherwise, it will run amok."

Aria's expression flickered—just a tiny shift—at those words.

"If you refuse that role," her mother said, "if you walk away, others will fill the vacuum. Aria. The others. They are extraordinary, but they lack something you have."

"What?" Celeste whispered.

"Doubt," her mother said, as if she'd heard. "Conscience. The willingness to feel pain on behalf of others. That makes you dangerous in a way they will never be." She paused.

"I won't tell you what to do," she said. "I have already controlled too much of your life. This message is not an order. It is a plea. If you can find a way to use what we built without becoming what we feared, do it. Conduct the chaos. Don't let the worst men in the room hold the baton."

The image froze for a second, then blinked off. The laptop screen returned to a simple login prompt.

Silence crowded the space where her mother's voice had been. Celeste stared at the dark screen, the after image of her mother's face burned into her vision.

"You see?" the Maestro's voice said. "You were always meant to be more than a blunt instrument. Your mother wanted you to lead. Harriman wanted you to obey. I am offering you the chance to fulfill what she began."

Celeste swallowed. Her tongue felt thick. "Who are you?" she asked, voice low.

"A collaborator," he said. "Someone who saw the flaw in Harriman's methods and the potential in your mother's vision. I am not important. You are."

"Spoken like every narcissist who's ever built a cult," she said.

"You've killed enough men to recognize one." His voice had a joking quality like he was amused. "And yet… here you are. Listening."

She looked at Aria and said, "You knew about this."

"Of course," Aria said. "We studied it in briefings. 'Morgan's message.' It was supposed to be shown to you once you had proven your reliability. You accelerated the schedule by killing Harriman and making a mess of their models."

"You were always so good at extra credit," Celeste said.

Aria's eyes sharpened. "I take no pleasure in this, you know. I like you. You're… interesting. But if you don't step into the role she designed for you, someone else will. And they won't be half as careful with the world."

"You think you're careful now?" Celeste said.

"We remove tumors," Aria said. "You've participated. Don't pretend you're innocent. Reznov. The general in Caracas. The banker in Zurich. The arms dealer in Lagos. You played for them, then killed them. Efficiently. Beautifully."

Lena made another muffled sound, eyes wild.

Celeste's hands shook once, then stilled. She slid the cello case off her back and set it down carefully, as if this were any other stage.

"You've made your pitch," she said. "Let me be clear in return." She stepped closer to the center of the platform, where the camera could see her fully. "You hurt a friend of mine," she said. "You used her as bait. You threatened to bleed her to force my hand. That was your first mistake."

The Maestro's chuckle echoed. "And the second?"

"You showed me my mother finally being honest," Celeste said. "And you thought that would make me grateful to you."

Aria frowned. "You're not?"

"No," Celeste's voice was steady and she kept her emotions under wrap as she said, "I'm furious." She lifted her right hand.

The ring on her finger caught the light. She pressed the small gem with her thumb.

For a heartbeat, nothing happened.

Then the air hummed. A faint, sharp crackle travelled through the space like invisible lightning. The laptop screen fizzled and went black. The red light on the camera cut out. Somewhere above, hidden electronics sizzled and popped.

One of the guards cursed, slapping his ear as his comm earpiece squealed and died.

The lights didn't go out completely, but they flickered, dimming for a second before stabilizing.

"What was that?" the Maestro's voice snapped, losing its calm for the first time.

Aria's head whipped toward Celeste. "What did you do?"

"Short-range EMP," Celeste said. "Courtesy of someone they shouldn't have underestimated."

She moved though she didn't have a gun. She didn't need one.

The guard to Lena's right reacted fastest, bringing his rifle up. Celeste closed the distance in three strides, grabbed the barrel, and slammed it sideways into the other guard's throat. He staggered back, gasping.

She drove her knee into the first guard's stomach, then twisted the rifle out of his grip. It slid toward the edge of the platform, clattering, but she didn't reach for it. She didn't want stray bullets ricocheting around a stone cavern above dark water with her friend tied to a chair.

Aria recovered quickly, hand going for the small of her back.

"Careful," Celeste said sharply. "You fire in here, you hit her."

Aria's eyes flicked to Lena, then back.

"You're not that sloppy," Celeste added.

Aria's hand stilled.

From somewhere deeper in the cistern, she heard movement—footsteps on a distant walkway, the splash of something dropped into water. The EMP had not reached that far.

Good. That meant Volkov's gear was probably still functioning. If he was still alive.

"Untie her," Celeste said, voice low and cold.

"Or what?" Aria asked.

"Or I walk away," Celeste said. "Right now. Off this platform, up those stairs, into the night. I disappear. You lose the central variable. You lose whatever piece of your puzzle you think I am. You get nothing but a hostage who will never forgive you for using her."

"Big words for someone unarmed," Aria said.

"Do you really believe that?" Celeste asked.

They stared at each other. It was like being back in the training room: two operatives, one problem, different solutions flashing through their minds like options on a screen.

"Enough," the Maestro's voice cut in, grim. "Kovalenko, secure her. If she resists, shoot the friend. We have other instruments."

Aria's jaw tightened.

For the first time, Celeste saw her hesitate.

"This is why she wanted you," Aria said.

"She wanted a conscience at the center," Celeste said. "You call it weakness. I call it a safety."

"A brake," Aria said.

"A choice," Celeste replied.

"Shoot the friend," the Maestro snarled. "Now."

Aria flinched, minutely. She turned toward Lena, gun in hand.

Lena's eyes went huge, frantic.

Celeste's heart stopped.

"Aria," Celeste said. "Don't."

Aria's hand trembled. Then she shifted her aim two inches and fired at the rope binding Lena's wrists instead. The shot cracked like thunder in the enclosed space, echoing off stone and water. Lena jerked, the chair skidding, but the rope frayed.

Before anyone could process the deviation, a shout came from the shadows between columns.

"Down!" Volkov's voice.

Celeste dropped instinctively.

The flash of light from the left came an instant later, blindingly bright. The thunderclap of sound that followed set her ears ringing—even as she realized it wasn't a gun; it was the pendant at her throat, triggered by a flick of her hand as she fell.

The world turned into noise and white.

She squeezed her eyes shut, counted three, then opened them again to a dimmer, chaotic scene.

The guards were stumbling, disoriented, hands to their faces. Aria blinked hard, teeth gritted, trying to track movement through the haze.

Volkov came out of the dark like a ghost, pistol steady, eyes narrowed. He fired once, twice, dropping the two riflemen cleanly by their kneecaps, not by kills. They went down screaming, weapons clattering away into the gloom.

"Lena!" Celeste shouted, half-deaf, lunging toward the chair.

The violin player was already twisting, working her hands free from the half-shredded rope. Celeste grabbed the tape at her mouth and ripped it away.

Lena gasped, then swore. "What the actual—Celeste, what is—"

"No time," Celeste said. "Can you stand?"

"I can do more than stand," Lena snapped, adrenaline blazing in her eyes.

Volkov moved to cover, positioning himself between them and the edge of the platform, gun tracking potential threats.

Aria had not fired again. She stood near the table, weapon in hand, eyes flicking between Celeste, Volkov, and the shadows where other Eidolon agents might be regrouping.

Through the ringing in her ears, Celeste heard the Maestro's voice, distorted, furious.

"Kovalenko," he snapped. "Kill them. All of them. Now."

Aria's jaw worked. Something cracked across her face, not physically, but like a mask slipping. "No," she said. The word was small, almost swallowed by the echoes. But it was there.

"What?" the Maestro hissed.

Aria lifted her gun.

For a horrible second, Celeste thought she might finally aim it at Lena, or at Volkov.

Instead, Aria shot the camera, blowing it off its tripod. Sparks burst. The smell of burning plastic and insulation mingled with damp stone.

"Lines are cut," Volkov said quickly. "They're blind. But not for long."

Celeste grabbed Lena's arm. "We're leaving."

"You're not going anywhere," the Maestro snarled. "You think your little display changes the architecture? We own this city's underbelly. We own your histories. We own—"

The rest of his sentence dissolved into static.

The EMP had killed their primary channels. Aria's bullet had taken out the backup. "We don't have long," Aria said. "He'll reroute. There are redundancies."

"And whose side are you on?" Volkov asked, gun never leaving her.

Aria gave him a look of pure contempt. "My own. Same as you."

"Right now, those align," Celeste said. "Don't waste it."

Footsteps pounded on distant walkways with the sound coming closer, uneven, organized.

"Exit?" Lena demanded, voice shaking but functional.

"Back the way I came," Celeste said. "But they'll expect that. They watched me enter."

"Drainage tunnel," Volkov said, jerking his chin toward a shadowed archway on the far side of the platform. "North side. Narrow, but it leads to a maintenance shaft."

"That's your route," Aria said. "I'll block this access."

"Why?" Celeste asked.

"So you'll owe me." Aria flashed a grin that reminded Celeste of a cat about to pounce on a sparrow.

"Celeste, move," Volkov snapped. "We don't have time to debate her redemption arc."

Lena was already staggering toward the tunnel, one arm slung around her ribs. "I vote we follow the man with the gun."

Celeste hesitated for half a second, looking at Aria. "You don't have to stay," she said.

Aria snorted. "I'm not doing this for free, *celistka*. When you decide what you are, remember who gave you the first clean note."

"Is that what you think this is?" Celeste said. "Clean?"

"Cleaner than what he wants," Aria said. "Go. Before I change my mind."

The footsteps were closer now, voices calling in Turkish and Russian, the metallic click of weapons being readied.

Celeste grabbed her cello case and a fistful of Lena's coat, dragging her friend toward the archway.

Volkov backed up with them, covering their retreat, eyes never still.

As they reached the tunnel, Celeste glanced back one last time.

Aria stood squarely in the middle of the platform, gun at her side, chin lifted. She looked like a performer about to step into a spotlight, not into a crossfire.

"Aria," Celeste said.

The other woman met her eyes.

"Don't die," Celeste said.

Aria smiled, sharp and sad. "I'll try not to disappoint your mother twice." Then she turned to face the oncoming storm.

Celeste plunged into the tunnel. The passageway was low and narrow, forcing them to duck. The air was colder here, laced with the stronger smell of stagnant water. The floor was slick under their feet.

Behind them, the cistern erupted. Gunfire hammered the stone, each shot a crack of violence that ricocheted down the tunnel. Shouts. Something heavy splashing into water. A scream that was short and then cut off.

Lena flinched with each sound. "What is happening?"

"Later," Celeste said. "Watch your footing."

"Somebody grabbed me off a street, tied me up, and now we're in a sewer with gunshot." Lena's voice trembled with rage. "You'll tell me now, or I'm quitting the orchestra."

"Please don't," Volkov muttered. "Your section is one of the few tolerable ones."

Lena threw him a wild look, as if just realizing he existed. "Who the hell are you?"

"Quality control," he said. "Left here."

The tunnel bent sharply, then widened slightly, opening into a vertical shaft with a rusted ladder bolted to the wall. Dim light filtered down from somewhere above. Volkov climbed first, moving with efficient speed despite the slick metal. Celeste helped Lena onto the ladder below him, then followed, one hand always ready in case her friend's grip slipped.

Halfway up, there was another echoing boom, a deeper sound, more like a small contained explosion than a gunshot. Dust rained down, making them cough.

"Was that—" Lena began.

"Probably something structural," Volkov said. "Good sign. Means they're as panicked as we want them to be."

"Your standards for 'good' are alarming," Lena said.

They reached the top of the shaft and pushed open a heavy metal hatch. Cold night air rushed in, tasting like freedom and exhaust. They emerged in a small walled courtyard behind an unremarkable building. Trash bins lined one side. A stray cat hissed at them and bolted.

Volkov shoved the hatch closed, dragging an old crate over it. It wouldn't hold long, but it might confuse anyone trying to follow.

"Where are we?" Lena blinked her eyes.

"Old city, north quadrant," Volkov said. "Close enough to traffic that we can disappear. Far enough that they can't risk a noisy pursuit."

Celeste's knees felt weak. Adrenaline was crashing, leaving her trembling.

Lena looked at her—really looked—and something in her face changed. "This wasn't random," Lena said. "This was about you."

Celeste exhaled. "Yes."

"Who are they, Celeste?" Lena asked. "What did you drag me into?"

Celeste opened her mouth, but Volkov's hand closed gently on her arm. "Not here," he said. "Not yet."

Sirens wailed distantly. Police, maybe, or ambulances. Maybe both. Istanbul was big enough to swallow a lot of noise, but not all of it.

"They'll be recalibrating already," Volkov said. "We need to move."

Lena's laugh was shaky. "Sure. We just escaped a secret dungeon under a world heritage site. Let's get ice cream."

"That's not a bad idea," Volkov said.

She stared at him.

"Sugar helps with shock," he explained.

"Are you a doctor now?" she demanded.

"No," he said. "I'm just not completely heartless."

Celeste touched Lena's face; her fingers were gentle on the bruised cheekbone. "I'm sorry, but we need to move. Are you able to go fast?"

"I can run," Lena said. "Especially if it's away from… whatever that was."

"Then stay close," Celeste said. "Don't talk. Don't look back."

They slipped out of the courtyard through a narrow gate and into a side street. The city was still alive around them: cars, voices, the distant glow from restaurants and shops. People walked dogs, held hands, dragged children who were too tired to be awake.

They reached a busier street, where the noise and movement of the city thickened. Lena eyed Volkvo openly. "Who the hell are you?" she asked again.

"Her extremely underpaid support staff," he said.

Celeste shot him a warning look.

He met it, something fierce and unspoken passing between them. "You walked into their teeth," he said, low, barely audible over the street noise. "You walked in with nothing but a few toys and a promise to yourself that you'd get her out. Do you understand how insane that was?"

"Yes," she said.

"Good," he said. "Just checking that you're aware."

"Would you have done it differently?" she asked.

He hesitated.

"No," he said. "That's what bothers me."

They moved together through the crowd, three people in ordinary clothes carrying the weight of choices that felt anything but ordinary.

Behind them, under the old city, water dripped, stone shifted, and a piece of Eidolon's architecture cracked. Not collapsed. Not yet. But cracked.

In some room far away, the Maestro would be reviewing what little data they still had, revising models, marking Aria Kovalenko as "unreliable variable," marking Celeste Morgan as something else entirely. Not asset. Not tool. Not yet leader. Something in between.

Celeste felt the shape of it forming around her, like a piece of music she hadn't meant to write.

"You don't have to become what she wanted," Volkov said suddenly, as if he'd read her thoughts.

"My mother?" she asked.

"Your mother. The Maestro. Eidolon. Any of them," he said. "You don't have to conduct their orchestra just because they put a baton in your hand."

"If I don't, someone else will. Someone like Aria was before tonight. Or worse."

"Then we break the baton," he said. "We burn the sheet music. We walk away and watch it fall."

"And what about the tumors?" she asked. "The Reznovs. The generals. The men who never faced what they did because no one can get close enough?"

"We'll find another way," he said.

"There isn't another way," she said. "That's why they built us."

He stopped walking.

Lena looked bewildered and halted beside them, scanning their faces like she'd somehow wandered into someone else's argument.

The street swirled around them with ordinary people, ordinary lives.

"Celeste," Volkov said. "Look at me."

She did.

"You are not a project," he said. "You are not a hypothesis. You are not a legacy. You are a person who has every right to say no to being turned into a machine, no matter how beautiful the casing."

"And if saying no means more people die?" she asked.

"They're already dying," he said. "You've saved some. You've killed some. You will never balance that equation by letting sociopaths define its terms." His eyes were rawer than she'd ever seen them.

"You told me once you'd stop me if I became what they wanted," she said.

"I will," he said. "Even if it kills me."

Lena's eyes widened. "Okay," she said. "Hi. Still here. Very confused and I can't believe she killed anyone. I'm also bruised. Could we maybe have this existential crisis somewhere with chairs?"

The spell broke, and Celeste exhaled, a tiny, unexpected laugh escaping her. "Yes," she said. "Chairs. And ice cream. Apparently."

Volkov nodded once. "We'll debrief later," he said. "For now, we get invisible."

They walked on, swallowed slowly by the city.

Above them, Istanbul glowed.

Below, in the dark, something had shifted. The cistern would not be the last underground space they faced. The Maestro would not give up. Eidolon's "cohort" would not all hesitate like Aria. There would be more tests. More traps. More choices that didn't feel like choices at all.

But for the first time, Celeste felt something like agency under her ribs. Her mother had built a system and expected her to conduct it. Eidolon wanted to own her. Volkov wanted her to walk away. Celeste wanted… something else. She didn't have a name for it yet.

But she knew this: she was done being only someone else's instrument. The next movement would be hers. Whether the world survived it or not.

Chapter 9

Dissonant Truths

THEY ENDED UP in the least dramatic place possible: a fluorescent-lit café wedged between a pharmacy and a currency exchange, three blocks from the hotel. The chairs were plastic. The floor was sticky. A television in the corner played a soap opera on mute while Turkish pop blasted from tinny speakers. A glass case near the counter held desserts that looked like they'd been slowly hardening since the Ottoman Empire.

Perfect, Celeste thought. Nobody was looking for clandestine meetings next to a display of suspicious baklava.

Lena sat across from her in a red plastic chair, both hands wrapped around a paper cup of tea she hadn't touched. Her curls were frizzed, her cheeks smudged, eyes huge in a face that now showed every bruise in unforgiving café light.

Volkov had claimed a seat at the table behind them, angled just enough to watch the door and the street. To anyone else he looked like a bored night-shift worker killing time. To Celeste he looked like a loaded weapon someone had forgotten to lock away.

"Start talking," Lena said. Her voice wasn't loud. It didn't need to be. There was more fury in those two words than in some men's entire manifestos.

Celeste stared at the tea between her own hands for a second. Her knuckles were raw, scraped where she'd grabbed the rifle, where stone and ladder rungs had bitten skin. "What do you want to know?" she asked.

"All of it," Lena said. "Like yesterday." She leaned forward, pain flashing briefly across her face as the movement pulled at bruised ribs. "Who took me. Why they took me. Why they left a note that basically said 'Dear Celeste, we have your violinist, come play.' Why there were armed men and cameras in a creepy underground Roman thing. Who he is." She jabbed a finger in Volkov's direction without looking away from Celeste. "And what the hell you've turned our orchestra tour into."

Celeste glanced at Volkov.

He nodded once. "Your call."

She looked back at Lena. The words lined up in her throat like notes in a piece she hadn't rehearsed enough. Saying nothing wasn't an option anymore. Saying everything might get Lena killed in a different way.

She chose a starting point. "You were taken by a group called Eidolon," she said. "They're… an organization. Private. Global. They interfere where governments won't."

"Like a charity?" Lena asked.

"Like a scalpel," Celeste said. "They cut out people they decide are dangerous. Crime lords. Arms dealers. Corrupt officials. They specialize in… removals."

Lena's eyes narrowed. "Assassins."

"Yes," Celeste said.

"And you just happen to know this," Lena said slowly. "Because…?"

Celeste swallowed. The words tasted like rust. "Because I'm one of them."

The café's hum seemed to dim around that admission, even though no one else had heard it.

Lena sat very still. "You're joking."

"I'm not," Celeste said.

"Celeste." Lena's voice went higher, strained. "You play Bach like your soul is on fire. You cry at rehearsal when the second oboe misses their entrance on the Mahler adagio. You organize people's birthdays in your phone. You are not—" She stopped, groping for a word. "You are not a cold-blooded killer."

Celeste almost laughed. It came out thin. "I'm not cold-blooded," she said. "That's the problem."

"How long?" Lena demanded. "How long have you been… doing this?"

"Since I was eighteen," Celeste said.

Lena blinked. "That's eighteen years, Celeste."

"I can count," Celeste said without malice.

"Does the orchestra know?" Lena asked.

"No," Celeste said. "Just Marcus. My manager. He… coordinated things."

"Coordinated," Lena repeated, flat.

"He's dead," Celeste added.

"Oh," Lena said faintly. "Of course. Naturally." She pressed her fingers to her temples. "You… you killed people. Between rehearsals. Between flights. While we slept."

"Yes," Celeste said.

"Who?" Lena whispered.

"Men like Reznov in Vienna," Celeste said. "You were there when the tycoon 'had a heart attack' during the gala. He didn't. A general in Caracas. A banker in Zurich who laundered money for militias. A trafficker in Lagos." The list tasted worse with each word. "People who hurt a lot of other people."

"So you're… what? A vigilante?" Lena asked. "Batman with better hair?"

"It's not that simple," Celeste said. "Eidolon picks the targets. Or did. My mother helped design them. I agreed because I thought… I was putting something right. Because I was angry."

"Angry about what?" Lena asked.

Celeste forced herself not to look away. "My mother was killed by a car bomb in Berlin when I was sixteen. They never found who did it. Eidolon told me they could use me to prevent things like that from happening to other people. That I could be precise where governments are clumsy."

Lena stared at her. "Your mother. I didn't— You never talk about her."

"I know," Celeste said. "I wasn't allowed to. Operational security."

"Oh, great," Lena said, a hysterical edge creeping in. "We're in an opera full of secret organizations and dead parents. We're one tragic monologue away from cliché."

A few heads turned at her tone. Volkov shifted slightly, scanning, then relaxed when no one lingered.

"I'm sorry," Celeste said.

"For what?" Lena snapped. "For not telling me? For being an assassin? For dragging me into your… whatever this is?"

"All of it," Celeste said.

Lena let out a shaky breath. "Start with why they took me."

"They're losing control of me," Celeste said. "I killed Harriman, the man who managed their assassinations. I've been… disrupting their operations. They wanted leverage. They watched us. They saw you.

They saw how you orbit me."

Lena's face crumpled momentarily, then hardened. "They used me because you care about me."

"Yes," Celeste said.

"And if you didn't come, they would've killed me to prove a point," Lena said.

Celeste nodded once. "Probably on camera. They like theatrics."

Lena leaned back, knuckles white around the tea cup. "I want to throw up." She said the words like it a normal part of a mundane conversation.

"Don't do it on the table," Volkov murmured from behind them. "People will notice."

Lena twisted to glare at him. "Who. Are. You."

He met her stare evenly. "Volkov. That's all you need."

"Do you have a first name?" she demanded.

"Not one that matters right now," he said.

"He's ex-intelligence," Celeste said. "Russian. Then independent. He helped me get out from under Marcus. He's helping me against Eidolon."

"So, he's also a killer," Lena said.

"Yes," Volkov said. "But unlike your friend, I don't play cello in public."

"This is not helping," Celeste muttered.

Lena turned back to her, eyes bright and wet and furious. "Why didn't you tell me any of this? All those nights on tour, all those hours in buses and hotel bars— I thought we were friends."

"We are," Celeste said.

"Then why?" Lena's voice cracked. "Did you think I'd be scared of you? Think I'd run? Think I'd tell the press? I know secrets, Celeste. I can keep my mouth shut."

Celeste stared at the cheap tabletop. "Because if you didn't know, they wouldn't target you."

Lena laughed once, harsh. "How's that working out for us?"

Celeste winced. "Not well."

"And anyway," Lena went on, words spilling now, "you're wrong. Knowledge doesn't make people targets. Proximity does. I was always close. I had your room numbers. Your itineraries. Your moods." Her jaw clenched. "They could've used me even if I thought you were just obsessed with scales and espresso."

"I know that now," Celeste said.

Silence stretched between them.

The TV in the corner flashed a melodramatic close-up of a man confessing something to a woman who slapped him in slow motion.

Lena huffed a sound that might have been a laugh. "The irony is ridiculous."

Celeste lifted her gaze. "I didn't tell you because I wanted one part of my life that wasn't full of blood and lies," she whispered. "The orchestra was… proof that I could be something else. That I wasn't only what they built. I didn't want to stain it."

"Newsflash," Lena said. "You can't keep stain out by pretending it's not there."

"I know that too," Celeste said.

Lena stared at her for a long moment, then looked down at her own hands. The rope-burn on her wrists stood out dark against pale skin.

"You said your mother helped design them," Lena said. "Eidolon. And they showed you something tonight."

Celeste's stomach twisted. "You heard some of it?"

"Not the words," Lena said. "Just her face on that screen. And your face looking at her. And the… atmosphere." She shuddered. "He was so smug."

"He calls himself Maestro," Celeste said.

"Of course, he does," Lena said. "Men in power always think they're conducting something."

"He worked with my mother," Celeste said. "He believes I should take the position she… intended."

Lena's head snapped up and her eyes met Celeste's. "What position?"

"Leadership," Celeste said. The word still felt like a foreign object on her tongue. "He wants me to run Eidolon."

Lena blinked three times. "Run the assassin cult that kidnapped me."

"It's not a cult," Volkov said.

"It's absolutely a cult," Lena snapped without turning.

"It's a network," he said.

"With a mythology and a theology and a high priest with a pretentious name," Lena said. "Cult."

She looked back at Celeste. "And he thinks you're going to chair the board?"

"Yes," Celeste said.

"What do you think?" Lena asked.

Celeste opened her mouth. Closed it again. *What did she think?* Her mother's recorded face flickered in front of her eyes. Not an order, a plea. *Use what we built without becoming what we feared.*

Volkov's words pressed in from the other side. *Break the baton. Burn the sheet music.*

Her own rage sat somewhere between them, coiled and contradictory.

"I don't know yet." Honesty infused her words.

Lena stared at her like she'd slapped her. "What do you mean, you don't know?"

"I mean I don't know," Celeste said. "If I take it, I might be able to change what they do. Redirect them. Stop things like what happened tonight from happening. Prevent idiots like the Maestro from using us as toys."

"Or you become him," Volkov said quietly.

"Yes," Celeste echoed. "Or I become him."

"And if you don't take it?" Lena demanded.

"Someone else will," Celeste said. "Someone like Aria. Brilliant.

Efficient. Less… conflicted."

"Aria," Lena repeated. "The one who shot at my ropes."

Celeste nodded.

"She saved you," Volkov said, "and made herself a liability in one move."

"Did she survive?" Lena asked, voice smaller.

"I don't know," Celeste said.

"Does it matter?" Volkov asked.

"Yes." The word shot from Celeste's mouth.

He studied her face. "You can't save everyone."

"I know," she said, "but I need to know which ghosts are mine."

Lena rubbed her face. "So, your options are: run a murder organization and hope you don't like it too much, or walk away and let someone worse have the keys."

"That's the shape of it," Celeste said.

"Those aren't options," Lena said. "That's a rigged game."

"Welcome to my life," Celeste said.

Lena looked at her for a long, long moment. Then she said, very quietly, "I wish you'd trusted me sooner."

Celeste felt something crack under her ribs. "So do I."

"Because I would've told you something you apparently missed," Lena said. "You're not the only smart person in the room. You don't have to solve this alone. You have… us."

"Us?" Celeste echoed.

"The orchestra," Lena said. "Your… friends. The people whose lives you think you have to protect by shutting them out while simultaneously putting them in proximity to snipers and bombs. It's rude."

"This isn't a string-section problem," Celeste said weakly.

"Everything's a string-section problem if you orchestrate it right," Lena said. A ghost of her usual mischief surfaced. "You're a conductor. You just keep pretending you're not."

Celeste almost smiled. "Now you sound like my mother."

"Scary thought," Lena said.

The café door opened, letting in a gust of colder air and three teenagers laughing about something on a phone. They grabbed takeaway cups, oblivious to the war being sketched in quiet words two tables over.

Celeste's mind floated to their itinerary. "We're leaving tomorrow," their manager had reminded them before the concert. "The flight to New York is at noon. You'll have a few days off before rehearsal starts again."

New York. Home base. Familiar streets. Less ancient underground architecture.

But Eidolon's reach was just as strong there.

Celeste flexed her hands, feeling the ache in her scraped knuckles. "The orchestra can't stay in this," she said. "They're not built for it. You're not."

"Apparently I'm build adjacent now," Lena said dryly. "Kidnapping does that."

"I'm serious," Celeste said. "If they realize Eidolon failed tonight, they'll escalate. They'll use you again. Or someone else."

"So, we go home," Lena said. "We keep moving. We adapt. We get better locks on the hotel doors. I start carrying pepper spray. You and Robin back there make contingency plans."

"Pepper spray is not going to help against people like this," Volkov said.

Lena turned just enough to shoot him a look. "It might make me feel better."

"Feelings are not——" he began.

"Don't finish that sentence," both women said at once.

He shut his mouth, but his lips twitched.

Lena set her tea down, untouched. "I should report this," she said. "To Esra. To the police. To someone."

"You can't," Celeste said instantly.

"I was kidnapped," Lena said. "There are bruises on my wrists. On my face. It's not exactly a misunderstanding."

"Any investigation will lead back to that cistern," Celeste said. "Which will lead to questions. And you don't know their cover names, their faces, their routes. You'll hand Eidolon a map of what you don't know. They're good at filling in blanks."

"And if I stay quiet?" Lena asked. "I just… pretend it didn't happen?"

"No," Celeste said. "You document it. Privately. With me. With him." She jerked her chin toward Volkov. "We build our own record. But we don't hand them a justification to bury things deeper."

"So, I lie?" Lena's eyebrows were raised.

Celeste nodded once. "Welcome to my other life."

Lena stared at her tea again moment, then let out a long breath. "I hate this," she said.

"I know," Celeste replied.

Lena looked up. "I won't quit."

Celeste blinked. "What?"

"The orchestra," Lena said. "Us. You. I'm not walking away. Not unless you make me. You're stuck with me, Morgan."

"You almost died because of me," Celeste said. The words came out rougher than she intended.

"I almost died because some cartel of morally confused overachievers decided you were interesting," Lena said. "That's not the same thing. And they're wrong if they think hurting me will make you docile."

A slow, dangerous smile ghosted the edge of Lena's mouth. "If anything, I'd pay to see what you do to them now."

Celeste's vision blurred for a second. She blinked it away. "I don't deserve you," she said.

"Correct," Lena said. "But you have me anyway."

Volkov made a quiet sound behind them that might have been approval. Or warning. It was hard to tell with him, Celeste thought.

Lena pushed her chair back, wincing. "I need a shower. And about eight hours of bad sleep. And a therapist. Several therapists."

"We'll get you one," Celeste said.

"Please, not one of their therapists," Lena said. "I don't want to wake up hypnotized and loving murder."

"No one in Eidolon is touching your brain." Celeste was emphatic.

Lena nodded once. "Good." She looked at Volkov. "You too, Tall, dark, and ominous. If I find out you messed with my head—"

"I don't do that," he said. "I only break knees."

"Reassuring," Lena muttered.

Celeste stood. Her legs felt less like stone now, more like muscle again. "I'll walk you to the hotel," she said.

"Oh, now I get a bodyguard," Lena said.

"You always had one," Volkov said.

She eyed him. "We'll unpack that later."

They stepped out into the night. Istanbul had that exhausted-late brightness cities get when they're too big to really sleep: streetlights, shop windows, headlights, a million small suns in a man-made sky. Cold air hit Lena's face. She flinched, then took a deep breath as if trying to reset her lungs. "Will we ever play a normal concert again?" she asked.

"Yes," Celeste said.

"You sound sure," Lena said.

"I'm writing it into the score," Celeste said. "I don't let anyone change my tempo onstage. I won't let them do it offstage either."

They walked in silence for a block. Volkov drifted a few paces behind, eyes scanning, posture loose but ready. If anyone watched them, it would look like three ordinary people heading home after too long a night.

At the corner, Lena stopped. "If anyone grabs me again," she said, "I'm biting them."

Celeste's lips quirked into an almost-smile. "Good."

"And if you decide to take that job," Lena added, "the murder-

CEO of Eidolon or whatever, you tell me first so I can hit you with my violin case."

"I'll keep that in mind," Celeste said.

"I'm serious," Lena said. "You don't get to just disappear into some shadow boardroom and come back speaking in cryptic phrases. You're my friend. You owe me honesty now."

Celeste's throat tightened. "I do."

"Good," Lena said. She hesitated. "And… Celeste?"

"Yes?"

"Thank you," Lena said. "For coming. For not… letting them decide I was expendable."

"I will never think that," Celeste said.

Lena nodded once, sharply, as if sealing a contract. Then she squared her shoulders, turned, and walked into the hotel lobby, head high despite the stiffness in her step. The glass doors hissed shut behind her.

Celeste stood on the sidewalk, staring at her own reflection in the lobby window: tired, pale, hair messy, dark sweater instead of concert gown. She looked less like a myth and more like a person.

"Polyphony," Volkov said next to her.

She glanced at him. "What?"

"Multiple lines at once," he said. "You said your life was divided. Orchestra here, assassinations there. Two scores. Tonight, they overlapped. It's messy, but… it's also real."

"You think I can keep both?" she asked.

"I think you already are," he said. "And I think that terrifies Eidolon."

"They'll go after others," she said. "If not Lena, someone else. Ayla also in first violins. Victor. Esra. They'll use any note they think matters to me."

"Then we change the melody," he said.

"How?" she asked.

He looked up at the hotel, then past it, toward the invisible point where the city met the horizon.

"Not here," he said. "Not while we're still on their board. We get back to New York. We get you somewhere familiar, somewhere you have home-court advantage. We find out who the Maestro really is. We hit his infrastructure. Hard. We make it more expensive to chase you than to leave you alone."

"Deterrence?" she said.

"Punishment," he corrected. "The kind that sticks."

"That's what they think they're doing to the world," she said.

"The difference," Volkov said, "is that you still care who gets caught in the blast radius."

She stared at her reflection a moment longer. "My mother wanted me to conduct," she said. "She thought I could hold the baton without becoming the man at the podium."

"What do you want?" he asked.

She didn't answer right away. Cars passed. A tram bell clanged in the distance. Someone laughed on the other side of the street. Finally, she said, "I want to be able to play a concert without wondering who in the audience is waiting to shoot me. I want to walk my dog someday without flinching at every van that slows down. I want Lena to complain about intonation instead of abductions."

"You could run," he said. "Change your name. Disappear. There are places I could hide you."

"And leave them with the system my mother built?" she said. "Leave Aria's cohort in their hands? Leave the Reznovs of the world to be killed or not killed based on someone else's whim? That's not peace. That's cowardice dressed up as self-care."

"You're allowed to choose yourself," he said.

"Not if choosing myself means handing them the baton," she said.

He was quiet for a moment. "You're going to say yes," he said eventually.

"I'm going to say something," she said. "But not on their terms."

He tilted his head. "What does that mean?"

"It means they want me to step into their idea of leadership," she said. "Invisible. Controlled. Answerable to no one. If I take any piece of what they're offering, I rewrite it. I drag it into the light. I make it accountable. I turn their scalpel into something with a code."

Volkov's mouth twitched. "You want to build ethics into a murder syndicate."

She shrugged one shoulder. "Somebody has to."

"That's not how systems like that work," he said.

"Then I break the system," she said.

He watched her for a long moment, something like reluctant admiration shown in his eyes under his skepticism. "You're going to get yourself killed," he said.

"Probably," she said. "But maybe I can kill some worse things first."

He huffed a quiet, humorless laugh. "You are the most reckless careful person I've ever met."

"I take that as a compliment," she said.

"It wasn't meant as one," he replied.

They stood there a moment longer, like two people at the end of a concert, listening to the last notes fade.

Finally, he said, "Get some sleep. I'll keep an eye on the hotel tonight."

"You need sleep too," she said.

"Later," he said. "I can sleep on the plane."

"What if they hit the plane?" she asked.

"Then I won't need sleep," he said.

She rolled her eyes. "Morbid."

"Realistic," he said.

She hesitated. "Volkov?"

"Yes?"

"If I become what they want…" Her voice was resolute with

purpose. "If I start sounding like him… you stop me."

"I already promised," he said. "Even if it kills me."

"Even if it kills me," she said.

He held her gaze. "Especially then."

There it was again: the terrible comfort of someone who had already accepted that they might have to hurt her to keep her from becoming worse.

"Goodnight," she said.

"Goodnight, Celeste."

She went inside. Up in her room, she locked the door, then locked the deadbolt, then slid the chain across. It was habit, not faith. Locks were suggestions to people like Eidolon. She set the cello case in its corner, then took the instrument out and sat on the edge of the bed with it. Her hands hovered over the strings.

She thought of the cistern and the columns and darkness and her mother's face on a screen. She thought of Lena tied to a chair. She thought of Aria's small, defiant "no." She thought of the Maestro, somewhere far away, realizing his leverage had slipped.

She played. Not Bach. Not anything from the tour. Something new. It came out halting at first, then surer: a melody that rose and fell in strange intervals, never resolving exactly where a listener might expect. There were jagged edges and sudden drops, lines that almost sang and then turned sharp.

It was messier than anything she'd ever dare bring to a stage. It was honest. The notes bounced off the hotel ceiling and walls, off the glass of the window, off the darker corners where shadows thickened.

Outside, Istanbul buzzed and breathed and went about its business.

Inside, a woman built for precision and violence sat on a bed and tried to write her way into a version of herself that wasn't dictated by the dead. When she finally set the bow down, her fingers ached. Her chest felt looser, emptier.

Her phone buzzed.

One new message. Unknown number. **Well played, *celistka*. The next movement will be harder. –A**

Aria.

Celeste stared at the screen.

Then she typed back, before she could talk herself out of it: **You switched sides. That has consequences.**

The reply came almost instantly. **I didn't switch. I improvised. See you soon.**

Celeste set the phone on the nightstand and lay back, the cello resting on its side beside her like a sleeping animal. She closed her eyes.

For the first time in weeks, sleep came. Not easily, not cleanly, but it came. Somewhere between dreaming and waking, she heard her mother's voice again, not from a laptop, not from a recording, but from memory. *You hold the bow. Remember that.*

"I remember," Celeste murmured.

Morning would come fast. Planes, airports, New York, new stages, new threats.

The Maestro would regroup. Eidolon would adapt. Aria would move in whatever direction best served her own private calculus.

And Celeste? She was determined to walk between her lives, cello case on her back, weapons in her hands and music in her bones, trying to find the line where she could stand without falling.

The score wasn't written. She'd always been good at improvising under pressure.

Chapter 10

Home Key

NEW YORK SMELLED like jet fuel, wet concrete, and burnt coffee.

Celeste stepped out of JFK's sliding doors with her cello case on her back and the orchestra's chatter swirling around her. The sky was low and gray, the kind that pressed down on the city and made the air feel heavier.

"Welcome home," Lena said dryly at her side. "We've gone from mosques and cisterns to overpriced pretzels and passive-aggressive honking."

"Comforting," Celeste joked.

Lena still moved gingerly, like her ribs were stiff under her coat, but the bruises on her face had started to fade from violent purple to jaundiced yellow. She wore sunglasses despite the weak light—not for glamour—but to hide the rest.

"Buses will take you to Manhattan," Esra, who have traveled with them from Istanbul, called over the group, already transitioning out of tour liaison mode and into "please stop losing your passports" mode. "First stop: Midtown hotel. Second stop: orchestra hall. Rehearsal is in three days; enjoy your rest."

A tired cheer went up.

Celeste's phone chimed.

Volkov: **Black SUV, far right lane, behind the white van with the dent. Don't get on the bus.**

She scanned the line of vehicles. There it was: black, nondescript, the automotive equivalent of a straight face.

Lena caught the glance. "Let me guess," she murmured. "Brooding Safety Man wants to whisk you away before the brass section convinces you to go to a dive bar."

Celeste huffed a tiny laugh. "Something like that."

"You're leaving?" Lena asked, and for the first time since the cistern, Celeste heard a thin thread of fear in her voice that had nothing to do with kidnapping.

"Not the orchestra," Celeste said quickly. "I just… need to be somewhere for a few days. To work. To plan."

"Plan what?" Lena asked.

"How to make it more annoying and expensive for Eidolon to chase me," Celeste said. "And how not to lose anyone else I care about in the process."

Lena studied her. "You're going to go after them."

"Yes," Celeste said. "Eventually."

"That Maestro man," Lena said. "And your mother's… ghost project."

"Something like that," Celeste said.

Lena sighed. "Okay. But you text me. If I find out you've been shot from someone else, I will never forgive you."

"I'll try not to get shot," Celeste said.

"That's not the bar I was setting," Lena muttered. "But it's a start."

The orchestra began loading into the two waiting buses. Cases went under, musicians went in, the low rumble of gossip and complaints about airline food already starting up.

Esra approached Celeste. "Do you need a separate car?" she asked. "Media are asking for you. I told them you'd gone mute after Istanbul."

"Keep me mute a little longer," Celeste said. "I'm going off-grid until rehearsal. Call it… creative recovery."

Esra's eyes narrowed. She was too sharp not to sense something bigger moving under the surface. "Are you in trouble, Celeste?"

"Yes," Celeste said. "But I'm working on it."

"You know I'm very good at trouble," Esra said. "Officially and otherwise."

"I do know," Celeste said. Volkov had let her know that Esra was loosely connected to *Milli Istihbarat Teskilati*, or Turkish National Intelligence. "That's why I'm asking you to let this one be unofficially invisible. For now."

Esra studied her face, then exhaled through her nose. "Three days," she said. "After that, if this still smells wrong, I am intervening."

"Fair," Celeste said.

They hugged briefly—unexpected, awkward, real. Then Esra went back to shepherding musicians, snapping at a trombonist who had somehow already misplaced his carry-on.

Lena squeezed Celeste's hand one last time. "Text me a stupid meme so I know you're alive."

"I'll find one with a violin joke," Celeste said.

"If it's out of tune, I'm blocking you," Lena said, then hauled her suitcase toward the bus.

Celeste waited until the buses pulled away and the crowd thinned.

Tourists surged forward to fill the gap. Taxis honked. Somewhere, a child started to cry.

She walked to the black SUV.

The driver's window rolled down a few inches. Volkov's eyes appeared above the edge, faintly amused. "You ditched music camp," he said. "Rebel."

"I'm an adult," she said. "And we need a war room."

"Get in," he said.

The inside of the SUV smelled like leather and faintly of gun oil. A laptop case was on the floor, a duffel in the back, and a stack of manila folders on the console between them.

"You brought homework," she observed.

"I brought reality," he said. "Where to first?"

"My place," she said. "I want to see if anyone's redecorated."

The city blurred past outside as they drove toward Manhattan. Bridges, gray water, the jagged, familiar skyline. New York had always felt like neutral ground to her, a place where she could be both Celeste Morgan, celebrated soloist, and something sharper, without either identity looking too out of place. But now it felt like a battlefield.

Her apartment was on the Upper West Side, in a building old enough to have character but new enough to have decent plumbing. The doorman, Henry, gave her a broad smile as she walked in.

"Ms. Morgan," he said. "Welcome back. I saw you on TV last week. My wife cried."

"I'm sorry," Celeste said automatically.

"Don't be," Henry chuckled. "She likes crying at fancy music. You want the usual deliveries brought up?"

"Just the mail," she said. "No flowers."

"There's a stack," he said. "I'll send it up."

The elevator ride felt longer than usual.

Her apartment was exactly as she'd left it: tidy, spare, mostly blank walls except for a few framed posters from early concerts, a stack of music on the piano, a plant on the windowsill bravely not dead yet. The cello stand sat in its corner like a patient animal.

She looked for signs of intrusion, small, almost invisible ones, such as a hair moved, a book slightly out of place, a faint scuff on the floor. Nothing was obvious.

Volkov did his own sweep, more thorough. He checked behind curtains, under the bed, inside cabinets. She knew his eyes sharp and economical. He paused near the piano, tapping one of the legs lightly with his knuckles, listening.

"Clean," he said. "No bugs. No obvious physical tampering. Either they respect your privacy or they're saving it for later."

"They don't respect anything," she said. "But they also like to come in through the front door when they can."

Henry buzzed, then came up with a stack of envelopes and packages. "All yours," he said. "Fan mail, probably. And some heavy envelope from a lawyer." He stuck his head back into the hallway while saying, "Did you hear that?"

"Hear what?" Celeste asked, moving toward to the door.

A small mewl came from down the hall. Henry was moving toward the crying.

He returned to her door carrying a small, fluffy gray cat who looked underfed. "Do you know this cat?" He was frowning, like he didn't understand how it got past him and into the building.

"No, I don't."

Volkov joined them at the door. "If it has no tags, she'll keep it."

"I can't keep a cat," Celeste protested. "I can barely keep a plant alive."

"You need something soft and comforting in your home," Volkov insisted, his eyebrows raised as if asking her to challenge him.

Henry said, "My wife and I would be honored to help you care for him… or is it a her?" He turned the cat up so he could see its underside.

"Maybe you should adopt it," Celeste suggested.

"Take the cat, Celeste," Volkov said. He reached for it.

"I'll keep it until you find its rightful owner, Henry. And if there isn't one, well, we'll co-parent it." She flashed her doorman a smile though the word co-parent twisted her guts. She wasn't qualified to parent anything. "Thanks, Henry."

When he left, Volkov set the cat on the floor and it raced into the other room. Celeste dropped the stack on the dining table. The heavy envelope was on top. No return address, just her name printed in neat block letters.

"Please," she said to the room at large. "Not another letter. And I can't believe you made me take the cat."

"Don't open it yet," Volkov said. "Let me check it." He examined the envelope, held it up to the light, ran a small device over it that hummed faintly. As he inspected it, he declared, "Pets help our humanity" before he turned professional again. "No obvious chemical signatures. No transmitter. Probably paper. Or someone's gotten more subtle."

She slit it open with a butter knife.

Inside was a single sheet of paper and a small, plain key. The letter was hand-written in tight, precise script.

Celeste Morgan,
Your mother left things here she didn't trust Eidolon to see.
If you want to know why she built you, come alone.
The key fits a storage locker at the below address.
Bring no one.
Tell no one.
She knew this day would come.
—M

A Manhattan address was written beneath, the location of a storage facility on the edge of Chelsea.

"'M'," Volkov said. "Maestro. Modest."

"Could be someone else," Celeste said, though her gut said otherwise.

"Your mother," he repeated, eyes narrowing. "She left something outside their reach."

"Or he wants me to think she did," Celeste said.

He watched her carefully. "You're not actually considering going alone."

"Of course not," she said automatically.

He didn't look convinced. "This could be a trap," he said. "A secondary one. Yesterday was about seeing how you react to personal threats. This could be about seeing how you react to promises."

"You think he forged her hand?" Her voice was barely above a whisper.

"I think he's capable of anything that gets you where he wants you," Volkov said. "And I think dangling your mother is the most direct route there."

She rolled the key between her fingers. It was small, cold, ordinary. "My mother helped create Eidolon," Celeste said. "She knew Harriman. She knew the Maestro. If she hid something from them, it might be the only thing in this mess that wasn't curated."

"Or they let her hide it because it served them," Volkov said.

"You're very good at worst-case scenarios," she said.

"That's why I'm alive," he said.

She walked to the window and stared at the city below. Yellow cabs, pedestrians, a dog walker with six leashes, a woman carrying a cello case that looked like a smaller version of hers.

She pressed her forehead lightly against the glass. "I can't not look," she said softly. "If there's even a chance that she left something for me…"

"You'll chase it," he finished. "I know."

She turned back to him. "Come with me," she said.

He opened his mouth to protest; she held up a hand.

"Not inside," she said. "You wait nearby. Not to stop me. To pull me out if things go bad."

He considered that. "That's a compromise I can live with," he said. "Barely."

"Barely is better than not at all," she said.

He nodded once. "Not tonight. You're exhausted. And if they're watching, they'll expect you to jump at the bait immediately. Waiting makes them nervous."

"Nervous people are dangerous," she said.

"Nervous people make mistakes," he countered.

She exhaled. "Fine. Tomorrow."

He picked up the stack of fan mail and flicked through it. "You know, normal people get letters that say 'thank you for your music, you changed my life,' not 'come to this ominous location, solve your trauma.'"

"I get those too," she said. "They're just less… actionable." She shrugged and flashed him a grin.

One postcard fell out of an envelope and fluttered to the floor. It was from Tokyo and was a photo of Suntory Hall at night. A familiar hand had written on the back in neat, looping letters.

You broke me and put me back together again. Thank you. —A listener

She stared at it a moment, then set it aside.

"Polyphony," Volkov said again, almost to himself.

"You keep saying that," she said.

"You're living in more than one key," he said. "It's messy. And it makes you harder to predict."

He set the letters down and moved to the table, opening the manila folders. "These," he said, "are what I was working on while you were playing for people who don't realize their assassins use the same door they do."

She sat across from him, the storage key still in her hand.

He spread out photographs, printouts, scribbled notes. "Eidolon's infrastructure," he said. "Shell companies. Donors. Contractors. Field offices they don't call offices. I traced Foundation Orfeó, the 'music philanthropy' front in Barcelona, back to a financial trust in Dubai. That trust shares a board member with a logistics firm in New Jersey."

"New Jersey," she said. "How glamorous." Sarcasm oozed from her.

"That firm," he went on, ignoring her, "has three warehouses in the tri-state area. Two are clean. One isn't." He tapped a photograph of an anonymous warehouse in an anonymous industrial park. "Eidolon moves equipment through it," he said. "Weapons, tech, fake documents. And probably people, when they want to disappear them locally."

"New York node," she said. "Their vein into my city."

"Yes," he said. "You wanted a war room. This is one of your battle maps."

"Why show me this now?" she asked. "When I'm half-dead from the cistern and contemplating Freudian storage units?"

"Because you said you were done just surviving their tests," he said. "You wanted to hunt. This is a start."

She stared at the photo.

In another life, she would've been preparing for a week of rehearsals at the hall, dinners with donors, interviews about "the emotional journey of the tour." Instead, she was planning operations against the people who had once pointed her at targets like a rifle.

"You realize what happens if we hit that warehouse," she said. "We'll be moving from defensive to offensive. That's… a line."

"You crossed plenty of lines in other directions," he said. "This one, at least, points toward the people who deserve it."

"We can't just blow it up," she said. "There could be workers there who don't know who they're really working for. Guards who think they're just doing security for crates full of electronics."

"We gather intel first," he said. "Watch. Listen. Find patterns. We don't have to move fast to move well."

She rubbed her eyes. "I'm tired of moving well. I want to move decisively."

"Decisive moves without information are how you become them," he said.

She hated that he was right.

A soft thump distracted her. Something had nudged against her calf. Celeste looked down. The cat—small, gray, smug—stood beside her chair, tail up, eyes unimpressed. "I forgot I was strong armed into having a roommate." She scratched under the cat's chin.

The animal meowed once, demanding tribute.

Volkov watched the exchange with an expression she couldn't quite parse. "What will you call it?"

"Fermata," she said almost instantly.

The cat hopped onto her lap, turned around exactly twice, and settled, purring like a small engine.

Volkov smirked. "A pause, huh. And you were just telling me you're not allowed to choose yourself." Volkov's voice was calm, even. "You realize you did, at least once."

"I chose not to put him back on the street or wherever he came from," she said. "That's different."

"It's not," he said. "You agreed to let something soft into your space."

She scratched behind the cat's ear. It butted into her hand with imperious affection. "He doesn't ask hard questions," she said.

"He might," Volkov said, "if he could talk."

The corners of her lips quirked into an almost smile.

The city lights outside dimmed as the sky darkened. Traffic noises shifted from evening rush to late-night rhythms. Somewhere above, a neighbor played a trumpet badly.

"Sleep," Volkov said eventually. "We'll watch the storage facility tomorrow. See who comes and goes. No heroics yet."

"You're staying?" she asked.

"For tonight," he said, "you shouldn't be alone."

"I have a cat now," she said.

He snorted. "Your cat would sell you for better food."

"True," she admitted.

"You take the bed," he said. "I'll take the couch. I've slept in worse places."

"Like sewers," she said.

"Stop bringing that up," he grumbled.

She stood slowly and realized she needed to fill a bowl with water and probably open a can of tuna for the cat. So, she walked into the kitchen and after she set the bowls on the floor, the fatigue hit her all at once, a wave that made her knees momentarily weak.

The cat gobbled the fish like he hadn't had a meal in weeks. She left him to it. But then she paused in the bedroom doorway and eyed Volkov. "What if the key is real? What if she truly hid something for me?"

"Then you'll have one more piece of her that isn't curated by the men who used her work," he said. "And maybe one more reason to choose your own direction."

"And if it's a trap?" she asked.

"Then we spring it on our terms," he said. "For once."

She nodded, half to him, half to herself. "Wake me if you see anything," she said.

"I always do," he replied.

She lay down fully clothed, too exhausted to undress. The cat curled into the curve of her knees, a small, warm weight.

Sleep came in stuttering waves. Somewhere between them, she dreamed of her mother standing at the front of an orchestra, baton in hand, except the musicians were faceless. Aria sat in the concertmaster's seat, gun instead of her drum sticks. The Maestro watched from the back of the hall, hands folded.

In the dream, her mother turned and held the baton out to her.

"You can put it down," she said. "Or you can write a different piece."

When Celeste woke, the room was dim with early morning light. The clock read 6:12 a.m. Volkov sat at the table, laptop open, eyes on some document. He looked like he hadn't moved all night.

"You watched the warehouse feeds," she said.

"Of course," he said. "I piggybacked on their security cameras. They're arrogant; they think their encryption is clever. It's not."

"Anything?" she asked.

"A few trucks," he said. "No faces I recognize. But the pattern's interesting. Data can wait. The key can't."

She sat up, joints stiff, mind spinning up. "Today, then," she said.

"Today," he agreed.

Outside, New York spun on as it always did with coffee carts opening, subways rattling, another ordinary day in a city that had no idea one of its residents was about to walk into yet another place someone else had chosen for her.

Only this time, she thought as she closed her hand around the storage key, the choice afterward would be hers.

The Maestro wanted to move to the next movement.

So would she. On her terms.

Chapter 11

The Storage Score

THE STORAGE FACILITY looked exactly like every storage facility Celeste had ever driven past and never noticed. Gray concrete, red roll-up doors, a small glass office with a bored clerk behind a desk, a coffee machine that had probably been stale since the Bush administration. The kind of place where people kept the things they couldn't quite throw away and couldn't quite live with.

Perfect place to hide someone else's mess, she thought.

She sat in the passenger seat of the SUV and watched the building through the windshield. A truck hummed by on the street. A woman wheeled a dolly stacked with boxes toward the entrance, earbuds in, oblivious.

Volkov sat behind the wheel, eyes on the side mirror, face in that neutral mask that meant he was cataloguing everyone within a fifty-yard radius.

"Still time to pretend we misread the letter and go get pancakes instead," Celeste said.

"I don't eat pancakes," he replied.

"Of course, you don't," she muttered.

He nodded at the glove compartment. "Last chance to leave the key in there and walk away."

She opened it, looked at the small piece of metal resting on the manual, then closed it again.

"We both know I'm not leaving it," she said.

"Worth trying," he said.

She pulled her phone from her pocket and typed a quick message to Lena: **Alive. Running boring errands. Don't practice today; your bow arm needs a break.**

A few seconds later: **I knew it. You're secretly my mom. Bring me back a fridge magnet from "boring errands."**

Celeste huffed a small breath that almost qualified as a laugh. She put the phone away. Some parts of her life felt almost normal. Others… not so much.

"All right," Volkov said, "let's choreograph this. You go in like a regular New Yorker finally dealing with the emotional detritus of her ex's vinyl collection. Don't linger in the office. Take the elevator if they have one. You go straight to the unit, open it, and look. No touching anything until I get eyes in there."

"How exactly are you going to have 'eyes in there' if the letter says I have to go alone?" she asked.

He held up a small, ugly little device that looked like a hybrid between a beetle and a paperclip. "Camera. Transmits to my phone. Stick it to something near the entrance when you unlock the door. I'll be in the hallway before you're halfway through."

"You're impossible," she said.

"You like that about me," he replied.

She took the device, turning it over in her fingers. "And if they've filled the unit with explosives?"

"Then I'll be glad you didn't go in without me," he said. "You're wearing the pendant?"

She touched the chain under her sweater. "Yes."

"The ring?"

She flexed her right hand. "Used the EMP in Istanbul. This one's empty."

"I'll get you a new one," he said. "For now, rely on your brain."

"That's always plan A," she said.

He watched her for a beat longer. "Remember," he said, voice lower, "this may be real. Your mother may have left something here for you. That's allowed to matter."

"Noted," she said. "Now stop being almost gentle. It's unnerving."

"Go," he said.

She stepped out of the car, the cold January air biting the edges of her face. The city felt different in this part of town, less polished, more industrial. Trucks, warehouses, the river not far away.

Inside, the storage office was warmer than it had any right to be. A heater rattled in the corner. The clerk, who was mid-twenties, with a nose ring and wearing a black hoodie, looked up from his phone.

"Can I help you?" he asked, tone saying he sincerely hoped she would say no.

"I have a locker here," she said. "But I haven't been by in a while. I think I still have the key." She set the small metal key on the desk.

He picked it up, glanced at it, then tapped at his computer. "Unit 5C," he said. "We still have it under 'Morgan, C.' Photo ID?"

She slid her driver's license across.

He compared, nodded, and slid it back. "You're good. Down the hall, elevator to five, follow the signs to C-block."

"That's it?" she asked.

He shrugged. "You want me to make it harder?"

"No," she said. "Thanks."

As she turned, he added, "We have moving blankets and boxes on sale if you need them."

"I'll improvise," she said.

The hallway beyond the office was lined with roll-up doors in identical red. The fluorescent lights hummed overhead. The air smelled faintly of dust, cardboard, and the chemical clean that never really masked mildew.

She spoke without moving her lips. "Office clerk matches database?"

"Nothing interesting," Volkov's voice murmured in her ear. "Local. Too bored to be dangerous."

She walked to the elevator at the end of the hall, pressed the button. It arrived with a complaining ding. The inside was metal and graffiti, the kind of claustrophobic box that made her wish she'd spent less time reading about building codes in old cities.

"Any other entries for unit 5C?" she whispered.

"Rental date, ten years ago," Volkov said. "List address is a PO box. No payment issues. Auto–draft from a bank account that goes through three shells before landing at an institution in Switzerland."

"So, yes, my mother," Celeste said.

"It fits," he agreed.

The elevator doors opened on the fifth floor. Rows of identical doors stretched in both directions with the numbers stenciled in black. The lighting here flickered a little.

She followed the arrows for C–block, boots silent on the concrete. 5C was halfway down, tucked between two larger units. A single overhead light buzzed above it.

Her pulse picked up. She took a slow breath, then knelt and fitted the key into the lock. Before she turned it, she palmed the tiny beetle–camera Volkov had given her and stuck it to the frame, as if steadying herself. The device vibrated once, a barely perceptible acknowledgement that it was live.

"Visual's up," Volkov's voice came through in her ear softly. "I'm in the stairwell one floor down. No movement in the hall. No thermal signatures beyond you."

Celeste turned the key, and the lock clicked with an almost anticlimactic neatness. She slid it free, lifted the latch, and rolled the door up.

The unit was about the size of a small bedroom. No bomb. No glaring lights. No ominous mannequins. Just boxes. Neatly stacked, labeled in crisp handwriting she knew too well.

CELLO – JUVENILE PIECES

ACADEMICS

FIELD NOTES

CORRESPONDENCE – PERSONAL

CORRESPONDENCE – EIDOLON

Her breath caught on the last.

"I'm in," she murmured.

"I see it," Volkov said. "Stay in the doorway. Let the camera drink it in. Don't touch the Eidolon box yet."

She stepped just inside, out of the hallway, leaving the door half–rolled as if she wanted light and air. The concrete floor was cold through her boots.

Her mother's presence leached from the cardboard in ways that had nothing to do with ink and everything to do with order. Even in storage, she'd organized her past.

"Anything weird?" she asked.

"Nothing wired," Volkov said. "No transmitters. No obvious trap signatures. It looks… mundane." He sounded almost offended.

Celeste moved to the box labeled ACADEMICS and lifted the lid.

Inside were notebooks, binders, old syllabi from universities they'd lived nearby. A photo of her mother in front of a whiteboard full of complex diagrams, smiling.

She swallowed.

FIELD NOTES held smaller notebooks, the kind you could tuck

into a pocket. Her mother's tight script filled page after page with observations, dates, names blacked out with careful strokes, coordinates.

CORRESPONDENCE – PERSONAL was full of letters. Some from colleagues, some from old friends, a few from a handwriting Celeste recognized as her own at twelve, complaining about scales and thanking her mother for a book.

She closed it gently.

Last was CORRESPONDENCE – EIDOLON.

"Now?" she asked.

"Now," Volkov said.

She lifted the lid.

Inside, instead of loose letters, Celeste found a single black binder and a sealed envelope. Her mother's handwriting on the envelope: FOR CELESTE. OPEN WHEN YOU ARE NO LONGER ABLE TO PRETEND.

Her knees almost buckled.

"Sit," Volkov said immediately. "On the floor. Now."

She sank down, back against the cool wall, the envelope in her hands.

"This is a bad idea," he said. "Emotionally. Tactically. Spiritually."

"I know," she whispered.

"You're going to open it anyway," he said.

"Yes," she said.

She slit the envelope carefully, as if any violence would hurt more than paper.

Inside was a letter. Not long. Two pages, single–sided.

She recognized the date at the top. Three months before Berlin. Before the car bomb. Before everything.

> My Celeste,
>
> If you are reading this, something has broken.
>
> Either I am dead, or you have discovered enough of my work to resent me, or both. I wish I could say I'm writing

to apologize, but I don't trust that word. It's too easy to say "sorry" and still believe the choices were necessary.

So instead, I will try to be honest in a way I have not been while alive.

You were not an accident. I chose to have you knowing the world I was working in. I believed—perhaps arrogantly—that I could build a life for you that integrated both music and violence without letting the latter devour the former.

Eidolon began, as all bad things do, with good intentions. We saw rot. We saw men who used their power to break lives. We saw governments look away. We wanted to act.

I built frameworks. Harriman built pipelines. Others built cover. We all told ourselves we were conducting necessary dissonance.

And then I had you.

I put a cello in your hands because I knew you needed a language that was not kill or don't kill. I taught you discipline because you were powerful even as a child, and power without discipline is cruelty.

I agreed to let them recruit you because I believed you would be better than we were. Better shot. Better judgment. Better heart.

This is where I failed. I convinced myself that because you had conscience, you could carry more weight than we could. That you could make the choices we flinched from. That you would not break.

I forgot that even the strongest instrument has a resonance point beyond which it shatters.

If you are reading this, you have likely reached it. You have seen enough blood that the stories Harriman told you about "targets" and "necessary evil" ring hollow. You have killed men who deserved it and men you suspect might not have. You have been used as both weapon and symbol.

You are tired.

You are furious.

Good.

You have two paths.

One: you take control of what we built. You become the Maestro they are whispering about in rooms you have not seen. You insist on transparency where there was none. You create rules. You will break yourself trying to enforce them.

Two: you burn it down. You dismantle networks, expose accounts, drag names into the light. You will break yourself watching what happens after.

I cannot tell you which path is right. I have argued both in my head, in meetings, in the bath, in dreams. Every argument ends with bodies.

What I can tell you is this: if you choose either path alone, you will end up worse than we were. Not because you are bad, but because no one can hold this much power and pain without warping.

You need people who know you as more than a blade. Musicians. Friends. Even men like the one reading this over your shoulder right now, if he has earned it.

Celeste glanced involuntarily at the tiny camera.

"Your mother was unnerving," Volkov said. "Remind me to never underestimate her retroactively."

She kept reading.

Do not cut yourself off from everyone who could say "no" to you. Harriman never tolerated dissent. That is why he had to die.

Yes, I know you killed him. I built you. I know how far you go when pushed.

If you lead them, lead with people who can walk away. If you destroy them, do it while someone holds your hand.

The binder beneath this letter contains things they don't know I kept. Names. Accounts. Weak points. I stole them slowly, over years, and hid them in plain sight. I could have used them myself, but I was not ready to accept what that would make me.

You may be.

Or you may choose to walk away from all of it. Change your name. Play cello in a small town. Get a dog. Teach children who will never know what you were capable of.

If you do that, I will not be disappointed. I will be relieved.

But if you stay in this fight, if you pick up the baton I was too much a coward to wield, do it on your terms.

Not Harriman's.

Not the Maestro's.

Not mine.

Yours.

I am sorry. I am proud. I am terrified of what I made, and I love you more than I fear you.

You hold the bow. Remember that.

—Mama

Her eyes blurred.

She blinked hard with her jaw clenched.

"Celeste?" Volkov's voice was softer than she'd ever heard it. "What did she say?"

"She admitted… all of it," Celeste said. Her voice sounded raw to her own ears. "That she built me. That she thought I could do what they couldn't. That she was wrong and maybe right and terrified."

"And?" he prompted.

"And she left us a map," Celeste said.

She slid the letter back into the envelope and reached for the binder. Inside, neatly ordered, were tabbed sections.

FINANCIAL

PERSONNEL

OPERATIONS

FAILURES

Pages of printouts, annotated in her mother's hand. Account numbers. Shell companies. Boards of directors. Cross-referenced with names Celeste recognized and some she didn't. A whole hidden score of Eidolon's structure.

"She stole from them," Volkov said, awe threaded through his voice. "Quietly. For years."

"She called it cowardice," Celeste said. "Not using it."

"She called leading them cowardice, too," he said. "Your mother had a strange relationship with bravery."

"She had me," Celeste said. "That complicates things."

She flipped to the section labeled FAILURES. Fewer pages, but the ink here was darker, angrier. Operations gone wrong. Collateral far outside acceptable parameters. Notes in the margin: H. insisted on proceeding despite intel gap. Civilian casualties. This cannot continue.

Page after page of the same pattern.

"Blackmail material," Volkov murmured. "On her own people."

"Insurance," Celeste said. "Against herself." She closed the binder.

For a moment, she let herself sit there on the cold concrete, back to stone, boxes full of her past around her, a stranger's camera watching through a beetle on the doorframe, her mother's confession in her lap.

Half musician. Half assassin. Daughter of a woman who'd tried to build a better scalpel and ended up slicing herself open.

"So," Volkov asked, "what does this change?"

"Everything," she said. "And nothing."

He made an impatient sound. "That's not helpful."

"It confirms what the Maestro said, but from her side," Celeste said slowly. "She wanted me to lead. She also wanted me to burn them down. She wanted mutually exclusive things and handed me the paradox."

"And gave you tools," he said. "Don't forget that part."

"No," she said. "I won't."

Footsteps echoed faintly in the hallway outside.

She stiffened. "What—" she began.

"Two people," Volkov voice was rushed. "Male, mid–weight. Walking past, not stopping. They're talking about sports. You're fine."

The footsteps receded.

She exhaled. "We can't leave this here," she said, tapping the binder.

"No," he agreed. "We copy it, digitize it, secure it, then move the physical somewhere they'll never think to look. Or destroy it completely once we've extracted what we need."

Some stubborn part of her rebelled at the idea of burning her mother's careful ink. "Not yet," she said. "This is… her handwriting. Her thought processes. I'm not ready to turn it into just data."

Volkov was silent for a moment. "Okay." His voice was low. "We'll find a place for it."

She stood, knees protesting, and slid the binder into the cello–shaped padded bag she'd brought instead of her usual hard case. It fit better than any instrument.

The letter stayed in her pocket.

She took one last look around the unit. Childhood music. Academic achievements. Field notes from a life she'd only glimpsed through redacted files. Correspondence from a world that had thought of her mother as an asset, not as someone who made grilled cheese and threatened to toss cellos.

"Lock it," Volkov said. "We'll decide later what else to salvage."

She pulled the door down, the metal rattling. For a second, as it closed, she had the odd feeling of leaving her mother in the dark again.

In the hall, Volkov waited, hands in his pockets, jacket unzipped. He looked like any other man killing time between domestic tragedies. His eyes flicked to the padded bag. "Congratulations," he said. "You've stolen from Eidolon."

"Familial tradition," she said.

They walked to the elevator. As they descended, he asked, "What did she call me?" He paused for a beat. "In the letter," he clarified, "she implied I'd be reading over your shoulder."

"She said, 'even men like the one reading this over your shoulder right now, if he has earned it,'" Celeste said.

He digested that. "She anticipated someone like me."

"She anticipated me not doing this alone," Celeste said. "She underestimated my stubbornness."

"Good," he said. "I'd hate to be a surprise footnote."

They stepped out into the ground–floor hallway. The clerk glanced up as they passed, then did a double–take at the bag.

"Did you just put a cello in storage?" he asked, mildly horrified. "My sister plays. She'd call that blasphemy."

"I took one out," Celeste said. "And I'm putting the past in."

He snorted. "Heavy."

She almost smiled.

Outside, the air felt sharper. They walked to the SUV in silence. Traffic hummed on the avenue. Somewhere, a siren wailed.

When they were inside, engine idling, Volkov said, "So. Your mother's binder. The warehouse. The Maestro. Aria. Eidolon's donors. Where do you start?"

"Not with them," she said.

He raised an eyebrow. "No?"

"With us," she said. "With rules."

"Rules," he repeated, nodding his head once.

"If I take even a piece of what she left—if I use those names, those accounts—I'm stepping into the game she and the Maestro were playing," Celeste said. "I refuse to do it without constraints."

"You want to write an ethics code for targeted killing," he said.

"You say it like it's absurd," she replied.

"It is," he said. "And yet… I've seen worse plans."

She looked out the window, at a woman dragging a reluctant bulldog across the crosswalk.

"I need people who can tell me no," she said. "Lena. Esra. You said she has skills. Maybe Aria, if I can get her to join any team but her own. You, if you can stop being allergic to hope for five minutes."

"I'm allergic to group decisions," he muttered. "And Esra was trained similar to you plus she has advanced degrees in computers. I found her dossier."

"Too bad you're allergic to group decisions," she said. "If I go after Eidolon with only your cynicism and my anger, we'll burn the world down."

"That's dramatic," he said.

"True," she said.

He drummed his fingers once on the steering wheel. "You're talking about… what? A council? A board?"

"A string quartet," she said.

He gave her a look.

"Not literally," she said. "A small group of people who know enough to be dangerous, who care enough to balance me. No one person gets a full score. No one holds the baton alone."

"And you think Lena is going to be willing to join your ethically ambiguous shadow committee?" he asked.

"She already is," Celeste said. "She got kidnapped for me and still hasn't quit. That's consent by trauma."

"That's not how consent works," he said.

"I know," she said. "I'll ask her. Properly. Let her say no."

"And if she says yes?" he asked.

"Then I owe her even more than I already do," she said. "And I'll spend the rest of my life trying not to get her hurt."

He sighed. "I'll make a list," he said.

"Of what?" she asked.

"Lines," he said. "Things we won't do. Targets we won't touch. Methods we won't use. You want rules? Start there."

"And if the rules cost lives?" she asked.

"They will," he said. "But so will the lack of them. At least this way, we know which ghosts belong to us."

Her fingers found the edge of her mother's letter in her pocket. *You hold the bow. Remember that.*

"I'll talk to Lena tonight," she said. "Esra after that. Maybe Aria if we decide we need her. Carefully."

"You understand that the more people you bring in, the more points of failure you add," Volkov said.

"Yes," she said, "but I also add more points of view."

He shook his head, half exasperated, half resigned. "You're building a committee to dismantle a death cult," he said. "Somewhere, Harriman is screaming in whatever miserable afterlife he earned."

"Good," she said.

He pulled away from the curb. "Where to?" he asked.

"Home," she said. "For now. I need to scan this binder, feed the cat, and call a violinist."

"A glamorous life," he said.

"I never promised otherwise," she replied.

As the SUV merged into traffic, New York rose around them, chaotic and indifferent. People rushed to jobs, to lovers, to errands, to nowhere in particular.

None of them knew that in a small apartment on the Upper West Side, a woman with a cello and a newly stolen binder was about to try something that had broken better people than her mother.

None of them cared. That was alright. They had their lives.

She had her score. And for the first time since she'd killed Harriman, since Berlin, since the first time she'd realized her music could be a weapon, Celeste felt a strange, fragile thing under her ribs.

Not hope. Not yet. But the outline of a plan that belonged to her.

The next movement was coming. And this time, she was done pretending she wasn't the one writing it.

Chapter 12

Terms of Engagement

CELESTE HAD NEVER been so painfully aware of the sound a scanner made. The machine on her dining table hummed and clicked, light bar sliding back and forth under the lid with mechanical indifference. Each pass captured another page of her mother's handwriting of numbers, names, cross–references and turned it into a PDF on Volkov's laptop.

"You're sure it's not connected to anything," she said for the third time.

"It's air–gapped," he said without looking up. "No Wi-Fi. No Bluetooth. No cables to the outside world. It's dumber than some toasters."

"That's not as reassuring as you think," she muttered.

He lifted the binder page, set the next one down, closed the lid. The scanner whirred.

They'd been at it for hours. The winter light outside had slid from thin gray to the darker bruise of early evening. Her newly adopted cat had abandoned them for the couch, offended that the warm rectangle of the scanner was not for him.

"We'll hit FINANCIAL and FAILURES first," Volkov said. "Those are the most leverage. Personnel can wait."

"I want the whole picture," Celeste said.

"You'll get it," he said. "But it's like sight–reading a symphony. Start with the themes, not the second bassoon line."

She paced between the table and the window, letter still folded in her pocket. "You need people who know you as more than a blade," she muttered to herself repeating her mother's words in the letter. Her mother, who had built the blade in the first place.

"Stop walking grooves into the floor," Volkov said without heat. "You're making the building nervous."

"I don't like being in one place when they know where I live," she said.

"They always knew where you lived," he said. "It was in your contract rider."

"Helpful observation," she said.

He glanced at the clock on the microwave. "Speaking of people who know you as more than a blade, don't you have a call to make?"

She checked her phone. It was just past seven.

Lena would have had time to nap, shower, maybe make herself look less like someone who'd been tied to a chair above an underground lake.

"You can listen," Celeste said, "but don't talk."

"That's my favorite arrangement," he said.

She dialed and Lena answered on the second ring, no greeting, just,

"If this is a butt dial, I'm hanging up."

"It's not," Celeste said. "Hi."

"Hey," Lena said. There was the rustle of fabric, a clink of glass. "You sound weird. More weird than usual."

"I found something," Celeste said. "I need to talk to you. In person."

"Please tell me you're not calling from another continent," Lena said. "Because my trauma budget is full."

"I'm in my apartment," Celeste said. "Upper West Side."

"Oh," Lena said. "Rich people land."

"You're the one who spends her per diems on artisanal coffee," Celeste said.

"Artisanal coffee is a human right," Lena said. "When?"

"Now," Celeste said. "If you're… up for it."

There was a longer pause this time. "Is this a 'you're about to reveal more life–altering espionage' meeting," Lena said, "or a 'you want me to water your plant while you flee the country' meeting?"

"First one," Celeste said. "Plant's fine."

"Traitor," Lena said. "I was hoping for the plant. Send me your address."

Celeste texted it.

"I'll be there in twenty," Lena said. "If I get murdered on the subway, I'm haunting you."

"If you get murdered on the subway, I will burn the MTA to the ground," Celeste said.

"See, that's friendship," Lena said, and hung up.

Volkov slid another page under the scanner. "You're sure about this," he said. It wasn't really a question.

"No," she said, "but I'm going to do it anyway."

He grunted. "I'll vanish before she arrives. She shouldn't see me here."

"You think it's safer that way?" Celeste asked.

"I think the less she knows about my movements, the fewer ways they have to get to her through me," he said. "For now, you're the only link."

"I don't like you disappearing," she said.

"You'll live," he said. "And I'll be in the neighborhood."

He lifted the next page, then paused. "She'll have questions I can't answer for you," he added. "Ones about you, not them."

"I'm aware," Celeste said.

He scanned, saved, closed the binder, and set it gently aside, as if the cardboard were a living thing. "I'll finish the rest at my place," he said. "Shadow copies. Off–site backups. All the paranoid things that keep me charming."

"You're not charming," she said.

He gave her a look that said *yeah, right,* then gathered the laptop and a small external drive. "I'll be two floors down in the lobby or three blocks away with line of sight," he said. "Text if you need an extraction."

"It's my apartment, not a black site," she said.

"With your life, those are synonyms," he said.

He shrugged into his coat, paused at the door. "You're doing the right thing," he said, "telling her. Asking her."

"It doesn't feel right," she said.

"Good," he said. "Things that feel righteous are usually dangerous."

He left, the door clicking softly behind him. The apartment felt bigger without him in it, and emptier in a way that annoyed her.

The cat emerged from the couch, stretching luxuriously. Celeste scooped him up and buried her face in his fur for exactly three seconds before he wriggled free with offended dignity.

"You're not on the ethics council," she told him.

He flicked his tail in a way that said: *obviously.*

Lena arrived twelve minutes later. Celeste buzzed her up, and in under a minute, there was a knock on the door. She opened it to find Lena in a long coat and a knitted beanie, curls stuffed underneath, eyes ringed with fading bruises and stubborn light.

"Wow," Lena said, stepping inside and looking around. "You have windows. And art. I was expecting… I don't know. A mattress on the floor and a wall of weapons."

"The weapons are in the closet," Celeste said.

Lena paused. "You're joking."

Celeste raised an eyebrow.

Lena exhaled. "Okay. Add that to the list of things I'll compartmentalize later."

She unwound her scarf, hesitating when she saw the padded bag on the table.

"That's not your cello," she said.

"No," Celeste said, "it's something my mother left."

Lena's eyes sharpened. "From the dungeon storage you mentioned in your vague text?"

"Not a dungeon," Celeste said. "Storage unit. Different flavor of unsettling."

Lena dropped her coat on the back of a chair and sat, wincing as she adjusted. "All right. Hit me. Though I'm questioning my word choice." She flashed Celeste a weak smile.

Celeste sat opposite her, the letter in her hand. "She knew," she said, "about Eidolon. About me. Obviously. But she also knew I might break."

"Useful," Lena said. "Moms who anticipate their children's mental collapse."

"She left me this," Celeste said, holding up the envelope. "And a binder full of information on Eidolon. Accounts. Names. Weak points. Things she stole from them without telling anyone."

Lena's eyebrows climbed. "So, your mother was secretly stealing from the secret murdering people. That's… on brand."

"She framed it as cowardice," Celeste said. "Not using it."

"What does the letter say?" Lena asked.

Celeste hesitated. The instinct to keep it private, to hold it to her chest like a last unbroken piece of childhood, was strong. *You need people who know you as more than a blade* echoed in her head.

She unfolded the letter. "She says she's proud and sorry and terrified of me," Celeste said. "She admits she built me. She admits she let them recruit me. She thought my conscience would make me better than they were."

Lena's face stayed very still. "That's… a lot to put on a kid."

"I wasn't a kid when she wrote it," Celeste said. "Not technically."

"You still are when it's your mother," Lena said quietly.

"She gives me two options," Celeste went on. "Lead them, or burn them down. She says either path will break me. She says doing either alone will make me worse than they were."

"She's not wrong," Lena murmured.

"And then she tells me to have people around who can tell me no," Celeste said. "Musicians. Friends. 'Even men like the one reading this over your shoulder right now, if he has earned it.'"

"Cryptic," Lena smirked. "And creepy accurate."

Celeste folded the letter again. "I want to do something with what she left," she said. "Not just hand it to some agency and hope they don't become Eidolon with better stationery. But I refuse to do it the way they would."

Lena tipped her head. "Okay. Translation."

"I'm going to fight them," Celeste said. The words felt different this time, less reactive, more deliberate. "Not just by dodging their tests, but by going after their structure. Their funding. Their ability to hurt people like you. People like my mother thought she was protecting the world from."

Lena's throat worked. "And you want… what from me?"

"Rules," Celeste said. "Perspective. Resistance."

Lena blinked. "You're asking a violinist to be your conscience?"

"Yes," Celeste said simply.

Lena's laugh was incredulous and shaky. "That's the dumbest, nicest thing anyone's ever asked me."

"I'm serious," Celeste said. "If I use this"—she tapped the bag—"I want people in the room who are not trained killers. Who think about collateral in musical terms, not acceptable ratios. I want… a council. Small. People who know me as more than a tool and aren't afraid to tell me to sit down."

"And you think I'll magically be good at this because…?" Lena prompted.

"Because you already told me you'd hit me with your violin case if I took the Eidolon job without telling you," Celeste said. "Because you were kidnapped and your first reaction was 'I will bite them.' Because you still haven't run."

Lena stared at the table. Her hands traced the grain of the wood.

"What would it mean," she asked slowly, "to say yes? Practically."

"It would mean knowing more," Celeste said. "About what I do. About what they do. About what we're going to try to do to them. It would mean being in danger in different ways. It would mean… having opinions on who deserves to be taken off the board and how."

"That sounds terrible," Lena said.

"Yes," Celeste agreed.

"Why do you want me to do something terrible?" Lena asked, not looking up.

"Because you like people too much," Celeste said. "You cry when the second oboe misses their entrance. You apologize to your instrument when you play sharp. You give stray dogs names and then argue with yourself about not being able to take them all home. You are not built for 'acceptable collateral.'"

Lena's mouth twisted. "You're weaponizing my softness."

"I'm asking you to use it," Celeste said.

Silence settled between them like dust.

On the floor, the cat chose that moment to jump onto Lena's lap. He curled there as if he'd done it a thousand times, purring. Lena's fingers went automatically to his fur, stroking.

"You always said music needed tension to be interesting," she said finally. "Dissonance resolving. Big chords, bigger releases."

"Yes," Celeste said.

"This feels like… playing wrong notes on purpose and hoping it somehow turns into jazz," Lena said.

"It might," Celeste said. "Or it might turn into noise that gets us killed."

"You're terrible at recruitment speeches," Lena said.

"I'm not trying to sell you," Celeste said. "I'm trying to give you a choice I never got."

"That's a low blow," Lena said, but there was no real heat in it. She took a breath that shivered on the way in. "If I say no," she said. "If I tell you to keep me in the orchestra lane and leave me out of your shadow committee… what happens?"

"Then we go back to being what we were," Celeste said. "I'll still protect you. I'll still show up when you need me. I'll just have to make these decisions without your input. I'll hate it, but I'll respect it."

"And if I say yes?" Lena asked.

"Then you get a vote," Celeste said. "On who we go after. On how we do it. On when we stop. Your vote will not be decorative."

"Who else is on this… council?" Lena asked, the word tasting strange.

"Volkov," Celeste said. "He has skills and information I don't. He's good at telling me when something is stupid."

"I've noticed," Lena said drily.

"Esra if she agrees," Celeste went on. "She understands security and optics and how institutions react. Maybe Aya, later. She knows money. And she knows me in ways I can't ignore."

"And Aria?" Lena asked.

Celeste swallowed. "Too volatile. Too aligned with Eidolon still. Maybe someday. Not now."

Lena considered that, stroking the cat, who had decided she was his now.

"You're going to do this regardless," she said. It wasn't a question.

"Yes," Celeste said.

"Then it's not really a choice," Lena said. "It's how close I want to stand to the blast."

"Exactly," Celeste agreed, eying her friend.

The cat rolled onto his back, paws in the air, demanding homage. Lena obliged automatically. "When they took me," she said, so quietly Celeste barely heard it, "I thought 'this is what happens when you orbit a star. You get burned.'"

"I'm not a star," Celeste said.

"You are," Lena said, looking up. "In the 'massive gravitational pull that warps everything around you' way, not in the 'pretty dress on a red carpet' way."

"That's rude," Celeste said.

"You like it," Lena said. She breathed out, a humorless puff of air. "I was angry," she said. "At them. At you. At myself for not seeing it coming. And then you walked in, and I realized I was more scared of what they'd do to you if you let me die than of dying."

Celeste's throat closed for a second. "That's not fair," she managed.

"Nothing about this is fair," Lena said. "Here's what is: if we're already in this, if my name is already on their board somewhere as 'useful leverage,' then I might as well pick up an oar."

"That sounds like a yes," Celeste said, heart thudding.

"It's a 'yes with conditions,'" Lena said.

"Name them," Celeste said.

"First," Lena said, holding up a finger, dislodging the cat, who glared and relocated to the couch. "No murdering my section. Ever. If any plan you come up with involves 'sacrifice a violinist,' the answer is no."

"I would never—" Celeste began.

"Not even as a thought experiment," Lena said. "They're mine.

You don't get to use them."

"Agreed," Celeste said.

"Second," Lena went on. "We don't get to decide who 'deserves' to die over wine in your living room just because we have a binder and a grudge. We need criteria. Actual, written rules. No 'vibes–based justice.'"

"We're drafting them," Celeste said. "Volkov's making a list of lines we won't cross."

"He would," Lena muttered. "Third: I get full disclosure. No half–truths. No omissions because you think you're 'protecting' me. If I'm in, I'm in."

"That's the hard one," Celeste said.

"I know," Lena said. "Take it or leave it."

Celeste closed her eyes for a moment. *You do not cut yourself off from everyone who could say "no" to you,* her mother's advice reverberated in her head. "I'll try," she said.

"Nope," Lena said. "Not good enough. This is yes or no. I'm not asking you to text me every time you pee. I'm asking you not to keep me in the dark about the things my life might depend on."

Celeste opened her eyes. "Full disclosure on operations and risks that touch you," she said. "No strategic lies. If I break that, you walk."

"And hit you with my violin case," Lena said.

"And hit me with your violin case," Celeste echoed.

They looked at each other across the table, before Lena extended her hand. "Council member, then," she said. "Against my better judgment."

Celeste took it. The handshake felt like a vow and a sentence all at once.

"Great," Lena said, voice too bright. "We're founding a murder–ethics committee. Do we get jackets?"

"We're not calling it that," Celeste said.

"Oh, we are absolutely calling it that," Lena said. "In my head, anyway."

Celeste exhaled a laugh she hadn't realized she'd been holding. Something in her chest loosened, just a little.

The cat jumped back onto the table, sat squarely on the padded bag, and stared at them both.

"See?" Lena said. "He approves. He knows I'm the only one here with sense."

"I thought you said you were joining against your better judgment," Celeste said.

"Exactly," Lena said. "I have sense. I'm just ignoring it."

Elsewhere in the world, the Maestro watched the recording without sound.

The image on his screen showed a cistern in Istanbul—columns, shadows, water like black glass. Figures moved: Celeste, Aria, the hostage. His tech had salvaged fragments from backups; the EMP and Aria's bullet had destroyed the primary feeds, but nothing stayed dead forever in a system as redundant as Eidolon's.

He tapped a key. The image froze on Celeste's face as she activated whatever device had knocked out his eyes.

The still frame captured fury and something like grief. The kind of expression people made when they were done being polite and not yet done being human.

"She's better than Harriman thought," he said.

The man standing at the edge of the desk shifted. He was lean, older than his posture suggested, with iron hair and the kind of gaze that took measure and gave nothing back.

"Harriman underestimated variables that made him uncomfortable," the man said.

"And you don't?" the Maestro asked mildly.

"I catalog them," the man said. "I don't pretend they don't exist."

The Maestro smiled faintly. "What do you make of Kovalenko?"

He tapped another key. The screen jumped to the moment Aria turned her weapon and shot the ropes instead of the hostage.

"Compromised," the man said. "Emotionally entangled. Dangerous to leave active. Wasteful to discard."

"Yes," the Maestro said. "She's ours by architecture, but no longer by reflex. She flinched when I ordered her to kill the girl."

"Some people balk at friendly fire," the man said.

"Friendly," the Maestro repeated, amused. "You overestimate their bonds. They were designed as a cohort, not as a family."

"Design and reality rarely match," the man said.

The Maestro watched the image flicker: flashbang, movement, chaos. Volkov appearing from the shadows like an unwelcome footnote. The three of them escaping into the tunnel.

"Volkov complicates things," he said.

"He's external," the man said. "Wrong training set. Wrong loyalties. He makes her harder to control."

"Harder for us," the Maestro conceded. "But perhaps more useful in the long run. A conductor needs a foil. Or she grows brittle."

"You're still assuming she'll take the baton," the man said.

"She will," the Maestro said. "Or she'll try to break it and discover it's more fused to her hand than she thought."

He turned to another screen, bringing up a live feed from a traffic camera in New York. It showed a corner near an industrial district, bland as bread.

"There's activity at the Newark node," the man said. "She may hit that next."

"Let her," the Maestro said. "It will make the donors nervous. Nervous donors listen."

"And if she burns their warehouse?" the man asked.

"We have others," the Maestro said. "What we don't have is another Celeste Morgan. Not one with her mix of skill and conscience. Her mother was reckless. She made a singularity."

"You keep calling it conscience," the man said. "I call it hesitation."

"Potato, potahto," the Maestro said.

He switched the screen again, to a still photo of Celeste's mother. Younger than in the video Celeste had seen, eyes bright, mouth set.

"You left us an interesting inheritance," he talked to the screen. "Thank you."

"She left it for her," the man said.

"Yes," the Maestro said. "Which is what makes it ours. Eventually." He leaned back in his chair. "Let her play with her little committee," he said. "Let her believe she can write rules that contain this. Every rule is an admission that the game matters. Once she commits to structure, she's halfway to running it."

"And if she surprises you?" the man asked. "If she refuses both paths?"

The Maestro smiled. "Then," he said, "we give the baton to someone less interesting." He switched off the feed.

On the dark screen, his own reflection stared back at him, the room behind him ghosting faintly.

"We're approaching the end of the second movement," he said. "Time to introduce a new theme."

Back in the apartment, Celeste poured Lena and herself a glass of water. They clinked, not quite like a toast.

"To murder–ethics," Lena said.

"Stop calling it that," Celeste said.

They drank.

"I should go," Lena said after a while, pushing to her feet with a little groan. "If I stay, I'll fall asleep on your floor, and that's a level of intimacy I'm not ready for."

"You can crash on the couch," Celeste said.

"I like my own bed," Lena said. "Also, I have to call my mother back before she starts imagining I joined a cult."

Celeste winced. "That's… complicated."

"Yeah, well," Lena said. "At least my cult has better music." She pulled on her coat, wrapped her scarf. At the door, she turned. "One more condition," she said.

Celeste braced. "Yes?"

"You don't get to decide alone when you're too far gone," Lena said. "If I tell you you're sounding like him—your Maestro friend—you don't get to argue. You step back. You let us pull you out."

Celeste's skin crawled at the thought. "I'm not—" she began.

"You're not now," Lena said. "But power warps. People bend. You're scary because you know that. Let that fear mean something."

Celeste swallowed. "Okay," she said. "If you say I sound like him, I listen. I step back."

"And if you don't," Lena said, "I'll hit you with my violin case. And then Batman will shoot you in the leg."

"His name is not Batman," Celeste said.

"It is until he tells me a different one," Lena said. She opened the door, paused. "We're not the good guys," she said. "You know that, right?"

"Yes," Celeste said.

"But we're not them," Lena added. "That's something."

The door closed behind her.

Celeste stood there for a long moment, hand on the knob, listening to the fading echo of Lena's footsteps in the hall.

Her phone buzzed.

Volkov: **How'd it go?**

She typed back: **She said yes. With conditions.**

His reply: **Good. I'd have been worried if she didn't have conditions.**

She hesitated, then added: **You're in, too. Officially. We're making rules.**

There was a longer pause this time.

Finally: **I figured. You're not allowed to write them without me. You'd put "no lying" on the list and then explode.**

She smiled, despite everything.

In the corner, the cat had reclaimed the padded bag as his throne. He blinked at her slowly, as if to say: *you got yourself into this.*

"I know," she said aloud. "I'm trying to get us out."

She walked to the window. New York at night was a sheet of black velvet pricked with light. Taxis, office windows, the distant glitter of midtown. Somewhere out there, a warehouse held boxes that fed a machine her mother had helped build. Somewhere farther, men like the Maestro made plans.

She set her palms flat against the cold glass.

Terms of engagement. She had them now: a letter, a binder, a council, a man who had promised to stop her if she became what they wanted. It wasn't enough. It was all she had.

"You hold the bow," she whispered, and this time, she meant not just her mother's voice, but her own.

Tomorrow, they'd start on the rules. After that, the warehouse. After that, the Maestro.

The score was still unwritten. But the opening bars had been laid down, and whether she liked it or not, the world had tuned to her key.

Chapter 13

Crescendo

CELESTE HAD LOOPED Esra in earlier in the day and was surprised how quickly the woman took to the idea and how grateful she seemed to be to be entrusted with information about Celeste's life. Celeste decided to mentally unpack Esra's reaction later.

But now they had work to do.

The rules started on sticky notes. Yellow squares, pink squares, neon green, stuck in a rough circle on Celeste's living room rug. Each one held a few words in different handwritings—Celeste's tight script, Lena's loopy capitals, Esra's efficient block letters, Volkov's angular scrawl.

NO CIVILIANS.

NO OPERATIONS DURING PERFORMANCES.
NO HITS FOR MONEY.
NO HITS FOR REVENGE.
DOCUMENT EVERYTHING.
UNANIMOUS VOTE FOR LETHAL ACTION.

"'Unanimous' is going to get us killed," Volkov said. "You're building a deadlock machine."

"Good," Lena said. "I like us not killing by default."

They were all crammed into Celeste's living room: Lena tucked into the corner of the couch with a heating pad on her ribs; Esra in an armchair, posture sharp despite the late hour; Volkov in the only dining chair that did not wobble, arms folded; Celeste on the floor, legs crossed, back against the couch, cat using her thigh as a pillow.

Outside, New York murmured with sirens, distant horns, the low rumble of trucks. Inside, it was warm, the air thick with the smell of coffee and something Esra had brought in a paper bag that might have once been a pastry.

"Walk me through your objection," Celeste said, tapping the UNANIMOUS note with a pen.

"You're assuming we'll always have time to argue," Volkov said. "Sometimes you have seconds. You see a target. You know what they've done. You know what they're about to do. You don't have time to convene a committee."

"This isn't about field improvisation," Esra said. "It's about planned operations. The ones we're talking about now."

"Planned ops need flexibility," he said.

"Planned ops need restraint," she replied.

Lena made a see-saw motion with her hand. "Look at that. Balance already."

Celeste smiled faintly. "The unanimity clause is for when we decide to target someone with lethal force on purpose," she said. "Not for split-second situations where someone's pointing a gun at a bus full of children."

"Fine," Volkov said. "Add an asterisk. 'Unanimity except in obvious emergencies.'"

"I'll write 'imminent threat,'" Esra said, reaching for a sticky. "If I see the word 'obvious' in a rule book, I'm quitting."

Lena squinted at the mess on the table. "We need a whiteboard," she said. "Or a wall we don't mind ruining."

Celeste glanced at her mostly bare walls. "We could use the hallway," she suggested.

"We are not turning your hallway into a murder-ethics mural," Esra said, "however therapeutic it might be."

"We need something more permanent than sticky notes," Volkov said. "And more secure. These are one good gust of wind away from becoming confetti."

Celeste picked one up that read NO USING ORCHESTRA AS COVER. "This one's aspirational at best," she said. "My travel schedule is part of their architecture. They're not going to stop watching concert halls because I put a note on my table."

"We can still commit to not doing it on purpose," Lena said. "You don't pick targets just because you're already in town to play Dvořák."

"That's already true," Celeste said. "I've turned down jobs that tried to piggyback on tours."

"Write it down anyway," Esra said. "Intent matters."

Celeste wrote NO TARGETS CHOSEN FOR CONVENIENCE and stuck it beside Esra's note.

The cat swatted at one that had fallen onto the floor, batting it under the couch.

"Symbolism," Lena murmured. "Look at him, burying our worst impulses."

Esra leaned forward, elbows on her knees. "Let's be clear about scope," she said. "What exactly are we doing with these rules? Are we reforming Eidolon? Replacing them? Competing with them?"

"Destroying them," Celeste said. The words came out without hesitation. "That's the end goal."

"And between now and 'destroyed'?" Esra asked, one eyebrow raised.

"We use what my mother left," Celeste said. "We hit their infrastructure. Quietly at first. Carefully. We make it harder for them to use people the way they used Lena. We make donors nervous. We make their operators doubt."

"The warehouse," Volkov said.

"Newark," Celeste said. "The one you traced through the fake music foundation."

"What's in the binder about it?" Esra asked.

Celeste opened the padded bag on the table and pulled out the black binder. The cat watched with interest, then decided it wasn't edible and went back to sleep.

She flipped to a tab labeled NORTHEAST LOGISTICS. Her mother's handwriting marched down the pages: addresses, shell company names, references to shipments.

"Here," Celeste said, running a finger under a line. "Morgan Logistics LLC—subtle—warehouse lease in aNewark industrial park. Designated as 'node 3A' in internal comms. Primary functions: storage, transit, occasional 'holding' of assets."

"'Holding,'" Lena repeated. "Like they held me."

"Probably more like equipment," Volkov said. "But yes. People, sometimes."

"Security?" Esra asked.

Celeste turned the page. "They upgraded after a break-in. Cameras at all exterior points. Minimal interior coverage. Two shifts of guards who think they're working for a regular freight company. At least one Eidolon-trained operator on-site at any given time."

"That was years ago," Volkov said. "We need current intel. I admit to watching their cameras for the last two days," he added. "Patterns haven't changed much. Truck schedules, guard rotations, one man who moves like he was born with a gun in his hand. That'll be your operator."

"What's our objective?" Esra asked. "We can't just blow it up. Fire departments ask questions."

"Our objective is information," Celeste said. "We go in, we copy whatever's on their internal servers about donors, operations, nodes. And we leave a message."

Lena perked up. "Like a post–it that says 'We were here, stop being assholes'?" She grinned like a Cheshire cat.

"Something that tells them their secrecy isn't absolute," Celeste said. "But not so loud that they go fully underground and we lose them completely."

"Needle to thread," Esra murmured.

"And while we do that," Volkov said, "we see what they're moving. If they're staging something big, we get early warning."

"Like what they did in Istanbul," Lena said, voice tightening.

"Or worse," Esra said.

"What could be worse?" Lena asked.

Esra looked at Celeste, then back at Lena. "Doing it during a performance," she said. "Onstage. On camera. Using an orchestra not just as cover, but as spectacle."

"Let's not give them ideas," Lena muttered.

"They already have them," Celeste said quietly.

They all fell silent for a beat.

"Back to rules," Lena said briskly, as if yanking them back from the edge of a thought too dark to examine for long. "We agree: no civilian casualties, no convenience kills, no operations that hinge on traumatizing unsuspecting oboe players?"

"Yes," Esra said.

"Yes," Celeste said.

Volkov hesitated. "Yes, with the emergency exception," he said.

Lena pointed at him. "Compromises. We're doing it."

Celeste took a fresh sticky note, wrote:

RULE 1: NO CIVILIAN CASUALTIES BY DESIGN.

RULE 2: UNANIMOUS CIVILIAN COUNCIL CONSENT FOR LETHAL TARGETS. She underlined civilian council.

"Civilian council," Lena said. "I like that."

"You're not a civilian anymore," Volkov pointed out.

"I'm first violin in a major symphony," Lena said. "I am peak civilian. You and Celeste are the weirdos here."

Esra cleared her throat.

"You sign things," Lena told her. "You file paperwork. That counts as civilian."

"In that case, I'm honored," Esra fake-coughed.

They spent another hour arguing over finer points: what counted as "civilian," how much risk they were willing to accept, what happened if they disagreed.

Celeste pushed for a clause that allowed her to act alone in extremis. Lena shot it down so hard the sticky note ripped. "No exceptions for 'I had a feeling' or 'it seemed necessary,'" she said. "That's how we get every dictator in history."

"He's not a dictator," Celeste said, nodding at Volkov.

"I'm talking about you," Lena said.

Celeste took it. She deserved it.

By the time they were done, the sticky notes had migrated into rough categories: WHAT WE DO, WHAT WE WON'T, WHAT WE'LL ARGUE ABOUT LATER.

"What we'll argue about later" was the largest cluster.

"Looks about right," Esra said, standing and stretching. "If anyone had told me my week would involve co-writing a kill policy with a cellist, I'd have laughed."

"If anyone had told me my week would involve getting kidnapped and then joining a secret council, I'd have asked for a raise," Lena said.

"Speaking of raises," Esra added, pulling her coat on, "I'll need a budget. If we're doing this, we'll need safe houses, transport, possibly bribes."

"Bribes?" Lena repeated. "You sound like you read too much Tom Clancy."

"Strategic gratuities," Esra amended. "New York runs on them."

"Use my concert fees," Celeste said.

"And alert every accountant within two miles?" Esra shook her head. "We'll do it through the binder. Some of these shell accounts can be redirected. Quietly. A little bit at a time."

"You're stealing from them," Lena said, a smile playing at her mouth.

"Of course," Esra said. "You're not the only one with talents, Celeste."

The meeting broke up in fits and starts. Esra left first, with a promise to send a draft of "Version 1.0" of their rules. Lena stayed a little longer, helping gather the stray sticky notes and occasionally rewording "NO TORTURE" to "NO BEING MONSTERS" and back again.

At the door, Lena turned. "Warehouse," she said. "When?"

"Soon," Celeste said. "Not tonight."

"You're not going without telling me," Lena said.

"I'm not going without you," Celeste said.

"That sounds like a threat," Lena said.

"It is," Celeste replied.

Lena grinned, quick and crooked, then left.

Volkov stayed. He leaned against the window, looking out at the city. His reflection overlaid hers in the glass, two faint figures amidst scattered lights. "Composition by committee," he said. "I didn't think you had it in you."

"It's not finished," she said. "It's barely a sketch."

"It's more than they ever had," he said. "Harriman's only rule was 'don't get caught on camera.'"

"Maestro?" she asked.

"His only rule is 'we're right,'" Volkov said. "Everything else is improvisation."

"You sound like you know him," Celeste said.

"I know his type," he said. "Men who think in movements instead of consequences. They're the easiest to predict and the hardest to stop."

"Because they keep escalating," she said.

"Because they're convinced the finale will justify the mess," he said.

She thought of the cistern, of Lena tied to a chair, of Aria's gun swinging away from the hostage.

"He's not the only one escalating," she said.

"No," Volkov said. "You are, too." He pushed off the window. "Come on," he said. "You need to see the warehouse with your own eyes before we go in."

"Now?" she asked. "We just spent three hours arguing about verbs."

"It's midnight," he said. "Their guards are at their laziest. You like night practice. Consider this part of your warm–up routine."

He wasn't wrong so she grabbed her coat.

The warehouse sat at the edge of the Newark docks, an immense rectangle of corrugated metal and faded logos, hunkered down among its own kind. Sodium lights bathed the lot in a sickly orange glow. A chain–link fence ringed the property, topped with razor wire.

"It looks like every other warehouse in the row," Celeste noted.

"That's the point," Volkov said, as they watched from the dark interior of a parked sedan across the street. "You want your illegal goods to dress like legal ones."

"Any movement?" Celeste asked.

He lifted his camera, the lens long and obscenely expensive. "Two guards at the front door. One smoking, one pretending not to notice he's smoking. Third one does a patrol around the perimeter every twelve minutes. Operator's inside, according to heat signatures."

"What about cameras?" she asked.

"Eight external," he said. "Four corners, two over the loading dock, two over the employee entrance. Blind spots near the northeast corner."

"Convenient," she said.

"I made some of them," he said. "Digitally, anyway. Their system thinks its cameras are working. A loop, nothing fancy."

She studied the building before she said, "When we go in, we don't kill anyone who doesn't know who Eidolon is."

"No civilians," he agreed.

"And the operator?" she asked.

"If we can neutralize him non–lethally, we do," Volkov said. "If he reaches for an alarm or a weapon and doesn't listen to reason, we do what we have to do."

"I hate that phrase," she said.

"I know," he said. "That's why you're not the one pulling the trigger unless you have no choice."

Her hands curled around the seat belt strap. "Don't patronize me."

"I'm not," he said. "I'm being selfish. You're more valuable to this fight alive and not drowning in fresh guilt."

She watched the warehouse lights, breathing slow. "Every time I've gone after someone," she said quietly, "it's been because someone else pointed and said 'that one.' Reznov. The general. Harriman. Even in the cistern, it was reacting. Getting Lena back. Surviving."

"Self–defense," he said.

"Revenge," she corrected. "Now we're choosing. Proactively. That's different."

"Yes," he said. "That's why we brought in people like Lena and Esra. To stop you from using your knives just because they're sharp."

"Or you," she said.

"I know what I am," he said. "I've never pretended otherwise."

"That's not a defense," she said.

"No," he agreed. "It's an admission. You can't scare me with what I already accept."

He pointed at the warehouse. "What scares me is that somewhere in there might be a shipment that's not guns or servers. It might be something like… sheet music and explosives, headed for a concert hall."

She turned to look at him. "You think they're going to hit a performance."

"It's the next logical escalation," he said. "Barcelona. Istanbul. Both were tests in semi–controlled environments. Now they know you're willing to break their architecture. They'll want to remind you how many people stand under your spotlight."

She thought of the sticky note Lena had written: NO BEING MONSTERS.

"They wouldn't," she started.

"Celeste," he said, "they tied your friend to a chair over an underground lake and played you a message from your dead mother. There is no 'wouldn't.' There is only 'haven't yet.'"

The cold seeped through the car windows. Somewhere in the lot, a dog barked twice and fell silent.

"We need to know what they're planning," she said.

"Yes," he said. "And the warehouse is our best shot before they move the pieces again."

She looked down at her hands. The faint scars from the cistern were still healing.

"We do this by our rules," she said. "No casualties. No fire. No grand statements. We get in. We copy. We get out. If anything goes sideways, we abort."

"You realize that is the exact opposite of every Eidolon op you've ever been on," he said.

"I know," she said. "That's the point."

They stayed another hour, watching. Trucks came and went. A vendor's van pulled up, dropped off a crate with 'vending machine snacks' written on it, and drove away. The guard on the front stoop smoked his way through half a pack.

Volkov collected patterns: plate numbers, faces, times. Celeste collected something more nebulous: the feel of the place. The rhythm of its breathing.

At one point, her phone buzzed.

Unknown number. Not Aria this time.

She opened the message. **You are moving faster than forecast. Impressive.**

No signature. No emoji. Just those words.

She showed it to Volkov.

He cursed softly.

"He's watching," he said.

"How?" she asked.

"Doesn't matter how," he said. "What matters is that he's telling you he sees you. That he wants you to know you're in his calculations."

She typed back before she could talk herself out of it. **Then your forecasts are wrong.**

A moment. Then: **Perhaps. That is what experiments are for.**

Her mother's letter burned in her pocket.

"Don't engage," Volkov said. "He wants to pull you into a conversation. Every word you send is data."

"I know," she said. But she'd already sent it.

The next message did not come immediately.

They waited.

"They know we're here?" she asked.

"Not physically," he said. "If they did, we'd see it. This is about the binder. The storage unit. Your mother's trapdoor. He's letting you know he expected you to find it. That this, too, is part of his 'score.'"

"Doesn't that make you nervous?" she asked.

"Everything makes me nervous," he said. "That's why I'm useful."

She looked back at the warehouse. In the middle distance, the Manhattan skyline glowed like a cluster of stubborn stars.

"This op," she said. "We bring Lena?"

"Yes," he said.

"You didn't hesitate," she observed.

"She demanded full disclosure," he said. "And you agreed. She isn't going to sit home and knit while we go on field trips."

"She doesn't knit," Celeste said.

"She'll learn out of spite," he said.

The phone buzzed again. **I will concede you one thing**, the text read. **You are more interesting than Harriman.**

She didn't respond this time.

Volkov watched her profile, the way her jaw set. "You still have time to walk away," he said without emotion in his voice. "From this. From him. From the part of your mother's vision that wants you at the center."

"No," she said.

"It would be sane," he went on. "To take the binder, hand it to someone else, vanish."

"It would be selfish," she said. "To drop a live grenade on someone else's desk and call it justice."

"You owe yourself something," he said.

"I owe my mother better than repeating her cowardice," she said. "And I owe Lena better than leaving her in a world where men like the Maestro move pieces while she tunes her violin."

He exhaled, a sound halfway between a sigh and a curse. "Then we hit the warehouse," he said. "Soon. Before he adjusts."

"Soon," she agreed.

They drove back to the city in tired silence. On the way over the bridge, Celeste watched the lights of Manhattan slide by, reflected in the dark water below. The skyline looked different now that she knew how many invisible wires ran through it—money from shell accounts, data flowing between safe servers, orders encoded in innocuous emails.

Underneath all of it, her mother's binder lay on the seat between them, a physical weight that felt larger than cardboard. She rested her hand on it.

You hold the bow, she thought, not sure if she was speaking to herself or to the woman who had written those words. For the first time, she felt the shape of the ending approaching, not as a surprise, but as something inevitable she was walking toward.

It wouldn't all resolve in the warehouse. She knew that. The Maestro wouldn't go down from one cut. Aria was out there somewhere, improvising her own line. Eidolon had roots in too many places to be pulled up in one movement.

But the Newark node would be the first real note in a new piece, a deliberate, rule–bound strike against the machine that had raised her.

And whatever happened there, it would reverberate. Through New York. Through the orchestra. Through every shadowed room where someone like the Maestro thought they were conducting.

She watched the city grow closer.

The next movement was coming. And after that… another score, another stage, another fight she hadn't yet seen. He thought he knew her tempo. He was about to find out how wrong he was.

The score was still unwritten. But the opening bars had been laid down, and whether she liked it or not, the world had tuned to her key.

Chapter 14

The Warehouse

THE NIGHT THEY chose for the warehouse wasn't special.

No storm. No blackout. Just cold air, low clouds, and a forecast of "light snow, possible accumulation." The kind of winter evening when most people huddled indoors with bad TV and better blankets.

Perfect, Celeste thought. The world at half–attention.

They met in Esra's borrowed conference room—an anonymous space on the twelfth floor of an anonymous office building in Midtown. It smelled faintly of toner and ambition. A whiteboard covered one wall; a view of glittering skyscrapers filled the other.

On the table sat the binder, a laptop, three paper cups of coffee, one cup of tea, and a bag of pretzels Lena was stress-eating. Esra stood by the whiteboard with a marker, crisp in a dark blazer and jeans. She'd drawn a crude rectangle labeled WAREHOUSE and ringed it with arrows and notes.

"Last chance to bail," Volkov said. He sat at the far end of the table, chair tipped back, arms folded. "You could all go home and watch Netflix. I'll break in alone, steal what we need, and you can pretend I never told you."

Lena snorted, crumbs on her lip. "You wish."

Celeste sat between them with her hands wrapped around a cup she hadn't sipped. The cardboard warmed her palms. The warehouse address was printed at the top of a single sheet in front of her. "I'm not letting you go in alone," she said. "If this goes sideways, you'll need someone to yell at you."

"I'm perfectly capable of yelling at myself," he said.

"Yeah, but you don't listen," Lena said.

Esra tapped the whiteboard with the marker. "Focus. Here's the plan as we know it."

She pointed to a small square she'd drawn at the edge of the warehouse box. "Personnel entrance: main security checkpoint. Two guards most of the time. They work for 'Morgan Logistics.' They don't know who they're really working for. We avoid them if possible. If not, we incapacitate non-lethally. Agreed?"

"Agreed," Celeste said.

"Fine," Volkov said.

"Loading bay," Esra went on, circling the larger opening on the drawing. "Trucks in and out. Camera coverage good, but loops ready, courtesy of Mr. Cynical." She jerked her chin at Volkov. "We go nowhere near here unless something goes very wrong."

Lena raised a hand. "Where am I in this doodle?"

Esra drew a little car icon near the road. "You and I are the exfil team," she said. "I drive. You monitor comms, watch the street, and argue with Celeste if she tries to hero her way into extra danger."

"That last part is my specialty," Lena said.

"Inside," Esra continued, "Volkov leads. He knows this kind of layout. Celeste follows. You both wear body cams and audio. We record everything."

"So, we can watch it later like a really messed up home movie," Lena muttered.

"Or so we can prove what we find exists, if we need leverage," Esra said.

Celeste looked at the crude rectangle. It felt too simple to contain what they were about to step into.

"What's our objective?" Esra asked, looking at Celeste, not the board.

"Get into their internal network," Celeste said. "Copy whatever's on their servers about donors, shell companies, operations, especially anything tagged with my mother's codes. Plant a marker so they know someone could get in again. Get out without blood on our hands."

"And if it goes wrong?" Esra asked.

"We abort," Celeste said. "No improvising new heroics. No 'just one more file.' No martyrdom."

"Say it again," Lena said.

"We abort," Celeste repeated. "We live to try again."

Volkov gave a small nod, as if she'd passed a test.

Esra wrote ABORT EARLY > WIN BIG in the corner of the board.

"That's not catchy," Lena said.

"I'm not writing it on t-shirts," Esra replied.

"What about the operator?" Volkov asked.

"The Eidolon one?" Lena said. "The guy who actually knows where the bodies are buried?"

"If we encounter him," Celeste's cadence was slow, "we neutralize without killing if at all possible. If he forces a lethal response, we log it and own it. But we do not go in planning to eliminate him as a primary objective."

"That's going to make everything harder," Volkov said.

"Yes," Celeste said. "That's why it's a rule."

Esra uncapped a different color marker and wrote: NO PLANNED ON-SITE KILLS. She underlined "planned" three times.

They went over the layout one more time, the timing, the signals. Five minutes inside if everything went perfectly. Ten if they were lucky. Beyond that, the risk curve climbed too fast.

"Any questions?" Esra asked finally.

Lena raised a hand again. "Why are we doing this instead of burning the place down and starting a commune in Vermont?"

"Because Vermont doesn't have a major international airport," Celeste said.

"Also, because if we burn it down blind, we lose whatever's inside that could help us dismantle the rest," Volkov added. "We're not here to make a point. We're here to steal their spine."

"Fun," Lena's monotone voice implied just the opposite.

Esra recapped the marker with a sharp click. "Then we move at twenty-three hundred," she said. "Plenty of time for you two to brood and for me to pretend this is just another unpleasant corporate audit."

The drive to Newark felt shorter this time. Esra drove, calm and competent, hands light on the wheel. Lena sat in the back, headset around her neck, staring out at the blur of warehouses and truck stops.

Celeste sat in front, dressed in black jeans, dark sweater, hair braided tightly down her back. A slim pack with the essentials lay at her feet: a laptop, a drive, two compact flash devices, a coil of fiber, lockpicks. Tools for a different kind of performance.

Volkov had gone ahead on a bike, preferring his own routes. He'd texted once: **In position. Cameras are yawning.**

"Who's watching the watcher?" Lena murmured when she read it over Celeste's shoulder.

"We are," Celeste said.

The warehouse district was mostly empty at this hour. A few trucks rumbled down side streets. Sodium lights buzzed. Industrial shadows pooled between buildings. Esra parked in a service lane behind a row of dumpsters half a block from the target.

"Sexy," Lena said. "Love what you've done with the view."

"This is the least camera–covered stretch," Esra said. "Get your headset on."

Lena slipped the earpiece into place, testing the mic. "Check, check," she said softly. "One, two, morally gray crew."

"Loud and clear," Volkov's voice came in her ear and Celeste's at once. "Almost too loud. Don't shout."

"Sorry," Lena whispered. "I don't do espionage volume."

Celeste pulled her own earpiece into place, then lifted the slim black body cam and clipped it to the front of her jacket.

"You look like you're about to give a TED Talk on murdering responsibly," Lena said.

"Working title," Celeste said.

Esra handed Celeste a small black box. "Network injector," she said. "Plug this into any live port on their internal switch. It'll do the rest. Encrypted feedback to my laptop. No button to press. No fancy interface. Just stick and pray."

"I prefer to have more control than 'pray,'" Celeste said.

"So do I," Esra said. "That's why I wrote the code myself."

"You have many skills. I had no idea," Celeste admitted.

Volkov's voice cut in. "Perimeter is quiet," he said. "Our patrol just rounded the west corner. You have twelve minutes until he's back. Door team is bored. Now or never."

Celeste closed her fingers around the injector. It felt too light. "I'm going," she said.

She opened the door. The cold hit her in the face, sharp and clean. The asphalt smelled faintly of oil and old rain. Somewhere nearby, a ship horn sounded on the river.

Lena caught her wrist before she stepped away. "Hey," she said.

Celeste looked back.

"You come back," Lena said. "Or I swear to God I will learn how to use a gun and come in after you."

"I'd rather not die of friendly fire," Celeste said.

"Then don't make me test my aim," Lena replied.

Celeste squeezed her hand once, then let go. She slipped into the shadows of the alley, feet almost silent on the grit.

Volkov materialized from behind a stack of pallets like he'd been grown there, dressed in dark gray from head to toe. "You're late," he said.

"I was being emotionally blackmailed," she said.

He jerked his chin toward the chain-link fence. "North side. Blind spot. Move."

They moved. At the fence line, Volkov produced a tool that bit through the bottom two links with barely a sound. He lifted a flap just high enough for Celeste to roll under. On the other side, the ground was packed dirt and gravel. The warehouse loomed, all corrugated metal and faintly humming lights.

"Camera loop engaged," he murmured. "We have four minutes before the system starts getting suspicious about identical pixels."

"Four minutes?" she echoed.

"It's a stupid system," he said. "Not a comatose one. Let's go."

They hugged the outer wall, moving toward the northeast corner where the blind spot began. Cold metal pressed against Celeste's shoulder as they sidled past a stack of plastic-wrapped pallets.

"External door," Volkov said quietly. "Secondary access. Probably alarmed. Stay."

He knelt, gloved fingers running along the frame until they found a small gray box disguised as part of the wall. He popped the cover, exposing a tangle of wires and a cheap circuit board.

"Esra," he said softly.

"Here," she replied in their ears.

"Your new best friend installed this," he said. "You're live."

"Give me a moment," she said.

Celeste watched the warehouse yard: the glow from the front entrance, the faint movement of a shadow where one of the guards was shifting his weight, not looking their way. The patrol would be halfway around the opposite side now.

Her muscles thrummed with contained motion.

There was a small click.

"Alarm looped," Esra said. "You're clear."

"Door," Volkov said.

It was locked, but the mechanism was standard. Celeste pulled a set of picks from her pocket, feeling the familiar faint resistance, the tiny give as metal met metal, the soft thud of tumblers aligning. The handle turned.

Inside, the air was warmer and smelled of dust, rubber, and the faint tang of cleaning chemicals. The hallway beyond the door was lit by strip fluorescents, scuffed by years of traffic. A red EXIT sign glowed at the far end.

"Body cams show clear," Esra murmured. "Right, then left."

They moved.

Voices echoed faintly from somewhere: two guards talking about a game, laughter, the scrape of a chair. None of it close.

At a junction, Volkov paused, listening.

"Server room will be near the interior," he said. "Fewer walls between it and the world."

"Romantic," Celeste whispered.

He shot her a look.

Esra's voice came through. "Right turn in ten feet," she said. "Door with keypad. That's your room."

At the end of the short corridor, a metal door waited, keypad glowing. Celeste eyed it. "Can you…?" she began.

"On it," Esra said. "Hold still. Let me see the model."

Celeste angled her body cam.

"Oh, this one," Esra said, almost insulted. "Give me thirty seconds."

Thirty seconds felt like ten minutes as Celeste listened to the building breathe. The hum of lights. The distant rumble of a forklift. Somewhere above, a faint vibration that might have been the HVAC.

The keypad beeped. The light turned green.

"You're welcome," Esra said.

Volkov opened the door. The server room was small and cold, walls lined with racks of equipment. Blue and green lights blinked softly, like subdued fireflies. A single chair sat in the middle of the room, empty, its wheels leaving faint tracks in the dusty concrete.

"No operator," Volkov murmured.

"On patrol?" Celeste suggested.

"Or on break," Esra said. "You have three minutes before anyone gets curious about that door."

"Injector," Volkov said.

Celeste crossed to the nearest rack, where a small switch panel bristled with cables. She found an open port, slid the black box Esra had given her into place, felt it click. The indicator light blinked once, then glowed steady.

"Got it," Esra said, a flicker of triumph in her voice. "I'm in. Mirroring directories now. You've got two minutes, thirty seconds before my activity starts to throw flags."

Celeste scanned the room. "Paper records?" she asked. "Logs? Anything physical?"

"Check the cabinet," Volkov said, nodding toward a battered gray unit in the corner.

She opened it and found it filled with folders. Labeled not with names, but codes: ORPHEUS, HYMN, ECHO, ORFEO.

Her fingers paused on ORFEO. Her mother's name for the Barcelona front. She pulled the folder out and flipped it open. Inside were printouts of emails, memos, shipping manifests. Names of donors blacked out with thick marker, but not completely. If you held the page at the right angle, light picked up impressions of the letters.

She snapped photos with her phone: page after page, angle after angle.

"Time," Esra said. "Two minutes."

"What's HYMN?" Celeste asked, pulling that folder.

"Donor initiative," Volkov said, skimming over her shoulder. "Funding for 'cultural preservation.' A cover for moving money into conflict zones."

"HYMN links to ORFEO," she said, eyes catching on a schematic. "And ORPHEUS. And something called CHORALE." Her stomach tightened.

"Chorale?" Lena's voice cut in. She'd been quiet until now, listening from the car. "That's a lot of music terms. I'm offended on behalf of composers."

"Chorale has a sub–designation," Celeste said, reading. "CHORALE–NY–01. Implementation window: March. Target environment: high–capacity concert venue. Cover: 'Fire safety inspection.'"

"Send me a photo," Esra barked.

Celeste did.

A second later: "That's a planning doc," Esra said. "Look at the bottom. 'Projected casualty band: 800–1500, depending on evacuation efficiency.'"

The words crawled across the page, obscene in their calm.

"Casualties," Lena repeated, voice thin. "In a concert venue."

"In New York," Celeste said. "NY–01."

"When's the implementation window?" Volkov asked.

"March," Celeste repeated. "No specific date. Just a range."

"It's January," Lena said. "That's… not far."

"Focus," Esra cut in. "You have ninety seconds. Grab what you can physically. We can analyze later."

Celeste yanked out CHORALE, ORFEO, HYMN, and a thinner folder marked EIDOLON – INTERNAL. She slid them into her pack, heart hammering.

Something else caught her eye: a small, unlabeled flash drive taped to the cabinet's interior wall.

"Hidden," she murmured.

She peeled it off and pocketed it.

"Sixty seconds," Esra said. "I'm pulling out. Their IDS is sniffing at me."

"Leave them a message," Celeste said.

"Already did," Esra replied. "It's subtle. They'll find it in three weeks and have a very confusing day."

"What kind of message?" Lena asked.

"A discrepancy in their own financials," Esra said. "Nothing public. Just enough to make them wonder if they're bleeding internally."

"Clock," Volkov reminded them.

They stepped back into the hallway, pulling the door closed behind them. The lock clicked.

As they rounded the corner, Celeste heard it: the faint whir of a rolling chair, the creak of a door somewhere further down. Someone was coming.

"Exit," Volkov murmured.

They moved quickly but not too quickly, like employees heading for the break room, not intruders fleeing a crime. The hallway stretched ahead, each step echoing.

A man turned the far corner. He was mid–thirties, stocky, wearing a company jacket. The operator, Celeste guessed. His eyes narrowed. "Hey," he said, in accented English. "Who—"

Volkov's hand shot out, dropping a small black object at the man's feet. It hissed once, releasing a puff of something that smelled faintly like menthol and acrid spice. The man inhaled, coughed, staggered, eyes watering.

"What the—" he wheezed.

"Relax," Volkov said in Russian. "It's temporary."

The man's knees buckled. He went down in a controlled sprawl, coughing violently.

Celeste grabbed his arm, easing him to the wall so he didn't crack his head. His breaths were loud but already easing.

"What was that?" Lena demanded.

"Non–lethal inhalant," Volkov said. "Short–term respiratory irritant. He'll wake up with a headache and new trust issues."

"Rule check," Esra said quickly. "No permanent damage, no civilian. He's Eidolon–trained. We're within parameters."

"Forty seconds," she added. "Front patrol about to turn the corner outside."

"Move," Volkov said.

They slipped back out the external door. The night air felt like knives after the server room's chill. They ducked under the fence flap, flattened themselves between two trailers as the perimeter guard's flashlight beam swept the yard. It passed over them, unseeing, and moved on.

"Go," Esra said. "Don't loiter. Don't run."

They walked.

Half a block later, they were back at the car.

Lena's face was pale in the dim light, eyes huge. "Well?" she demanded.

Celeste slid into the front seat, pack still on one shoulder. "We got it," she said. "Servers, planning docs, something called Chorale that I'm going to have nightmares about."

Esra pulled them away from the curb, driving like someone obeying every traffic law for the first time in her life.

"Any tails?" Volkov asked from his bike; he had fallen in behind them now.

Esra checked the mirror. "Nothing obvious," she said. "If they noticed anything, they'll be looking inward first. The operator will assume someone monkeyed with his systems while he was on a smoke break."

"I'm not sure that's comforting," Lena said.

Celeste opened the pack; her fingers were numb now with adrenaline letdown. The folders felt heavier than paper. She pulled out CHORALE and slid it into Lena's lap. "Read," she said. "Tell me if I'm overreacting."

Lena scanned the first page, then the second. Her hands began to shake.

"This is…" she swallowed. "They're planning to hit a concert hall. They've modeled audience capacity, exit routes, average evacuation times based on 'panic scenarios.' They've even factored in whether the conductor is famous enough that people linger for extra bows."

"They're turning your world into a target," Volkov said.

"They already have," Celeste said. "We just didn't see the crosshairs."

She took the folder back, eyes jumping to the last page.

IMPLEMENTATION PARAMETERS:

– Target must be symbolically resonant (internationally broadcast or easily framed as "attack on art/Western decadence").

– Casualty count must be sufficient to justify subsequent "security regime" measures.

– Assets in place in security, crowd control, and logistics.

– Operative "C. Morgan" considered potential variable; keep informed enough for plausible deniability, uninformed enough to avoid interference.

Her name in that clinical list made bile rise in her throat.

"Let me see," Esra said, reaching one hand back for the folder, eyes still on the road.

Celeste handed it to her.

Esra read it at red lights, lips pressed into a thin line. "The line about 'security regime measures' bothers me," she said. "They're not just planning an attack. They're planning to profit from the aftermath."

"How?" Lena asked.

"Increased funding for their clients," Esra said. "Contracts for security consulting. Influence over policy through fear. Classic shock doctrine, with violins."

"They want chaos so they can sell order," Volkov said.

"And they were considering using you as cover," Esra added, glancing at Celeste. "Or at least as plausible deniability. 'Who, us? We work with the famous cellist who survived the incident.'"

Celeste stared at the page in Esra's hand. "My mother," she said slowly. "She wrote that they wanted me at the center. I thought she meant leadership. This is… something else."

"They want your face in the narrative," Volkov said. "Either as a hero or as a witness. Maybe as a regretful instrument. They're plotting in movements. You're their recurring motif."

"I'm going to be sick," Lena muttered.

"Not in the car," Esra said automatically.

They drove in heavy silence for a few miles. The city lights grew denser as they returned to Manhattan—the bridge, the river, the sharp glitter of midtown.

"What do we do?" Lena eventually asked. "We know they have a plan. We don't know where. We don't know when. We only know it's 'March' and 'concert.' That's not enough to call the cops with."

"We're not calling the cops," Esra said. "We're smarter than that. And less fond of paperwork."

"We have my binder," Celeste said. "We have their warehouse logs. We have Chorale. We cross-reference. We figure out which venue fits their criteria and where their 'assets' are in place."

"Lincoln Center," Lena said immediately. "Carnegie. The Met. Anywhere big and shiny enough to make headlines."

"And anywhere Celeste is scheduled to play," Esra added. "Don't forget that part."

Celeste closed her eyes briefly. "New York Philharmonic's gala in March," she said. "Carnegie has a festival. Met season is in full swing. There are a dozen options."

"Too many," Volkov said. "They like controllable variables. They'll pick one where they can plant their own people in security."

"We start there," Esra said. "We pull public records on staff changes. We use your mother's list to see where their shell companies intersect with venue contracts. We narrow it down."

"And in the meantime?" Lena asked. "We just… keep rehearsing? Sit on stage under lights and pretend we don't know someone's writing casualty projections about our audience?"

"Yes," Esra said. "Until we know more, you go to work. You don't suddenly start cancelling performances or changing behavior. That would tell them we're onto this."

"Business as usual," Volkov said. "With better exit strategies."

Lena let her head fall back against the seat. "I hate this," she said.

"I know," Celeste replied.

Esra pulled up in front of Celeste's building, flashers on. "Out," she said. "I'll circle the block, then drop Lena at her place. Then I'm going home to mainline coffee and parse these files until my eyes bleed."

Celeste put a hand on her arm. "Thank you," she said.

"Don't get sentimental," Esra said. "You'll make me regret my life choices."

Lena leaned forward from the back seat, resting her chin on the headrest. "Text me when you find anything," she said. "Even if it's three in the morning."

"You'll be asleep," Celeste said.

"Oh please," Lena said. "As if anyone is sleeping after tonight."

She grabbed Celeste's sleeve before she could open the door. "Hey," she said. "We did it. We went in, we stole from them, we didn't kill anyone, and we came out. That counts for something."

"It counts for the first cut," Celeste said. "They're going to bleed.

They're also going to strike back."

"Let them try," Lena said. "Now they're not the only ones with a score."

Celeste stepped out of the car; the pack was heavy on her shoulder.

Volkov waited by the building entrance, helmet under his arm. "You looked good on camera," he said. "Minimal panic. Excellent lock work."

"You sound like a teacher," she said.

"I am," he replied. "Unfortunately."

They rode up in the elevator in silence.

In the apartment, the cat greeted them with his usual offended meow, as if they'd left without signing the proper forms.

Celeste set the pack on the table and sank into a chair.

Volkov leaned against the counter, watching her.

"You okay?" he asked.

"No," she said. "Yes. I don't know."

"Pick one," he said.

She rubbed her eyes. "I thought the warehouse would be… a small victory. A notch. A step. Instead, it feels like we opened a door with more doors behind it."

"That's what systems look like from the inside," he said. "One root leads to ten more."

"Chorale," she said. "They're planning to turn a hall into a graveyard, and they wrote my name into the margins."

He nodded once. "At least now you know. Ignorance didn't protect you; it only made you easier to use."

She thought of her mother's letter. *You may choose to walk away from all of it. Change your name. Play cello in a small town.*

"That option of moving to a small town, of walking away is gone," she said.

"It was gone the moment you killed Harriman," he said. "This just made it official."

Her phone buzzed.

Unknown number.

She opened it.

You're playing the wrong piece, *celistka*.

Aria.

Before Celeste could respond, another message: **Chorale isn't just NY–01. It's bigger. You're out of time if you stay in that city.**

Her heart stuttered. She didn't have to ask how Aria knew. She understood they all knew or could anticipate her moves.

But she wanted to see if Aria would be on her side. She typed: **What do you mean, bigger?**

Three dots blinked, then vanished. Then: **Check your mother's binder. Page marked with blue. And get ready to move. Maestro just jumped to the next movement.**

Celeste looked up.

"Aria," she said. "She says Chorale isn't just one target."

"Of course, it isn't," Volkov said. "Why use one bomb when you can use three?"

"Don't say bomb," she snapped.

He held out a hand. "Binder."

She slid it across.

He flipped, fingers sure, until he found a page with a thin strip of blue tape at the top she hadn't noticed before.

The heading read:

PROJECT CHORALE – GLOBAL IMPLEMENTATION.

Sub–entries:

CHORALE–NY–01

CHORALE–PAR–01

CHORALE–TKY–01

Target environments:

NY–01: North America – high–capacity symphonic venue

PAR–01: Western Europe – opera house

TKY–01: East Asia – concert hall complex

"Three at once," Volkov's voice was steady like a warm breeze. "Coordinated."

"A global chord," Celeste whispered.

"Timeline?" he asked.

She read.

Implementation window: March–April, aligned with cultural festival calendars.

Key assets in place by end of February.

H–1 triggers staggered within sixty minutes to maximize media saturation.

Esra's voice came through the earpiece she still wore, faintly crackling. "I'm seeing it," she said. "I just opened the same file from the server mirror. It's Chorale multiplied."

"They're going to hit three cities," Lena said, exhaling sharply. "New York, Paris, Tokyo. All in one night."

Celeste's phone buzzed again.

You can't save them all, Aria's text read. **That's the point. He wants to see what you choose.**

"Turn it off," Volkov said.

She did, fingers shaking.

The cat jumped onto the table and curled up on the binder, as if trying to smother it.

"Get off," she said weakly.

He blinked at her, unimpressed.

"Okay," Esra said, her voice steady in a way that felt like a handrail. "We're not going to panic in the first five minutes. We have information we didn't have three hours ago. We know Chorale is global. We know approximate windows. We have donor lists I've already started cross-referencing. That's more than anyone else on the planet who isn't in that document."

"We're three people and a cat," Lena said.

"Four," Volkov corrected. "You're forgetting me."

"Three civilians and two killers," Esra amended. "Plus, a cat and a binder. It's not nothing."

Celeste stared at the blue-marked page. "What if we tell them?" she asked. "Interpol. CIA. MI6. Whatever acronym is in charge this week. We hand them Chorale and let them handle it."

"And watch them do what with it?" Volkov said. "Arrest a few middlemen. Leak nothing, because it's classified. Fail to believe that someone would coordinate attacks on three cultural hubs on the same night because it's 'too ambitious.' Or worse: decide to let one happen as a sacrificial lesson to justify their own budgets."

"Cynical," Lena said.

"Experienced," he replied.

"We can't be the only line of defense," Celeste said.

"We're not," Esra said. "Remember your mother's note: you don't do this alone. That doesn't mean we trust everyone. It means we choose allies carefully."

"Who?" Celeste demanded. "Who do we trust with this?"

Esra was quiet for a moment. "Someone like me," she said. "But higher up. With access. With morals. Maybe an investigative journalist who's not afraid to get burned. Maybe a politician with a conscience. We build a small circle, like we did here, but in other spheres."

"More committees," Volkov muttered.

"Better than one madman with a baton," Esra said.

Celeste closed the binder. Her reflection in the window looked pale, eyes too bright, shoulders tense.

Three cities. Three stages. Three nights that could become funerals.

Her mother's voice whispered in the back of her mind: *You will break yourself trying to enforce them.*

"Chorale is their third movement," she said.

Volkov looked at her. "And?"

"And we're not going to let them premiere it," she said.

"Ambitious," he said.

"Necessary," she replied.

He studied her, something like a question in his gaze.

"New York first," she said. "It's ours. Then Paris. Then Tokyo. We find where they're rooted in each city. We move faster than their forecast. And we do it by our rules, or not at all."

"You know what that means," Volkov said.

"Yes," she said. "It means I'm leaving sooner than planned. And it means this"—she tapped the binder—"isn't just about my mother or Eidolon anymore. It's about a lot of people who thought music was the safest place in the world."

Lena's voice in her ear was very small. "Where are you going?"

Celeste looked at the skyline. "Wherever their sheet music leads," she said. "And if I'm lucky… to the man who thinks he's conducting."

The room felt suddenly too small. She opened the window an inch. Cold air rushed in, tinged with exhaust and snow.

Down below, New York moved, oblivious: taxis, pedestrians, late-night dog walkers. People making plans for March. Tickets to concerts. Trips to Paris. Business in Tokyo.

They didn't know yet that, somewhere, a man had written their lives into a calculus of risk and reward.

Celeste watched a couple crossing the street, laughing at something on a phone.

"You hold the bow," she whispered to the glass.

Then, louder, to the room, to Volkov, to the voices in her ear: "This doesn't end here. The warehouse was the overture. Chorale is the next act. And after that…"

She didn't finish. She didn't have to. They all knew. After that would be another city, another hall, another line in the score she hadn't read yet. And somewhere beyond the last bar of this movement, waiting just out of sight, was a third book, a new piece, a different battlefield.

The Maestro wanted to see what she'd choose. He was about to find out.

Chapter 15

The Chosen Hall

THREE DAYS LATER, the rules were already fraying at the edges.

Not because anyone had broken them—yet—but because reality was pressing against them like a storm front pushing on flimsy windows.

Esra's email, when it came, was short and to the point.

Subject: Chorale – NY-01

Found it. Lincoln Center. Your gala.

They were sitting in a corner of a noisy coffee shop when she said it out loud. Lena nearly choked on her cappuccino.

"You're kidding," Lena sputtered, coughing. "Please tell me you're kidding. Make a joke, Esra. Any joke."

Esra slid a folder across the table. Her nails were neatly manicured; her eyes looked like she hadn't slept in days.

"Cross-referenced shell companies from the binder with vendor contracts for every major hall in the city," she said. "Security, crowd control, fire inspection, cleaning services. Three venues had overlap with Eidolon fronts. Lincoln Center has the most. A 'fire safety consultant' company whose parent corporation sits on the same board as Orfeó's main shell. And—" She flipped to a spreadsheet. "—a logistics firm that just got a contract to handle backstage freight for the Philharmonic's gala series," she finished. "Also tied to Morgan Logistics. That's not a coincidence. That's choreography."

"My name is on the gala posters," Celeste said, staring at the list of contractors. "Front and center."

"Exactly," Esra said. "Symbolically resonant. Famous soloist, beloved home orchestra, big donors, live broadcast. If you were a megalomaniac with a taste for theatrics, you'd pick it."

Lena leaned back hard enough to bump her chair into the wall. The teenager at the next table glared; she ignored him.

"They're going to hit the gala," Lena said. "Like, explode something? Gas? What are we talking about?"

"Chorale planning docs suggest fire," Esra said. "Or something that looks like fire at first. The 'fire safety inspection' angle gives them access to systems. Sprinklers. Alarms. They don't need to bring in a bomb when they can turn the building on itself."

Celeste's stomach knotted. "This is what my mother meant," she said. "They embed themselves in structures, then pull strings."

Lena's fingers trembled around her cup. "Can we cancel?" she asked. "Call in sick? 'Dear patrons, tonight's program is postponed due to asshole terrorists'?"

"If we cancel, they pick another date, another venue," Esra said. "Or they react by accelerating. We'd lose the only advantage we have: knowing where and roughly when they want to act."

"So, we… what?" Lena's voice shook. "We play? On a stage they've wired? With a fire they can start whenever they want?"

Celeste looked at Esra.

"Options," she said. "All of them." Esra took a breath. "Option one: we go to the authorities with everything. Binder, Chorale, donor links, shell companies. We push until someone listens. Best case, they quietly beef up security, scrub contractors, put plainclothes everywhere. Worst case, they smile, nod, say 'thank you for your concern' and file it under 'conspiracy theories.'"

"And Eidolon?" Celeste asked.

"They find out we talked," Esra said. "They adapt. They go quiet. Chorale moves to a plan B that we don't know the shape of."

"Option two?" Lena asked.

"We handle it ourselves," Esra said. "We let the gala go ahead. We quietly replace compromised contractors where we can. We insert our own people behind the scenes. We monitor every system. And when they try to pull the trigger on Chorale, we're there to cut the wires."

"Like a bad heist movie," Lena said. "But with more bassoons."

"Option three," Esra said, "we cancel the gala and also leak enough of Chorale to certain journalists with enough credibility and enough paranoia. We cause a panic, maybe. We also force agencies to act publicly."

"And turn every concert in the world into a suspected target," Celeste said. "We make people afraid to walk into halls. We destroy the very thing my mother thought she was saving."

"We also maybe save lives," Esra said.

Silence settled over the tiny table.

Behind them, the espresso machine hissed and clanked. Someone's phone rang with a ridiculous jingle. A child somewhere laughed too loud, then was shushed.

Lena set her cup down carefully. "Okay," she said. "Council vote time, I guess. But before that, I have a question."

"Ask," Celeste said.

"What do you want?" Lena asked simply. "Not 'what do you think you should do' or 'what would your mother do.' What does Celeste Morgan, human disaster and cello goddess, want?"

Celeste stared at her. She thought of the stage with its warm honey light, the applause swelling like surf. The feeling of the orchestra breathing with her, all the messy, beautiful human chaos focused into one chord. She thought of the cistern, cold and echoing, Lena tied to a chair. She thought of her mother's letter. *You may choose to walk away. If you do, I will not be disappointed.*

"I want them out of my halls," she said. "Out of our world. I want my audience to be able to sit down, breathe in, and only have to worry about whether the horn comes in on time. I want…" She swallowed. "I want to play and know that if someone dies near my music, it's because their body gave up, not because someone decided they were a pawn."

Lena's eyes shone. "Same," she said.

Esra folded her hands. "Then option two," she said. "We protect the gala without canceling it. We use it to hit them, not as bait, but as a shield we strengthen."

"That's not how shields work," Volkov's voice cut in. He'd been listening remotely, once again refusing to sit in the cafe and "pretend to enjoy latte foam." "Shields don't have stages and donors and board members who throw tantrums if you rearrange their seating."

"Is that a no?" Lena asked.

"It's a warning," he said. "If you choose option two, you're walking into the fire with your eyes open. You can't control every variable. People might still get hurt."

"And option one?" Celeste asked. "Authorities, handoff, hope?"

"Then you're outsourcing your soul," Volkov said. "If they fail, you get to blame them. If they succeed, you never know how close it was, because no one will tell you. And Eidolon stays in the walls."

"Option three?" Lena pressed.

"Panic," he said. "Chaos. Short–term safety for some, long–term victory for fear. Maestro would love that. He thrives in it."

Celeste looked at Esra. At Lena. At the flimsy paper coffee cup in her hand. "Council," she said quietly. "Vote."

"Option two," Esra said. "Handle it ourselves. Minimal exposure. Controlled leak to allies later, if needed."

"Same," Lena said. "We play. We protect. We document. We rub it in their faces if we live."

They both looked at Celeste.

She thought of Aria's text: *He wants to see what you choose.*

"Option two," Celeste said. "We fight on our stage."

"Unanimous," Esra said. "No turning back."

Volkov sighed in their ears. "Of course," he muttered. "You're all insane."

"You are part of 'all,'" Lena said.

"I'm here for the catering," he replied.

The rehearsal hall at Lincoln Center felt different when you knew it was sitting on top of a powder keg.

Musicians milled about onstage, tuning, noodling, gossiping. Cellos hummed low, violins chattered, someone in the brass section tried to see how many notes from a video game theme they could sneak into their warm–up.

"The energy is weird," Lena muttered, sliding into her chair into her section. "Can they sense it? Do orchestra players have threat radar now?"

"They're sensing jet lag and too much coffee," Celeste said. "Not your murder anxiety. Breathe."

Esra stood at the back of the hall, talking to the venue's head of security, a compact woman with a buzzcut and a scar on her jaw. They'd already had one "routine" meeting that morning, going over ingress, egress, emergency protocols.

The head of security had been unimpressed with much of the existing plan. "Too many assumptions," she'd said. "Too few drills. I'll fix it."

Esra had glanced at Celeste over her shoulder as if to say: one ally identified.

Volkov was somewhere in the building, in a way that made Celeste's skin crawl. He'd gotten himself hired through one of the "replacement" security contractors Esra had slipped into place. Officially, he was just another guy in a black suit with an earpiece. Unofficially, he was a knife in the walls.

Celeste tuned her cello automatically as the conductor, Maestro Duret, a man whose ego was sphinx–like and whose hair was increasingly transparent, took the podium.

"Welcome back," he said. "We have a glorious program tonight. Donors. Cameras. No pressure. From the top of the Mahler. Ms. Morgan, whenever you're ready."

She felt eyes on her: the orchestra's, Duret's, the invisible ones in the walls. She drew her bow across the strings, and the first note filled the hall, rich and deep, vibrating bones and wood and air.

For a blissful moment, everything else blurred—the warehouse, Chorale, Maestro's texts, Aria's warnings. There was only sound, the lines of Mahler's despair and hope threading together under her fingers.

Then her bow caught on a string for half a heartbeat, and she was back.

At break, she went to the wings. The backstage areas of Lincoln Center had always been a second home: narrow corridors, practice rooms full of stray notes, the faint smell of rosin and dust. Today, it also smelled faintly of fresh paint and something chemical.

"New." Volkov stepped out of an alcove.

"What?" she asked.

He jerked his head toward a panel on the wall labeled FIRE CONTROL. "Swapped last week," he said. "According to Esra's records. Old unit was fine. New unit's from our friends at 'Titan Safety Solutions.'"

"Eidolon front," she said.

"Yes," he said. "I've scanned it. No obvious foreign hardware. No additional lines. Whatever they're doing, it's in the software. Remote controls. Timed overrides."

"You can't crack it?" she asked.

"I can," he said, "given time and root access and a non–suspicious IT guy. We have none of those things."

"Then what do we do?" she whispered.

"Esra's working on a manual override," he said. "Mechanical. If they trigger something, we kill power to the system entirely. It'll mean no sprinklers, no alarms, no nothing. Just an old–fashioned evacuation nightmare."

"That sounds worse," she said.

"It sounds like control," he said. "Some, anyway."

She rubbed her temples. "How are you so calm?"

"I'm not," he said. "I'm compartmentalizing."

A second figure stepped out of the shadows and Celeste nearly dropped her bow.

"Hello, *celistka*," Aria said. She wore a black jumpsuit and a backstage crew badge she absolutely had not earned. Her hair was scraped back; her eyes were wary and amused.

"Security sucks," she said. "I've been here for an hour. I've already rearranged three of their prop closets."

Volkov's gun was half–out of its holster before Celeste could blink.

"Don't," Aria said mildly. "You'll get brains on the timpani, and we all know that's frowned upon."

"What are you doing here?" Celeste hissed. "If they see you—"

"They won't," Aria said. "They think I died in a cave in Istanbul, remember? Or at least that I'm on a very long 'reconditioning' trip. I've got a very small window before Maestro realizes his prodigal daughter is in your fly tower."

Volkov didn't lower the gun. "Give me one reason not to drag you out of here in handcuffs and dump you at the nearest federal office," he said.

"Because I'm the only one here who's actually seen the Chorale–NY–01 plan in full," she said. "And Maestro just moved up your timeline."

Celeste's pulse spiked. "What do you mean, moved up?"

Aria looked at her, and for the first time since their Istanbul training days, there was something like uncertainty on her face.

"He's not waiting for March," she said. "He's doing it tonight."

Chapter 16

Prelude

THREE SECONDS OF silence followed Aria's words, thick as curtain velvet. Then the world slammed back in.

Celeste grabbed her arm and yanked her deeper into the shadow of the fly tower, away from passing stagehands and violinists wandering off for coffee.

"Explain," she hissed.

Aria didn't fight the grip, but her gaze flicked to Volkov's gun, then back to Celeste. "Maestro accelerated Chorale after Istanbul," she said. "You embarrassed him. He doesn't like improvisation he didn't write."

"Details," Volkov said. The muzzle of his pistol stayed low, but his focus was surgical.

Aria's jaw flexed. "NY–01 was scheduled as part of the larger triad. PAR–01, TKO–01, all in the same window. He's moved New York up as a 'prelude.' His word, not mine."

"How?" Celeste demanded. "What's the mechanism?"

"Fire," Aria said. "But not fire. He wants panic more than flame."

She pointed up, toward the maze of ducts and pipes above the stage. "They're going to trigger a 'fault' in the fire system just after interval. Foam release in some zones, nothing in others. Alarms misrouted. Exits locked 'automatically' by a safety override. People will surge toward the wrong doors. Crush injuries. A few strategically placed ignitions to make it look real on camera."

Lena's voice crackled in Celeste's ear. "Crush injuries," she repeated faintly. "On purpose."

"You knew this," Volkov said to Aria. "And you didn't tell us sooner."

"I didn't know about the timing change until an hour ago," Aria snapped. "I'm not sitting in Maestro's lap these days. I'm on the 'observe and be evaluated' list. I got access to one update. I stole what I could and came here."

"How are you here?" Celeste asked. "Badges, clearances—"

Aria rolled her eyes. "Please. I wrote half their access protocols. Getting into a concert hall is kindergarten."

A door banged somewhere down the corridor. Footsteps. A trumpet player laughing too loud.

Celeste forced her breathing to slow. "Where's the trigger?" she asked. "Is it remote? Inside the panel? In the control booth?"

"Two stages," Aria said. "Primary trigger is remote, its offsite, encrypted. It sends a signal through that 'Titan Safety' box your friend is so worried about. Secondary is a local override in case the remote fails. That's in the main control room with the building's fire panel."

"So even if we cut the local panel," Celeste said, "he can hit remote."

"If you cut the panel properly, you sever the connection," Aria said. "But you have to do it without making the system scream. If the system screams, there's a 'fail–deadly' mode. Sprinklers dump where they shouldn't, doors lock. He gets what he wants anyway."

"Of course, he built a fail–deadly," Volkov muttered. "Paranoid bastard."

"And the local?" Celeste pressed.

"Keyed switch, guarded," Aria said. "Routine fire inspections have been a convenient excuse to add hardware."

"And the key?" Volkov asked.

Aria smiled humorlessly. "With someone who doesn't know where he got it. He thinks he's upgrading safety. He's wrong."

Celeste pinched the bridge of her nose. "Showtime is in one hour," she said. "We don't have time for a full rewire."

"Yet here you are," Volkov said. "And here she is. Fate loves being dramatic."

"In my experience," Aria said, "fate is just lazy planning."

Lena's voice came through again, tighter now. "Celeste," she asked, "do I need to fake appendicitis? Because I will. I will throw up on the concertmaster's shoes if it gets people out."

"No," Celeste shot back.

"No," Volkov echoed. "Any obvious disruption before we're ready will just make them pull the trigger early. We need control, not chaos."

Esra cut in, her tone clipped. "I heard everything," she said. "Control room is two floors down, east wing. Head of security is there now, running checks. I can get her alone for sixty seconds if I tell her there's an issue with the donor entrance."

"Looped cameras?" Volkov asked.

"For the room itself, yes," Esra said. "For the hallway leading to it, not yet. Aria, can you patch into their network without setting off alarm bells?"

"Of course," Aria said. "This place is a museum with Wi–Fi."

"Then here's the plan," Esra said. "Aria gets in and gives me eyes on the panel. Volkov and I disable the fail–deadly mode from the control room, physically if we have to. Celeste, you play the first half of the concert like nothing is wrong."

"What?" Celeste said.

"We can't tip our hand too early," Esra said. "They're watching to see if you flinch. If the gala goes weird before interval, Maestro pulls out of his chair and hits his contingency. We get an earlier, sloppier version of Chorale, possibly elsewhere."

"You're asking me to sit onstage for an hour knowing something could blow," Celeste said.

"Yes," Esra said, "because your presence and apparent calm are part of our cover. And because if we pull this off, we can redirect their 'accident' into a non–event before anyone gets hurt."

"And if we don't?" Lena asked.

"Then we improvise," Esra said, "and hope we've built enough redundancy to keep people alive."

"This is insane," Lena whispered.

"This is what we voted for," Celeste said.

Aria watched her with an unreadable expression. "You're going to conduct from the cello," she said quietly. "Just like your mother wanted."

"Don't make this about her," Celeste snapped.

"It's always been about her," Aria said. "For him. For Eidolon. For you. The difference is you're the only one trying to write a different ending."

A stagehand poked his head around the corner. "Ms. Morgan?" he said. "Fifteen minutes."

Celeste forced her shoulders down. "I'll be there," she said.

The stagehand vanished.

Volkov holstered his gun.

"I go with Esra," he said. "We gut the panel. Aria, you're our saboteur inside their code. You betray us, and I swear—"

"You'll shoot me," Aria said. "I know. Get a new line. It's boring."

She turned to Celeste. "Play like your life depends on it," she said.

"Because it does. And so does everyone else's."

Celeste swallowed. "Lena?"

"I'm here," Lena said. Her voice trembled but held. "I'll stay on the headset. If I see anything weird in the hall, I'll scream in your ears."

"Good," Celeste said. "If all else fails, you throw your violin at the fire panel."

"Gladly," Lena said.

They dispersed.

Onstage, the world shrank to lights and faces and sound.

The hall was full with patrons in black tie and jewel tones, donors glowing, families in their best clothes, students in the cheap seats craning to see. Cameras dotted the balcony rail, red lights winking.

Celeste could feel the invisible gaze behind some of those lenses— someone, somewhere, watching her for signs of doubt.

She sat, adjusted her endpin, nodded once to Maestro Duret.

He raised his baton.

Mahler began. She played. Every phrase, every bow change, every shift felt like walking a tightrope over an unseen drop. Part of her soared—this was her element, after all, this dialogue between cello and orchestra, pain and beauty. Another part of her was counting exits, watching the aisles out of the corner of her eye, tracking the faint glow of the fire exit signs.

In her ear, a quiet flicker of voices.

"Entering control room now," Esra murmured. "Security chief is getting coffee. We have sixty seconds before anyone gets suspicious."

"Panel's live," Volkov said. "Aria, talk to me."

"Yes, Father," Aria's dry voice replied. "I see your ugly box. There's a piggyback controller attached to the main board. That's Maestro's toy."

"Can you disarm it?" Esra asked.

"Disarm? No," Aria said. "Divert? Maybe. If we cut the right lines, we can isolate the piggyback without triggering fail–deadly. But I need a steady hand."

"I have two," Volkov said.

"And a knife, presumably," Aria said. "Use it on the yellow and blue wires, not the red. Red is the failsafe. Yellow and blue are his control feeds."

Onstage, Celeste reached a quiet passage, her solo line riding above a murmuring string bed. Her fingers moved on autopilot, each shift precise. Her brain split with one half submerged in Mahler's melancholic lilt, the other listening.

"Blue first," Aria said. "Careful. Don't nick the shielding on the neighbor."

"I know how to cut wires," Volkov said.

"Your personality suggests otherwise," Aria said.

Something pinged at the edge of Celeste's vision: a shimmer by the back of the hall, the security chief returning with coffee, scanning the exits with a professional eye.

"Thirty seconds," Esra said. "Chief's back."

"Blue is cut," Volkov said. "No alarms. Yellow next."

Celeste's bow hand tightened. She forced it to relax. She thought of the letter in her desk drawer. *You will break yourself trying to enforce them.*

"Now," Aria said. "Yellow."

There was a tiny sizzle sound over the comm, followed by silence.

"Panel status?" Esra asked sharply.

"Main system still green," Aria said. "Piggyback is dark. Remote access severed, as far as I can tell."

"As far as you can tell," Volkov repeated. "Comforting."

"You want certainty, talk to a priest," Aria said. "I deal in probabilities."

Maestro Duret cued the brass. The orchestra surged into a stormy section. The hall vibrated.

In her ear, Lena whispered, "No one's panicking yet. Donors are just checking their phones during the quieter bits. Humans are gross."

"Security chief?" Esra asked.

"Looking at the panel," Volkov said. "She sees a flicker. She thinks it's a glitch. Esra, do your thing."

Esra's voice shifted, took on her professional charm. "I'm telling you, the donors' entrance is a mess," she said. "If we pull a fire drill tonight, they'll mutiny. Can you assure me your systems are really as safe as you say? I need something I can tell the board."

A pause.

Then the chief's low, irritated rumble. "They're fine," she said. "We just upgraded. I'll run a silent test after the show. No alarms. We're not in the habit of roasting billionaires."

"Thank you," Esra said warmly. "I'll tell them the same."

Celeste almost laughed. Almost. But ever the professional, she played.

The first half of the concert felt both endless and far too short. When they reached the final chord before intermission, the hall erupted in applause. People stood. Donors beamed. Duret bowed, basking.

Celeste rose with the orchestra, bowed, smiled the practiced small smile that said, *I'm grateful, I'm distant, I have more music in my head than words on my tongue.*

In her ear, Esra said, very quietly, "Primary line is cut. Remote trigger is gone. But the local override is still live."

"And Maestro will have failsafes," Volkov added. "He won't trust a single access point."

"So, we're not safe," Lena said.

"We're safer," Esra said. "And we know more than he thinks we do. That's something."

As the orchestra filed offstage, Celeste slipped into the wings instead of heading straight to her dressing room.

Aria waited in the shadows with her arms folded.

"Well?" Celeste asked.

Aria shrugged. "You bought yourself a variable," she said. "He can't hit the kill switch the way he planned. That doesn't mean he won't try something else."

"Like what?" Celeste asked.

Aria tilted her head toward the house. "He doesn't just want bodies. He wants you. If he can't make you a martyr, he'll try to make you a villain."

"How?" Lena asked. Celeste hadn't heard her approach, but there she was, clutching her violin and a water bottle, face pale.

"Video," Aria said. "Audio. Narrative. 'Famous cellist miraculously guides people to safety while fire alarms fail' becomes 'famous cellist knew about safety issues and didn't tell anyone.' He'll seed just enough truth to make the lie stick."

"I hate him," Lena said.

"Get in line," Aria replied.

Somewhere in the building, a bell chimed: five minutes to curtain.

"We can cancel the second half," Lena said suddenly. "We can go out, tell the audience there's been a technical issue, send them home."

"And trigger whatever backup he's wired in," Volkov said. He had appeared on the other side of the corridor, as if the building itself had coughed him up. "He wants a disruption. Doesn't matter if it's fire or panic. Chaos is chaos."

"Then what do we do?" Lena asked. "We can't just… do nothing."

"Who says we do nothing?" Esra's voice said in their ears. "Celeste, there's a manual announcement script for emergencies. Fire, bomb threat, power outage. It's all boilerplate. But the PA system itself is just a microphone and speakers. No one can hack your tongue."

Celeste looked between them. "You want me to talk to them," she said.

"Not about Chorale," Esra said. "Not about Maestro. About exits. About paying attention. About staying calm."

"They'll think I'm doing some weird arts–as–life speech," Celeste said.

"Good," Esra said. "Let them. You've pulled audiences through death and resurrection in Mahler. Do it with actual logistics."

Lena's lips twitched. "You're going to conduct an evacuation drill without evacuating," she said. "New career."

"Can she do that?" Aria asked. "Won't Maestro smell something?"

"He'll think she's indulging her inner activist," Esra said. "He underestimates sincerity. Narcissists always do."

Maestro Duret bustled by, nodding at Celeste. "Five minutes," he said. "Don't be late. The cameras are hungry."

"I'll be there," she said. She moved.

Onstage again, the second half program—short, flashy, designed for donors—waited on the stands. A contemporary piece, loud and percussive; a crowd–pleasing encore.

She stood, instead of sitting.

"Ladies and gentlemen," she said, stepping toward the front of the stage.

The murmur in the hall quieted in waves. Cameras turned.

In her ear, Esra said, "You're live on at least two networks. Choose your words."

Celeste took a breath. "I know you came here tonight to hear music," she said, voice amplified, floating over the hall. "And I promise, you will. But before we begin the second half, I want to ask you for something unusual."

A ripple went through the audience. Duret shifted behind her, confused.

"We live in strange times," Celeste said. "We carry so much noise in our pockets—alerts, news, fear. For the next hour, I'd like us to do something different."

She gestured toward the exits, the aisles. "I want you to look around. Really look. Note where the exits are. Note the people in your row. Note the ushers. If you needed to leave quickly—not because of any danger, but because life is unpredictable—how would you do it calmly? Who would you help?"

A few frowns. A few nods.

"We come to concert halls to feel," she went on. "To remember we're human. Part of that is looking after each other. Music is only as powerful as the community that listens to it. So tonight, I'm asking you to add one more layer to your listening: awareness. Not fear. Attention."

She let the words hang for a moment.

"In return," she said, softer now, "I promise I will give you everything I have in this music. All the discipline my teachers demanded, all the passion my mother wanted, all the stubbornness my friends tolerate. That's my side of the bargain. Yours is to be here. Fully. Eyes open, hearts open. Deal?"

Someone in the front row started to clap. It spread, hesitant at first, then surer. A few people rolled their eyes. More smiled. A woman in the balcony dabbed at her eyes.

Backstage, Aria made a low whistle. "Nice," she said. "You just turned a safety briefing into a TED Talk."

"Maestro will hate it," Volkov said.

"Good," Esra replied.

Celeste sat.

Duret stared at her for a beat, then shrugged dramatically for the cameras and lifted his baton. The second half began. Time stretched.

In the control room, Esra watched numbers and lights, Volkov at her shoulder. The fire panel stayed green. No unexpected alarms. No sudden lockdowns.

In the rafters, Aria hunched over a borrowed tablet, eyes flicking across lines of code. "He's probing," she mumbled. "He can't see his piggyback. He's sending pings. They're dying at the panel."

"He knows something is wrong," Volkov said.

"He suspects," Aria said. "Knowing requires evidence. Right now, all he has is a feeling and an ego bruise."

"Do you think he'll pull the trigger anyway?" Lena asked.

"He's impulsive, not stupid," Aria said. "He'll cut his losses. He doesn't want a 'technical glitch.' He wants a spectacle. Without full control, the risk of looking incompetent is too high."

"God forbid," Esra muttered.

Onstage, Celeste's solo in the contemporary piece blazed, all jagged rhythms and sudden lyricism. She poured herself into it, feeling sweat between her shoulder blades, the slight bite of the string under the bow.

At the last note, the hall exploded in applause.

She stood, bowed, met the eyes of the front row, the second balcony, the cheap seats. Faces. So many faces. Alive.

When the encore ended and the final chord hung, then dissolved, she felt something loosen in her chest.

In her ear, Aria said, "Remote triggers stopped. No more pings. He's pulling back."

"He's not going to try anything?" Lena asked.

"Not tonight," Aria said. "Congratulations. You just flubbed his premiere."

Afterward, the backstage area was a swarm: donors pressing hands, board members gushing, journalists lurking with microphones like weapons. Celeste endured the gauntlet with practiced poise, Lena at her side, Esra hovering like a quiet shield. Volkov faded into the background, just another security presence.

The head of security pulled Esra aside. "About that panel," she said quietly. "I'm calling in my own people. 'Titan Safety' can take their boxes and shove them. I don't like black boxes in my walls."

"Good," Esra said. "If you need documentation, I have some… concerns in writing I can send you."

"Send them," the chief said. "I like having more ammo."

Later, when the donors had migrated to the reception and the cameras had followed, Celeste slipped back onto the empty stage. The hall felt different now. Still, but not heavy. Charged.

Lena joined her, violin case slung over one shoulder. "They're alive," Lena said. "All of them. No one even spilled their champagne."

"Some of them cried at my speech," Celeste said. "I'm going to get so much heartfelt email."

"Better than condolences," Lena said.

Volkov came up the side aisle, hands in his pockets. "Well," he said. "You survived your own concert."

"You sound disappointed," she said.

"I'm relieved," he said. "It's an unfamiliar feeling. I don't like it."

Esra appeared behind him, binder tucked under one arm. "New York is off the table for now," she said. "Chorale–NY–01 is a dead plan. They'll have to rebuild from scratch if they want to try again."

"They won't," Aria said, emerging from the wings. "Maestro doesn't repeat failed experiments. He moves on."

Celeste turned to her. "And the others?" she asked. "Paris. Tokyo."

Aria's smirk faded. "They're still live," she said. "He'll adapt their timelines based on how tonight went. If I had to guess? He'll accelerate them, too. He'll want to prove he can still play a chord without you."

"Can you get us access like this there?" Esra asked. "Floor plans. Contractor lists."

"Maybe," Aria said. "Paris is easier. I have more friends there. Tokyo… more complicated."

"And your position?" Volkov asked. "Eidolon will notice you were gone tonight."

"They already have," Aria said. "I burned a bridge to get here. Maestro locked me out of some channels when he saw the pings fail. I'm… off–roster."

"You're on ours now," Lena said.

Aria blinked. "Excuse me?"

"You helped," Lena said. "You didn't have to. That earns you a chair at the weirdest table on Earth."

"This isn't a table, it's a council," Aria said. "And I don't do councils."

"Too bad," Lena said. "We're recruiting."

Celeste watched Aria's face closely.

"You can walk away," she said. "You could vanish. Change your name. Sell yoga mats in Bali."

Aria snorted. "I'd last three days before I strangled a tourist."

"Or you can stay in between," Celeste continued. "Feed us what you know. Help us hit them. You don't have to be in the room every time we vote. But you'll have a hand in this, one way or another."

Aria looked at her, something raw flickering in her eyes and gone. "You really think you can out-conduct him," she said. "From outside the podium?"

"Yes," Celeste said simply.

Aria studied her for another beat, then shrugged. "Fine," she said. "I'll play along. For now. But if your ethics get in the way of efficiency, I reserve the right to ignore you."

"That's not how councils work," Lena said.

"Then don't call it a council," Aria replied.

Celeste felt tired down to her bones. The adrenaline was fading, leaving a hollow ache. She walked to the edge of the stage and looked out over the empty seats. For a moment, she let herself imagine another timeline: the same chairs, charred. The same aisles, littered with shoes and programs. The same stage, warped by heat.

She closed her eyes, let the image fade.

"We won," Lena said quietly, coming to stand beside her.

"Tonight," Celeste said.

"It counts," Lena insisted.

"Yes," Celeste agreed. "It counts."

Celeste turned back to them—Lena, Esra, Volkov, Aria. The strangest quartet she'd ever stood with. "This book is closed," she said quietly, more to herself than them. "This hall. This plan. This night."

"And the next one?" Esra asked.

Celeste looked up, up, as if she could see through the roof, across the ocean, to a city of narrow streets and a river, to another of neon and towers. "Paris," she said. "Tokyo. He thinks he's shifted the movement away from me. He hasn't. He's just changed the key."

Volkov's phone buzzed. He glanced at it, then froze.

"What?" Celeste asked.

He turned the screen so they could see. A news alert from an international wire service. UNUSUAL SECURITY DRILL AT PALAIS GARNIER CAUSES PANIC AMONG TOURISTS – NO INJURIES

Below the headline, a photo of the Paris Opera house, cordoned off with tape, crowds milling.

"Maestro testing the waters," Esra murmured. "A dress rehearsal."

Another alert popped up. Same source. Different headline. MINOR ELECTRICAL FIRE DISRUPTS REHEARSAL AT TOKYO CONCERT HALL – OFFICIALS INVESTIGATING

Celeste felt the ground tilt.

"He's moving," she said. "Already."

Her own phone buzzed.

Unknown number.

She didn't have to open it to know who it was.

Still, she did.

You saved your little stage tonight. Bravo. Now let's see how far your reach really goes.

– M

Her reflection in the dark screen looked strange—part musician, part something sharper.

Lena touched her arm. "You don't have to go," she said, voice rough. "We can find people there. Call in favors. You don't have to fix everything yourself."

"I know," Celeste said.

Her mother's letter burned in her memory. *You may be the only one who can.*

She slipped the phone into her pocket. "I'm not going alone," she said. "We'll build something there like we did here. Allies. Councils. Rules. But I have to go."

"Paris first," Esra said. "Their schedule is tighter. I'll start reaching out tonight. Old colleagues. A few politicians who owe me favors."

"And Tokyo?" Volkov asked.

"After," Celeste said. "Or during. We'll divide. Conquer. Overschedule ourselves like a tragically ambitious quartet."

"You're terrible at rest," Lena said.

"I'll nap on the plane," Celeste said.

She looked out over the seats one last time.

Outside, snow had started to fall, soft against the windows. Somewhere in the city, people were posting videos of her speech, arguing about safety and art, making jokes, making meaning. None of them knew why she'd really said the words she had.

Behind her, her council stood, unsteady, contradictory, flawed. Human.

Ahead, another movement waited.

"Pack a bag," she said to Volkov. "We leave for Paris tomorrow."

He nodded once. "Already done."

"To Tokyo after?" Aria asked.

"Yes," Celeste said.

Lena made a small sound that was half laugh, half sob. "You're going to chase music and murder across continents," she said. "You're insane."

"Probably," Celeste said.

Lena swallowed, then forced a smile. "Bring me back a fridge magnet," she said. "From everywhere. And I'll take care of your cat."

"I will," Celeste said. She stepped off the stage, cello case on her back, binder under her arm, phone heavy in her pocket.

As she walked into the wings, the hall lights dimmed behind her, then brightened for the cleanup crew. Life went on. Programs were swept, seats straightened, microphones packed.

Somewhere above, the fire system blinked in bewildered safety, its hijacked veins severed.

Outside, in a room full of screens, a man watched footage of a woman on a stage telling people to look at the exits. He smiled, fingers steepled.

"On to Paris," the Maestro murmured. "Let's see how well you travel, *celistka*."

Chapter 17

Movement Then Rest

THE NEXT MORNING, New York looked exactly the same. That bothered Celeste more than she expected. Cabs honked. Dog walkers cursed at leashes. Coffee shops bustled. The headline about the "unusual safety announcement at the Philharmonic gala" sat three scrolls down on most news sites, below gossip about an actor's divorce and above a piece about subway delays.

Most people thought she'd done a bit.

"Very moving," one columnist wrote. "And very on-brand for an artist increasingly interested in social commentary."

No one mentioned Chorale.

Good.

In her apartment, suitcases lay open on the bed. She packed with the efficiency of someone who'd done this a hundred times: concert black, rehearsal clothes, passports, scores. Weapons went in last, nested in false bottoms and innocuous cases. The cat watched from the dresser, tail flicking.

"You're going to stay with Henry," she told him. She had decided after last night's concert that Henry was the best choice. She might need Lena.

The cat blinked. He clearly considered this beneath him.

There was a knock at the door.

Lena. She came in without waiting for an invite, as she always did now, holding two coffees and a folder.

"This is for you," she said, shoving the folder into Celeste's hands before she could protest.

Inside: printouts. Headlines about Chorale–adjacent incidents. Notes scribbled in Lena's messy hand. A page titled RULES v. 1.1 with new additions in the margins:

NO USING TRAUMA AS AN EXCUSE.

NO FORGETTING WE'RE DOING THIS FOR PEOPLE WHO DON'T KNOW OUR NAMES.

Celeste's throat tightened. "You updated the rules," she said.

"Someone had to," Lena said. "You were busy saving the world with a G string."

"That's not how that works," Celeste said.

Lena's smile was quick and fragile. "You're really going," she said. "Paris. Tokyo. The whole 'catch the Maestro on his world tour' thing."

"Yes," Celeste said.

"Good," Lena said. "I'd be more offended if you stayed."

She set one coffee on the nightstand. "I made you a playlist," she added. "For the flight. It's all flute concertos so you remember things could always be worse."

Celeste laughed, startled. "Sadist."

"You love me," Lena said.

"I do," Celeste said.

Silence stretched for a beat.

"Come with me," Celeste blurted.

Lena blinked. "What?"

"Paris," Celeste said. "Tokyo. Be there. In the room. On the stage. On the council. I don't want to make these decisions with you an ocean away."

Lena's face did something complicated. "I have a job," she said. "A salary. An angry conductor. A mother who already thinks I live too close to danger because I ride the subway."

"We'll find covers," Celeste said. "Guest residencies. Exchange programs. The orchestra owes you time after Istanbul. After Lincoln."

Lena chewed her lip.

"Also," Celeste added, "if you're there, I'm less likely to do something stupid, because you'll yell at me."

"Flattery will get you everywhere," Lena said.

She looked at the open suitcases, at the cat, at the binder on the chair.

"I can't go to both," she said at last. "My mother will show up in person and drag me home. But… Paris. I can swing Paris. It's culture. It's croissants. It's a city where violinists wear scarves and pretend to understand philosophy."

"Paris, then," Celeste said. Relief loosened something inside her she hadn't realized was clenched.

"Tokyo after," Lena said. "We'll figure that out. One continent at a time." She grabbed Celeste in a hug that was fierce, tight, smelling of coffee.

"Don't get dead," she whispered into Celeste's shoulder. "I'm not done yelling at you."

"I'll do my best," Celeste said.

"Do better than your best," Lena said. "Do my best. It's superior."

When Lena left, the apartment felt emptier, but less lonely.

Volkov arrived ten minutes later, carrying two small bags and an air of grim readiness. "Esra's already at the airport," he said. "She's charming her way into upgraded seats using donor miles."

"And Aria?" Celeste asked.

"Will meet us there," he said. "She doesn't like being seen in daylight near you. Says it's bad for her mystique."

Celeste snorted. "Of course."

They rode the elevator down in silence. Henry the doorman met them in the lobby and took the cat carrier from her.

"I'll take good care of him, Ms. Morgan," he said. "My wife's already bought him a bed he's going to ignore."

"He likes to sleep on expensive sheet music," Celeste said. "Consider yourself warned."

Henry laughed. "Go make more of it," he said. "The world needs it."

Outside, the air was sharp, the sky a flat winter white. A car waited. Celeste paused on the sidewalk, looking up at the building, at the slice of window that was hers.

This part of the story felt frighteningly familiar: bag on shoulder, instrument at her back, a mission in another country, danger layered under concerts. But something was different this time. She wasn't just a weapon being pointed. She was choosing.

She slid into the car. As they pulled away, her phone buzzed one last time. A message from an unknown French number Esra had forwarded. It was a photo of the Palais Garnier, bathed in morning light. In the foreground, a spray–painted message on a barricade:

LA MUSIQUE N'EST PAS UNE ARME

Music is not a weapon.

Underneath, in smaller letters, someone had added: *ELLE EST UN CHOIX*

It's a choice.

Celeste smiled.

When the plane lifted off, New York dropping away beneath a blanket of cloud, she took out her mother's letter and unfolded it one more time.

You hold the bow. Remember that.

"I remember," she whispered. She looked out the window, toward an ocean and two cities where Chorale's shadow waited. Behind her, this book—the one that began with Vienna and Istanbul and a cistern, that moved through storage units and warehouses and a gala—was closing, its last notes still resonating.

Ahead of her, another score unspooled—Paris, Tokyo, Maestro, global chords of terror and resistance. She didn't know yet how that piece would sound, how many movements it would have, whether it would end in triumph or tragedy or something in between.

She only knew she would play it on her terms. And that somewhere, in a room full of screens and plans, a man who thought himself a conductor had just realized his soloist had started writing her own music.

That realization, she thought, was the inciting incident of something much larger than this book. Something that would stretch across borders and stages and lives.

"Next movement," she said to the clouds. Then she closed her eyes, wrapped her fingers around an invisible bow, and began to imagine how to turn Chorale into a rest.

To join the mailing list to know when *The Shadow Requiem: A Shadow Concerto #3* releases, add your email to the form at www.jillferguson.com

Author's Note

This book and the series is dedicated to Dr. Adrian Fung, who taught me that a cello can do so much more than play classical music. We are like-minded souls who know people can be "not just one thing." For that and so much more, I am grateful. Thank you for the inspiration, the artistry, and the reminder that what we don't say can resonate the longest.

About the Author

Jill L. Ferguson has been a fan of mysteries and thrillers since she read the books of Scott Corbett and Carolyn Keene as a child. She is an entrepreneur and consultant and an award-winning author who has written more than three dozen books. With her brother, she writes the Whiskey Dog Mystery series under the pen name Faith Walker. Like Celeste Morgan, airports are places she finds moments of stillness and clarity amidst chaos.